AILEEN LA TOURETTE
sixteen years. During that time she has
waitress, script reader, lecturer and journalist as well as
raising her two sons and writing. Her previous work includes
three radio plays broadcast by the BBC, a theatre play, and
short stories published in *Walking on the Water* (Virago) and
in *Mae West is Dead*, a collection of lesbian and gay fiction.
Weddings and Funerals, short stories by Aileen La Tourette
and Sara Maitland, was published earlier this year.

She was born in New Jersey in 1946, the oldest of seven
children. She now lives in south London with her sons, and
is working on her second novel.

NUNS
AND
MOTHERS

Aileen La Tourette

Published by VIRAGO PRESS Limited 1984
41 William IV Street, London WC2N 4DB

Copyright © Aileen La Tourette 1984

British Library Cataloguing in Publication Data
La Tourette, Aileen
  Nuns and mothers.
  I. Title
  813'.54 [F] PS3562.A75/

  ISBN 0-86063-555-1
  ISBN 0-86068-560-8 Pbk

Printed in Great Britain by litho at
The Anchor Press, Tiptree, Essex

for Georgia

Both nuns and mothers worship images,
But those the candles light are not as those
That animate a mother's reveries,
But keep a marble or a bronze repose.
And yet they too break hearts – O Presences
That passion, piety or affection knows,
And all that heavenly glory symbolise –
O self-born mockers of man's enterprise:

Labour is blossoming or dancing where
The body is not bruised to pleasure soul,
Nor beauty born out of its own despair,
Nor blear-eyed wisdom out of midnight oil.
O chestnut tree, great-rooted blossomer,
Are you the leaf, the blossom or the bole?
O body swayed to music, O brightening glance,
How can we know the dancer from the dance?

W. B. Yeats

1

Coldwick got its name by accident. In the beginning, it was Aldwych. But Aldwych was English, and didn't transplant to the red clay hills of New Jersey. Tongues tripped and twisted over it, the American eye resisted it in print. '-wych' conveyed little to mind, eye or tongue, especially when teamed with 'Ald' out of 'Auld' meaning old, which was an insult in the New World. Something short and to the point was required. But the serpentine tongue has a mind of its own, it gives more away than its keeper might wish. Particularly, it seems, when engaged in the making of names.

The hills themselves were called the Red Genesis Hills until they were tongue-trimmed and tipped the Red Jennies. By the time millionaires came and built their mansions in the lush russet foliage, they had evolved, or devolved, into the Pennies. Call it a change for the worse, a reflection of materialism spreading like gold fever, backed by a bastardised Calvinism. Call it a sentimental fondness for the smallest coin of the realm, made of copper in the New World as it had been in the old, copper which reflected the complexion of the hills, as the coins reflected their curves and the disc of the sun as it yo'yo'ed behind them.

Whatever fates or foibles lay behind it, the township of Coldwick sat upright and sober in the lap of the low-slung crimson mountains, and in time my father would be born

1

there. And so, accidentally, would I.

He would endow my mother, just in time, with his name. I would grow up wondering where in my all-too-robust frame was buried the ghost of the frail, premature infant I was said to have been. Eventually, it would dawn on me that my prematurity, and consequently my frailty, were mythical. That is, they both hid and expressed a truth. Premature, but not according to the moon. A resultant frailty of fit in the world, but not according to the bone.

My name was itself a source of some childhood anxiety. Carnet baffled American tongues and eyes much as Aldwych had done. My first name, Helena, didn't help. I got away with the 'a' at the end, impatiently tolerated as an affectation, or, worse, an exoticism. But 'Carnet' invariably became 'Karnett'.

My ancestors were anonymous Huguenots. That is, they had names, but they discarded them when they fled from the Catholics, into the Pyrenees. They changed their names overnight, took the title of things around them in their little mountain fortress, which sat in the stonier lap of the Pyrenees much as Coldwick sits in the flabbier Pennies. They could have chosen to name themselves after any phenomenon or feature of the landscape, inner or outer. My ancestor chose 'carnet', – notebook.

Why? Perhaps he – the Adamic task of naming must be assumed to have fallen to a male of the species, much as I would like to think otherwise – had a weakness for notebooks. Perhaps he lugged them everywhere, even – especially – into hiding. From hiding to hiding, of one sort or another, since childhood. Notebooks represented potential to this brooding ancestor, male though he was, who clutched them to his bosom and waited for them to hatch, someday, into something finished and whole. Litanies of dreams lived there, lists of possibilities and price-lists of fears alongside them. Parallel secret lives hid in du Carnet's notebooks, meant to flower from the paper one day, like origami, and he with them – 'du Carnet'. While he was at it, he ennobled himself. If he were noble before the escape and change of destiny, identity, and address, he'd have dropped the ennobling syllable and travelled lighter without it. A mug on the make who lives in a blizzard of notebooks and gives himself a 'du' like tucking a carnation into his buttonhole, is doomed to travel light, with only the flourish of magic behind the syllable. Hard to distinguish from illusion, and that from self-delusion, but that, perhaps, is where the notebooks come in. Or where I do, with Georgia Manion in tow, on another sort of pilgrimage, escape and odyssey, across the sea to Coldwick, just as he came those draughty centuries ago, pursued, as he was, by phantoms and fears, and who's to say his were more real? I know why I'm here with Georgia, if not why I'm here, period; though Coldwick isn't an obvious choice of a place for a lesbian honeymoon.

Georgia alone in the world knows about the ingredients I'm trying to blend together, smoothly; or at least together. Georgia knows about Wall, my father, about Coldwick, about me. And Georgia knows about names.

Her name's an accident. Her father swore in his cups to name his firstborn after himself, George, of course, after the father of our country and the dragon-slaying saint. When Georgia was born he made the best of it and saved face, and she's been making the best of it, and saving face, ever since. Named after her home state as well as her fathers, biological and patriotic, Southern womanhood isn't exactly her style. She's big and brash and somewhat butch, at least on the outside. What she is on the inside, I like to think I know, approximately and alone.

Meanwhile, back in Georgia, she set about making herself a belle without being a dumb-belle; not easy. She set about finding the one dressmaker in all of Dixie who understood how to dress a Big Girl for a cotillion; not easy. She eventually persuaded herself into Yankee business, where her Southern accent would prove an unequivocal advantage in dealing with the customers, foes and friends of Sabine Chemicals. Of the design of that particular name, nothing need be said. Georgia slurred her way to partnership, syllabically and alcoholically; not easy.

An actress on the side, she knows which roles are not for her. Not Scarlett O'Hara, not Blanche DuBois. Not self-proclaimed lesbian Amazon *guerillère*, either, whatever need of mine it might fulfil, however neatly it might replace the old 'Virgin and Martyr' in our worn Bible Missals, mine a gift from her.

She squirms behind the wheel, in her early fall ensemble, wheat-coloured. Georgia's all earth tones, with hints of coral or raspberry at heightened moments. Her body's opulent, ornate, Corinthian; but she dresses it down, dresses it Doric. It overflows, it stretches her tailoring. Right now it's stretching her white silk shirt and camel cashmere cardigan and fleshing out the linen of her camel slacks as it was never intended to be fleshed.

She looks over suspiciously. 'What're you grinning at?'

'Your thigh.'

'Cut it *out*,' she reaches for a cigarette. 'Are we close?'

'Oh Georgia, we're so close,' my hand threads her linen thighs.

'Close to Coldwick,' she sputters, batting the hand away. 'Helena, I have to drive.'

'We are, yes,' I assent, but vaguely, my mind on other things. Thighs, to be precise. 'You know what? You don't have a skin.'

She exhales a mouthful of Malboro smoke and smiles confidently. 'Don't you believe it. I'm as thick-skinned as they come, for all that I scorch in the sun.'

'I was speaking literally.'

'You? Speaking literally?' she laughs.

'Yes,' I insist, smoking my own brand of seductively packaged Gitanes, even more seductively named. Gypsies! I live my life virtually immobilised by scruple and anxiety, so I smoke gypsies. 'You don't have a mere skin, Georgia, that's what I mean. You have a pelt.'

She wrinkles up her stub Irish nose. 'A pelt? Reminds me of the smell of the cathouse in the zoo. Is that an insult?'

'I was thinking of the big cats' coats, not their smell. All striped or spotted with gold, like you.'

She smiles again, more shyly. A raspberry flush begins to underlie and underline her markings. Her hair's a rich strawberry gold, just — *just* — going the least bit strawberry grey at the temples, a professional touch. She's decorated with odd little legends and logos all over her skin, as if the goddess who made her couldn't resist signing her initials all over, in a billion different arcane scripts. And who could blame her? Not me.

Her eyes change colour constantly. She strives to give an impression of utter stability, particularly strives to give herself that impression. But her eyes give her away. They go from grey to blue to green, every day. Confederate eyes. Yankee eyes. Martian eyes. She's a gypsy, all right, much as she'd hate the description for its implication of scrappiness, hurly-burly, and fire.

But her face is a bit scrappy, with its ever-escaping wisps of gold flax on the forehead, its gold dots and dashes, its essentially rakish bones. She doesn't add up to herself, any more than I add up to me. Maybe that's what draws us to each other. She thinks so, anyway. Once we add up, respectively, she thinks, we'll fall apart.

'Oh my god, there's the Walsh's,' we're passing a huge mansion set on a hill outside Coldwick. 'Walsh's Galoshes.'

'Walsh's Galoshes?' Her thin pale lips quiver.

'They used to be — big.'

'Well I'll be,' she drawls. 'And did you folks — uh — fraternise with these rubber barons?'

'Not exactly fraternise,' I laugh to show her her pun hasn't gone to waste. 'My grandfather painted their mansion. He painted most of the mansions around here. And the Methodist church in Coldwick, including the steeple.'

Silence. We ponder the anomaly of class in the U.S. or at least I do. Georgia's sort of a snob but I'm not sure what sort. Come to think of it, am I? What about the dropped-out 'du' in du Carnet, a rumour carefully preserved in the family memory like the distant glow of better days? Then there are ladders and paintbrushes, overalls, good honest labour. It all works out upright and sober and WASP, on this side of the

5

tribe, but I'm not quite sure how.

'On the other side,' I muse aloud, drawing her into my quandary, or trying to, 'My great-grandfather was a jockey who left home in Ireland because his parents wanted something better for him.'

'What could be better than a jockey?'

'He settled down eventually in Pennsylvania, to train horses on a huge estate and have ten kids, of which my grandfather was one. Whenever Pom used to talk about his childhood, he used to refer to these people he called "Miss Evelyn" and "Master Peter", and I could never figure out why.'

'The owners of the estate?'

'And their kids. Right. And they called him Patrick.'

They strained like the English language, the class distinctions of the old world, faithfully carried over the water. But did they ever, finally, break?

'I never know what to think about all that,' Georgia ventures.

'Neither do I. Especially after living in England. They have separate bars in pubs for the working class and all the rest.'

'Is that the difference?'

'In the workers' one, the beer is cheaper and the decor scruffier. And the newspapers are actually divided into what they call "popular" and "quality".'

We contemplate the baldness of it in awed American wonder. Perhaps hypocritically, it stuns us. I contemplate other features of the English landscape, while I'm there, such as my husband and two children, at this moment, I establish with a quick look at the watch on Georgia's freckled wrist, just about stirring. Jonathan stirring in our big half-empty bed. Contemplating the empty half, perhaps. The children stirring to their half-parented Monday morning, with what questions forming and unforming like waves in their minds? With what questions in his?

With what questions in mine? Unanswerable and hence unaskable. I turn my attention to Coldwick, which we're rapidly approaching.

'Georgia, slow down. We're almost there. We're coming up

6

to the corner.'

Approaching it through fields of little cedar trees on both sides of the road, stubby little trees like green furled umbrellas. I cast my mind back over years of approaching this corner every Thanksgiving, every Easter, every summer. The summer approach was best because it was mine alone, unshared by my brothers and sisters, undiluted by my parents' tension as they pitched their last cigarettes from car windows and prepared themselves to deal with a day in Coldwick.

The magic corner. Once we rounded it, we'd changed worlds, the everyday fell away, the drab was no more. That street, Main Street, is the prototype, Main Street, Eden, U.S.A., and prototypal people live in every large, shaded house, or at least they used to. But what's become of the old gas station on the corner? Magic used to smell like petrol because of that gas station. I could close my eyes at any gas station anywhere and pretend I was rounding the corner into Coldwick.

It's become a white, pretentious mausoleum with 'Antique Barn' scrawled across it in that wrought-iron script that's like bird crap.

'Antique Barn,' I sputter. 'It isn't a barn. It's an old gas station. I remember the smell.' Gone. 'How could they do that?'

'Lament for a gas station,' she slows almost to stopping. 'Can we continue, or do we have to have a moment's silence?'

'Filling station,' I sigh. 'Coldwick is big on euphemisms.'

'Sure is. "Coldwick" for example – what's that a euphemism for?'

'Limp prick,' I snap back. 'What d'you think? Let's go on.' The corner's magic stubbornly sustains, even without the smell of gasoline. So does hers. I'm stitching two magic halves together. Surely they'll make a whole? Then I can go back and know where I am. Then I can make a life for myself, for the kids, then – we crawl along the street. The Wilsons', the Crumps'. Then. Who lives there now?

Where do you go when you're lost? You retrace your steps.

It never occurred to me you could just end up more lost.

'My Mummy's depressed so she's going home to America,' I hear Sam, my seven-year-old son, say in his precocious English voice. Not that he's precocious, perish the thought, it's just that accent, and only to my ears. Only right now the simplicities of England seem less treacherous than this mishmash of past and present, this voyage into absurd little Coldwick with Georgia.

She's watching me, impatient but tolerant. You wanted this, kid, and I chauffeured you here, her seagreengrey changeable eyes say. What now?

'Okay,' I say tersely. 'We can stop here.'

We've gone right past the house – but I couldn't take it in, except minimally, after all that time. I wanted to make sure it was still there, or that it had ever been there. Now I can make my way back.

'Here', where I've told Georgia to stop, is the schoolhouse. It, too, has been cosmeticised in the course of time, but less offensively. It's a library now.

'Wall went to school here,' I inform Georgia. Walter Carnet, deceased, walks the spongy fields behind the little building, as I look up, sharing his history with me and Wally and Marcelle, his three oldest kids, in a rare burst of confidentiality.

'It was Thanksgiving,' I might as well do my Intourist bit aloud, guiding us through the strange frowning land of the past. 'Wall told us how he went to school here from the age of six to thirteen, in one room, crammed full of farm kids and the occasional glass-eyed misfit, like him.'

'Your father wore glasses?' She wrinkles up her face, trying to remember.

How I love her for that effort of remembering! Maybe I cling to her because she can remember. She's one of the few who can, in my uprooted life. Uprooted, but not transplanted?

'No. Not when you knew him. He wore them as a kid, after he was in an accident. He was getting off the school bus – high school bus, he lived just up the street from here –'

8

We mulch around to the back of the schoolhouse, just as we did that day, getting mud on our new Thanksgiving patent leathers. There was an unseasonal thaw that year, instead of the usual snow, just as there's an unseasonal chill in the air now, instead of the usual August glare.

'He got off the school bus and stepped out in front of a car. It hit him head-on, left a dent in his head, damn near killed him. Then they'd thought he'd be blind, but he wasn't,' I finish lamely, helplessly. How can I begin to stem or to share the flood of memories unleashed by that simple tale? To share is, maybe, to begin to stem. 'He was shy all his life about that dent in his head, but it didn't stop him getting his super-short American businessman's haircut,' I throw in, for good measure.

'Of course it didn't.'

'When he woke up in the hospital and they told him what had happened, that he'd walked out in front of a car, he said, "That was a stupid thing to do"–'

'Smart kid.'

We walk around the back of the building to the front again, and stand surveying it. It's your classical one-room schoolhouse, painted red to preserve a sense of its history, an antique, but a real one. I think Wall would like the fact that they made it a library. I like it.

'Some of the kids stayed here up into their late teens, a few into their twenties,' I take her arm to lead her around again, towards the field. 'Wall told us this story about how they wrote their names on the blackboard when they had to go to the outhouse – there it is.'

'My, my, I certainly am glad we came here to view your relics. An outhouse!'

'Shut up. Anyway. The girls wrote their names in one column and the boys in another. Well, this one boy wrote his name and lumbered off, and when he came back and went to erase it, a girl'd written her name in the opposite column alongside his and he said, "Who called me a peenalope?"'

'That's funny, Helena? That's a joke? You brought me here to show me an outhouse and tell me a joke about a peenalope? Who was a girl called Penelope, I presume.'

'Oh, Georgia.'

'What?'

'I like you in brown.'

'Brown? Brown?' She raised her eyebrows, smoothing her sweater. 'Brown is for outhouses. This is camel, this is wheat.'

'How about earth?'

'Earth,' she says in her inimitable Georgia drawl, 'Earth is dirt.'

She's still brown against the blue sky, warm against me.

'I've never been kissed behind an outhouse before,' she murmurs against my teeth. 'I don't suppose I will be again.'

'You never know. You peenalope.'

We trudge on. She's brown, I'm blue, earth and sky I'd say if it didn't mean arrogating to myself the better part; but she's always played Martha to my Mary. Or Mary to my Christ, Christ!

'Once I climbed up there,' past the baseball field up the low rolling hills, pale with buff grasses. 'I was afraid I'd be disappointed. I'd looked out on it for years, out of my bedroom window. They always gave me Wall's old room –'

'Natch.'

'But one day I climbed up, and it was so beautiful,' I smile and squeeze her hand, trying to pass on the hilltop to her in some sort of Braille, to transplant the whole of it into the palm of her hand just like I try to transplant the whole of me right up into her core, so she'll know everything I can't tell her. But what I want to plant there in the smooth oasis of her palm, with its wavy lines like palm trees, is a sort of perfect perspective, the perspective of a child awake to self-important solitude, independently setting out, watched and wanting to be watched, then pulled from self-importance into the thing itself, pulled by the roll of the hill and the huge enveloping blue of the sky like two inimical forces between which she seems to fit and also to be lost, like living meat in a sandwich of earth and sky, not in a frightened way as if about to be gulped down some troll-god's gullet, just central. One morsel of a self tasting itself, at the same time, a mouthful of joy; like

10

having your cake and being it. Not to consume or be consumed, but to taste and be tasted with the lips and the tongue, like a lover.

How can I tell Georgia? I plant a moist kiss, finally, in the palm of her hand.

'Helena,' she wipes her hand on her camel haunches with a grey cloud-eyed look of disgust. 'This is hardly the time or the place.'

'It's always the time and the place,' I inform her, drawing out a Gitane, macho and loving it as much as she does. 'There used to be a baseball game here every Sunday.' I steer her from the hills, towards the house. 'Wall wasn't supposed to watch it, because of it being Sunday. But he did anyway.'

'With binoculars, if necessary.'

'He said he never did figure out what you were supposed to do on Sunday. Play with yourself, he guessed.'

'Your father had a neat turn of phrase.'

'Gallows humour. He had. That day, that Thanksgiving he brought us here, he told us about a poem he wrote in high school with the immortal lines, "Old Lem, he got so mad his face looked like a red hot pad" – '

She chortles, her laugh another mark against her in the line of succession from Olivia de Havilland through scores of Southern belles whose laughter is meant to sweetly, chastely peal. Georgia's is altogether too juicy, a deep, lubricious laughter down in her throat, a cross between something masculine and something porcine. Her eyebrows join her widow's peak when she laughs, almost, giving her a truly insane look, a look she perfected at sixteen and has worn to great advantage ever since. Her face says everything. Everything. She looks faster than she thinks, does Georgia, and she's a fast thinker. Her face, too, is a load of morse code dots and dashes. The dots have been with her from birth, the dashes are wrinkles, extending with the years, enriching or at least elaborating the message as they do so. Georgia has a rubber face, and though I'm not aware of being into rubber otherwise, despite Walsh's Galoshes, I am really into that face.

11

'Gallows humour,' she says thoughtfully. 'I favour gallows humour.'

'There's something incestuous about this relationship.'

'Of course there's something incestuous about this relationship!'

She's right to be impatient. It's transparently obvious. But I am, as she's fond of telling me, fond of stating the transparently obvious.

'Hey, Georgia. You know that old saying, "Like father, like daughter"?'

'Seems to me I've heard something along those lines. Only a little different.'

'Yeah, well. Maybe you learn it differently down South. I just thought of a poem not that different from "Old Lem". Only longer.'

'Shoot.'

She sighs, but it's a patient sigh. She can feel me tightening up inside, I'm sure, as we approach the house. She can feel me shrinking, awaiting ambush from the past. If that's what I came here for, it's also what I'm most afraid of. What if the past swarms and obscures the present, forever? I look to her for attention and approval, and I get it in good measure from her green eyes, signalling, Go on, kid; that's enough to hold the present firm and focused.

'The moon is my shepherd—'

'We learn that slightly differently down South, too.'

'I shall want everything.'

She smiles.

'She maketh me to fly from green pastures. She leadeth me beside the shrill waters. She—'

'She deploreth my soul,' she contributes, making a deplorative face, shepherding me into her arms, where I want to be. 'Well? Your turn.'

'Umm . . . skip some.'

'Okay.'

'I shall fear no evil,' I stare into her mossgreen eyes, praying it, 'for thou art in me,' wishing she were, feeling she is. 'Well?'

'Skip some,' she says thickly.

12

'Okay.'

'My breasts thou hast anointed with oil.'

'My cunt runneth over.'

We stand clasped, the sun flooding the landscape now, the present as present as present can be, making a present of itself. And yet – it feels blasphemous to allow a shadow, and yet, the house looms and with it, Wall, far off and aloof and lost. It's his face I see as I open my eyes from our kiss, his face as I last saw it, the antithesis of Georgia's, closed and blank and removed. Her arms loosen with mine, she stands helpless as I turn, somehow knowing I have to say hellogoodbye alone.

2

'Your father died last night.'
'That was a stupid thing to do.'
I didn't say that at the time, didn't even think it. Didn't even think. But I'm thinking it now, and I don't know whether I mean him, stupid for detaching himself from me, for going away alone and dying, or me, stupid for detaching myself from Georgia, for going away alone, and dying this other sort of minor secondary death, if there is such a thing, by choice.

Instead, I screamed. Screamed and went on screaming and the worst thing was, I registered my protest without coming near to real hysteria. I wanted to be hysterical. I wanted to be out cold. But consciousness hung grimly to me, or I to consciousness, and over and above the clamour of my screams, I was already beginning to accept it, sitting there with the phone in my hand through which the news had come via the Atlantic cable.

Died.

It was such a stupid word. You had no way of knowing what it was, until it happened to you, therefore we who had not yet done it (and had no intention of doing so) had no right to pronounce it. But somewhere, in what my old theology teacher had called the depths of my being, I *knew*, and knew that to refuse or otherwise refute the knowledge would be another kind of death, in those depths, of those depths, and that death definitively mine. Somewhere I chose life for me, right then, and if that meant surviving him, then I chose that, and that was the betrayal.

The best I could do by way of denial and insanity was to keep a few senseless, chattering, semi-minds alive, little scattered fragments of split-off consciousness that didn't know. I didn't inform them. One was the mind I was to wake up in, day after day, for months, a clear tabula rasa which would rouse itself with a childlike confidence only to be summarily dismissed by an older, sterner mind, a mind that knew, as soon as I blinked, stretched, or performed whatever ritual action sent it scurrying tearfully away. I was never sure. If I had been, I would never have performed it, or at least I would have had a choice, and without knowing there was no choice involved.

But that was much later. And much earlier, than this grim moment walking across the Coldwick fields cursing the crazy whim that brought me here. It's as if there's a child-me, still innocently enjoying festivals and summers here, someone who still doesn't know, whose joy I am about to disrupt forever; and I came back here to gather that joy in and make it mine, replacing grimness!

There's the house, so different now and so much the same. I don't know which it is that sticks little knives in me, the difference or the sameness. How can it be so heartlessly the same? How can it be so heartlessly changed.

It's changed, but not draped in black, not changed because of Wall or me or anything. I'll never bring my children here. I stand still. Now where did that thought come from? It never occurred to me I would bring them here. Except that it evidently did. Right now it did, because right now I want them here with me. I want to hold them and then let them scramble back into the fields and listen to their voices from a distance and feel the present filled instead of feeling this dumb, blunt emptiness.

They're not here. Georgia's there, waiting, and I must go on, I can't turn back now. I chose to come here without them, and I'd better make it worth something that I made

15

that choice.

White and green is still the colour scheme of the house, but green awnings have been added. Don't know why, the house is dark and shady and cool enough, inside. They give it a shady look in a different sense, like a gambler's green eyeshade. My grandfather, devout methodist that he was, would never have approved of that.

Three things happen to the glorified body after death. That was tucked away at the back of the Baltimore Catechism No. 2, with a terse question on abortion and suicide, linking them together, damning the sinner who did either, or both.

Radiance, bi-location, and the ability to walk through walls. Those were the three things that happened to the glorified, etc. The nuns avoided esoteric topics like glorified bodies, abortion and suicide. They were assigned for homework, if at all.

It sounded okay at the time. Radiance, or being turned on indefinitely (though that phrase hadn't come into existence yet) might be tiring, but no doubt glorification brought stamina. The ability to walk through walls could come in handy, provided you could control it and not go lunging through them all. And bi-location sounded wonderful.

Some nasty little demigod must've caught me at my musings, some evil genii granted that last aspiration. Because it seems to me I've been bi-located most of my life, to a point where I can't seem to be in one place at one time any more.

One foot on either side of the Atlantic, with the ground constantly turning soggy under my feet. One foot in straight domesticity and motherhood and one in wild wanton lesbian love with Georgia. That couldn't have been what they had in mind when they wrote the catechism. But then my body, as I sit down suddenly on a well-known rock in the backyard, isn't exactly glorified, either. It's flabby and toxic with alcohol. And utterly awash with so many feelings I can't decide which to express, let alone work out how. So I sit. Then I stand. Both actions are meaningless, like the endless sitting and standing in church, once those actions lose their original meanings. Sit. Stand. Why? Because it was time to

16

sit, and now it's time to stand. Why?

I approach the house, feeling invisible. The house is blind, now, it's not even the awnings, it just doesn't see me or recognise me. It used to. We'd drive up and it would practically vibrate with welcome. I would positively vibrate with recognition. But not now.

I do recognise it, but not in the old sense, not with vibration. Not with love. With a dull thump in the chest. It's the right one, all right. Memories are dry and flat as pictures pasted in an album. Wouldn't it be a joke if instead of scribbling fantasies and hopes and fears as I've imagined, my ancestor was some sort of philatelist? I wonder if 'carnet' also means 'stamp album' in French?

Every now and then I can feel Georgia's presence behind me. If it weren't for that, I wouldn't be here. I couldn't have come here alone. One of the first things I did when I found out Wall was dead, before I left England, was to write to Georgia, a hurried frantic letter, just telling her. And in the few frantic days before I left, I had time to get a letter back. She must've known before I wrote. Her letter was even briefer than mine. It just said 'Helena, I know. Love, Georgia.' Did she even say 'Love'? I can't remember. It was her knowing I needed, somehow, as I need it now.

I sit down again, this time on the cellar door, and hear my grandmother's high childish voice:

> *Playmate*
>
> Come out and play with me
> And bring your dollies three
> Climb up my apple tree
> Look down my rain barrel
> Slide down my cellar door
> And we'll be jolly friends
> Forevermore.

The cellar door is under the dining-room window. For one fanciful moment I imagine I'll look in and see us all at Thanksgiving dinner. I'll be the ghost, like the Dickens ghost of Christmas future, and they'll be safe and snug in unknowing innocence. Then the moment passes and I want to pitch a rock through the window. Just to spit some of the hard-pressed anger out. A rock would do.

But I don't. It might save me to throw that rock but I don't. I only act out against myself, like most females, not against property or other living flesh. Wall did, like most males. Break things, occasionally, that is. Come to think of it, Marguerite, my mother, is a breaker.

Wall broke a window once. I wasn't there. It was the week before he died. When I got there the window was still broken. The broken pane hung there, still in place, like a spiderweb, radials spiralling out from a central break. It seemed the only message he'd left in *that* empty house.

I stand up. Georgia must be wondering. She'd be terribly upset and embarrassed and angry if I broke the window, though she'd pay for the damage, like she paid for the damage the night she took me out to get drunk, the week after Wall's funeral. I walk round to the side of the house. I called her up, when I could resist the temptation no more. It seemed a desecration, to think of anything but Wall, but my concentration mercifully failed and I dialled the number with a shaking hand.

'Georgia. It's Helena.'

I can hear her voice as it was then, as it burst into my stale, sad eardrum, someone not family, someone connected and not, at the same time; a miracle. Friendship is one of the miracles. Wall thought so, too. Oh go away, Wall, please, I want to think about Georgia. I prayed the same prayer then, and he obeyed.

'How are you, Helena?'

We use each other's names a lot. It's one of the thrills of the miracle within the miracle that's love within friendship, friendship within love, indistinguishable except at the moments of passion. We used each other's names a lot then, too. Until we don't anymore.

'I'm okay. Getting – bored.'

She chuckled her deep rich chuckle, then abruptly stopped. '*Where* are you?'

'In Upper Middleburo.' Upper Middlebrow, for those, like Georgia, who knew; but this was a formal moment.

'I'll come and see you.'

Joy to the godforsaken world, too great to admit.

'Well – I mean, I wouldn't want you to come all this way just for me.'

'You wouldn't?'

Georgia lives in New York City, an hour's drive from Upper Middlebrow.

'Well I would but – I can't do much. I mean –'

'You never could,' she's laughing again.

'I mean, I have to stay with Marguerite.'

'Mothersitting. Sounds like fun. Doesn't she let her sitters have their friends over while they're there?'

Teasing, flirting on the brink of a precipice. Will I or won't I take it one step further, in my mother's silent, glittering house?

'Only their boyfriends, Georgia. Only their boyfriends.' The die is cast.

'I'll be there tomorrow afternoon.'

That left the night. Michael, five months old at the time, was restless and colicky and I sat up with him, most nights, stricken and fearful, baffled by my fear. The dead are foes of the living, at least the newly dead, the untamed dead. You fear their bony fingers, long before their fingers are even bony, beckoning you where you don't want to go. Into the dark, where they are. I sat trying to talk myself out of my fear of poor Wall, whose presence, after dark, seemed huge and sinister in the big house with its glinting glass, its many picture windows uncurtained.

But when I went to bed that night, exhausted from Mike's crankiness and my fears, my eyelids clanged open as if they had cymbals attached, and I sat up in bed, listening, watching. There was something in the room, besides Michael tossing in his crib.

Something moved along the wall above me, a small dark spot like a tiny blot or a very small dark cloud. It moved slowly, and it gave off a gust of sadness, like an aroma, very strong. It was like a ball of sadness, as if there were so much

19

sadness in the house that it had to take a palpable form.

It was oddly flat, for a ball. More like a spotlight, I thought groggily. Then I was plummeted back into childhood, back down the years till I found myself in an audience at Madison Square Garden, watching the circus. The smell of sadness at the circus was similar, but different, also sharp, and connected to a spotlight that the clown Emmett Kelly was trying to sweep under a rug. The old clown shuffled like a bear, baffled by the elusiveness of the circle of light, or huge pale rind of dust. The act went on and on, uncertain laughter rang from the bleachers where we sat, and then the audience dissolved into distance and I was the clown, sweeping and sweeping at the recalcitrant light, or bulge of darkness. Till the birds woke me, silvery with reproach. I had swept the small lost beam of Wall's spirit, my hesitant visitor, under the wonderful carpet of sleep. But Georgia was coming! I had a day off from mourning.

Marguerite looked pale and interesting, in her grief. I just looked pale. Georgia didn't seem to mind. She hugged Marguerite dutifully and me not at all, just looked. That look knew something – then it vanished, and the knowledge along with it. Swept under another carpet. No wonder Emmett Kelly's act with the spotlight was so popular! We were all at it, constantly, lights after lights under bushels after bushels. My mind teemed and travelled; I steered it back. It was time to pay attention.

We drank a glass of white wine together, the three of us. Georgia suggested that we Go Out, looking at me over the top of her glasses. My heart skipped, almost stopped. She'd had it skipping and almost stopping with that mock-strict look when we were both sixteen. Delicious danger.

I dumped Mike on Marguerite as a sort of occupational therapy, and out we went, into Georgia's car. Perversely, no sooner had we set off down the road when I began seeing Wall everywhere. There he was, driving past us on the other side of the road, going home, in his station car, a little Renault. There he was, picking up the mail from the mailbox down in front of the house, on a Saturday. There he was.

Georgia sat behind the wheel, growing quieter and quieter, her mouth thinning out into the absolutely shortest distance between two points which is, in fact, a pucker. I realised, finally, that she was sitting there literally smoking with fury as she drove, and for the first time in a week I felt laugh bubbles in my belly.

She glanced at me. 'What's so funny?'

'You are.'

'I am?'

'Yeah.'

'Why, pray tell, am I so funny?'

'Because you're so angry.'

'I see. And why, pray tell, am I so angry?'

'Because I'm not paying any attention to you.'

'But that's unreasonable.'

'That's right.'

'You know how reasonable I am.'

Laugh bubbles rose and floated through my thoracic cavity now. She was flirting. It was time for me to deflect the conversation teasingly back towards grief. Good grief, I was using my poor father as bait to snare Georgia! Using him to keep her sweet and solicitous, as I had done at sixteen when he lay in the hospital. But he'd used me as bait to get Marguerite, in a literal sense.

There he was again, conjured by guilt, going about his Saturday chores posthumously. There he was in the little delicatessen, buying smoked this and that, trying odd treats, wearing his old car coat. I pointed him out to Georgia.

'I remember that car coat. He wore it when he came to pick you up from school the day JFK was assassinated.'

She remembers that car coat, that spectral Wall, that spectral afternoon. She is unique and irreplaceable. No one else remembers.

'Saturdays smelled like men. Out of all the week, only Saturday. A sad-happy smell. Sad because that was its only day. Shit and Witch Hazel and gasoline and grass.'

'Which kind of grass?'

'Green.'

21

She nods. 'What did the rest of the week smell like?'

'Black serge and starched handkerchiefs and maternity clothes.'

'A black surge, did you say?'

No; that was last night.

'What did maternity clothes smell like?'

'I don't know. They smelled fat. Milk? Resignation? It was a parallel smell to the black serge, or whatever the hell that stuff was that habits were made of. The rest of the week smelled like nuns and mothers. And Sunday smelled like nuns and mothers and men, all mixed up.'

'And God.'

'And God. Remember that old joke? "Mother? If Nun, write None".'

'That's a joke?'

Fog made soft shapes against the windows, pressed like the vaporised noses of wistful ghosts against the pane separating them from us. We were safe inside the glass, inside the car. Safe from the fog. Almost safe from the ghosts.

She was heading up the New York thruway to Glass Mountain. It sat like a huge fishbowl on the side of a cliff, all glass. Ghosts could beat their heads against it, gasp like goldfish splashed out of water, while we swam, or drank, inside.

'Wall loved his Saturdays. But he gave them up to fly to Texas and teach. Why did he do that? How could he forfeit the only human thing he did all week, what for? To go to Texas and die?'

'How come only car coats and delis qualify as human? Wall Street's human. You may not like it, but it's human. Ambition's human. You may not have any, but it's human.'

'You red-eyed son-of-a-bitching misfit, Sabine Chemical's missionary to the fertile, bringing sterility. Among other things.'

'Oh, yeah. And when are you starting on your next fifteen kids? Or do you prefer celibacy?'

'I have a coil.'

'Oh, that's very healthy, Helena. Very healthy. Just as bad

as the pill −'

'It is not −'

'And besides, the pill isn't the only thing we manu-
facture−'

'I'm sure not. There's Valium and Librium and −'

'Oh stop snowing me with slogans! Or trying to. You house-
wives are all alike. Consciousness-raising in the kitchen−'

I grab a fistful of her spun-gold hair and pull, as hard as I
can. We're in the Glass Mountain parking lot by now, so I'm
not risking life and limb, at least not directly.

She lets me pull till my wrists suddenly go limp, my hands
relax and then start to shake.

'Okay, kid,' she holds me, loosely, lightly, as the tears
come. 'I'm sorry. I had to do that. Come on, cry, damnit.
What're they all doing up there in Upper Middlebrow, sitting
around with gags on, or what? Come on, kid. Cry!'

'They say lots of things about letting out your feelings, lots
and lots but they don't want you to,' I blurt somewhat
incoherently into her shoulder. 'They all don't want
Marguerite to be upset. Why shouldn't they all be upset?' My
fists hammer her shoulder. 'Why shouldn't they all be upset?
Wall's dead,' my dam bursts. She holds me against her and
lets it rush, bolt, pour, the flood, the wrenching waves
breaking against her over and over till it's past, for the
moment at least. I feel empty, tired and awed; it's the first
time in my life I can remember suffering under the eyes of
another person without having those eyes shift, or film.

Mopped and mollified, I walk with her to the mouth of
Glass Mountain, an oversize revolving door that gulps and
delivers us into a cocktail lounge hung with glass-bead
curtains. Glass is certainly the theme of the evening. Sat in a
curve of the fishbowl, an alcove reminiscent of the alcoves in
the refectory of Stella Maris Academy. I turn to Georgia over
a welcome scotch on the rocks with a laugh.

'When I was fourteen or fifteen, I forget, much too old, I
wrote something about somebody called Melanie whose
heart broke "with a faint tinkling sound, as of breaking
glass".'

She shudders. 'Broken glass doesn't even tinkle. It crashes.'

'Like hearts.'

'I wouldn't know.' She raises her glass, 'If you say so, kid.'

The scotch evokes a fogbound world of its own in my head. This is a closed-off, separate moment in the long day of mourning, unrecorded, except by her. Unjudged, even by her, and thanks to alcohol, even by me. Anger, fury spill out and over, grief and bitterness and that blank terror of last night.

'I can even envy her a bit, with half my mind,' I comment at one point, of Marguerite. 'I have fantasies of widowhood sometimes.'

'Not very likely to come true, in your case.'

'I guess not. But the thing is about the fantasies, they feel so clean. It's such a perfect solution. You'd get out of it without having to disrupt or disturb or hurt anyone – '

' – only kill them off –'

'But you wouldn't. That's the beauty of it.'

'But don't you think you'd feel guilty? I mean, you feel guilty now.'

'Oh, probably,' I lean on a wobbly elbow to agree, wearily. Even my elbows are drunk. 'Guilt would probably ruin the whole damn thing, it usually does.'

'Poor Jonathan.'

'Poor *Wall*.'

She nods. 'Okay,' she says softly.

Suddenly it feels to me as if Wall somehow ordered the fog the way we ordered our drinks. As if he's behind it, literally and figuratively. Why? To give me a rest, to throw up a smokescreen, or smokesignal, maybe, telling me it's okay to let go of him for a night? It feels like that. A gentle, wistful signal, the unravelling of that tight, sad ball on the wall of my room last night. This is what was inside. Fog – miles and amorphous miles of it, the stuff of sadness itself, cold, blind and endless.

'Hey, come back,' Georgia says, more firmly. 'Let's talk about the other days of the week. Besides Saturday.'

'Remember those little-girl underpants with the days of the

week on them?'

'Of course. That's better.' She chuckles and tries to keep the momentum going, the ball rolling; another sort of ball from the one unrolling outside.

'You know what I think? I think we made other mothers of the nuns,' she says confidingly. 'I think your joke has it backwards.'

'How d'you mean? They certainly made daughters of us, or tried to.'

'I mean especially people like us,' she says determinedly.

'How d'you mean, like us?' Does she mean gay, queer, lesbian? Even in my drunken state I sit up and take notice. But of course, she doesn't.

'I mean oldest girls in large families. And probably youngest, too. The ones our mothers didn't want, and the nuns did.'

I know what she means. We came first in the egg-and-sperm race, and we weren't supposed to. The oldest child was supposed to be a boy. And alternatively, once a mother had gone through her seventh or eighth summer kneeling back on her heels at Sunday Mass with her belly filling the space between her and the pew in front, swelling a maternity smock that'd done the rounds of the Rosary Altar Society, there was only one justification for her monotonous reproduction. That this time she'd reproduce not herself but her father, whom she adored, being herself a mistaken first or last female child and hence rejected in turn by her own swollen mother. The sins of the mothers were certainly visited upon us, with the difference that we had the nuns.

They taught us what it was to be wanted. Oh, how they wanted us! We firsts and lasts were the prime catch. We had an over-developed sense of responsibility if we came first, built from years of baby tending, and an over-developed sense of guilt similarly built, from years of baby hating, practical if not emotional. We who sat in rocking chairs holding down a baby's fluttering eyelids to make the brat sleep, we who stuck pins into the waxy baby buttocks of the first-born male, when he duly arrived, had plenty to be guilty

25

about.

The last-born – what made them so desirable? An over-developed sense of helplessness, I suppose. The first daughters had to have someone to push around, behind those convent walls.

The nuns were our Superior Mothers. They didn't like little boys much, which was fine with us. Little boys got far too much liking at home. And if the mothers couldn't find much to like in their little girls, well, that was their loss; we had the nuns.

They wanted us, all right! They used every device in the book to persuade, seduce and blackmail us into joining up. All of the most pious sort, of course. They had enormous influence. They were God's way of compensating us for our mothers.

'I used to write off to so many orders for information, Marguerite still gets catalogues from some of them.' Georgia snorts appreciatively. 'Little Sisters of This, Big Sisters of That, Charities, Cruelties, I'm on every religious sucker list there is. The pictures in their little brochures! I used to pore over them. Like travel brochures, you know? A Cook's Tour of the Order. Little pink-cheeked postulants in short white veils and nightgowns, baby nuns.'

'Goo goo. I remember seeing them on Vocation Days. They'd let them out of the incubators.'

'They were cute. And then Novices, very romantic, engaged to God. Postulants were just sort of Going Steady, or Pinned. Novices in black, longer veils, very serious. Adolescent nuns. And best of all, behind them all, Mother Superiors galore.' I sigh deliciously. 'Reverend Mothers, beyond them. And – at the top of the heap – Mother General. What a figure to look up to! What a –'

'Wait a minute, kid.' She sounds worried.

'What?'

'What if – knowing the way first-born daughters tend to boss people around –'

'Some first-born –'

'What if, just what if, you started climbing the hierarchical

26

ladder of which ever lucky order you decided to grace with your membership –'

'Why would I do that? I'd stay a Novice forever if they'd let me. The highest I'd ever like to climb would be Mistress of Novices.' I flash her a lascivious grin from behind my latest scotch. The ruins of the typical bar meal, steak, baked potato and salad, lie around us, ruins by virtue of much mud-pie playing during my fits of regression, echoed by similar playing by her, rather than because we'd actively tasted them. 'Imagine that, Mistress of Novices. You could be one of my novices.'

'Oh, *one* of your novices, thank you,' she grins back maliciously. 'But wait. They wouldn't let you stop there, kid. In fact if they knew you wanted to stop there they'd promote you so fast it'd make your head spin, just to mortify the flesh. No, I see you as a natural for the long climb all the way up the mortifying ladder – till you get to the top, and then, you know what? You're Mother General. That's where you'd end up.'

'Georgia,' I say after a pause, my voice theatrically tremulous, 'That's why I didn't do it.'

She waits.

'I couldn't risk it. Losing everything. Losing Mother General. So I decided to just be a general mother, instead.'

'Good thinking, kid,' she says seriously. 'Know what? I think we should go home. If I can drive, that is. Christ, I'm drunk.'

We stand. We reel. We've sat inside that fishbowl for seven hours, swilling its contents the entire time, copiously. We're goldfish now, solid gold through and through, scotch running in our veins and arteries. Outside the fog's so thick we couldn't see even if we could see, which we can't.

'I'm blind as Oedipus Rex.'

'Oedipus Rex didn't have to drive,' she answers, soberly, taking my arm. 'Maybe we should get a room for the night –'

Glass Mountain has Glass Cabins behind it, with rooms for the night. Made of glass, needless to say, they are not. But glass or not, I feel a distinct sense that they're not for us. This

27

is not how I want to consummate my passion for Georgia, not how, not where, and not when, while to risk staying and not consummating it, the likeliest possibility given our mutual drunkenness, was to risk an indefinite postponement I didn't want to give my consent to, either.

'I should get back, for Mike, if I can.'

'Okay, kid. Give me your arm.'

The blind led the blind and we both fell into the car, in a heap from which we untangled in delightful drunken slow motion.

Coldwick comes back through the fog of indistinct time, time meshed and myrrhed. My memory begins to unwind itself in past tense instead of present, I'm revisiting instead of reliving. Almost disappointed, I listen, now audience, not participant, to my own story. I'm back here on the rock, in the cold sun, remembering.

It was too soon for an overnight. Too soon for us and too late; between times. We wended our way down Glass Mountain in an atmosphere thick with lust and laughter, delicate and precious, disruptable any moment by grief, by a new cascade of tears, by plain old simple fear, our old bugbear. At least, I didn't want the lust or the laughter disrupted by regret. I wanted that drive home with her through the fog more than I wanted a premature, spurious night with her in a cabin vacated by a clandestine couple some hours, or minutes before. We would not be clandestine. Such a night could bring no blessings. It was still too soon for me. I was too afraid of Wall, too guilty. Let a decent interval intervene.

Jonathan had gone back to London by then, taking Sam with him. He had to go back and start work again, and it was thought best that Sam go, too, rather than stay for the longer mourning period. It was thought better for him, and for me, and it probably was. He was old enough to notice and receive emotions he couldn't begin to comprehend.

But I wasn't thinking of Sam, or Mike, or Jonathan, not that night. Or of Wall, except superstitiously.

We stopped for a red light looming up at us out of the fog,

still thick once we were down from the mountain, if less dramatic on level ground.

'C'mere,' Georgia said huskily, not comfortingly this time, as I slid into her arms across the seat.

I wanted the light to stay red. Wall could go to hell, they could all go to hell, for the space of that particular spotlight. I didn't really care if I saw another day, sitting there against Georgia, and not because I wanted a double-quick reunion with Wall either. I'd waited ten years for that moment.

I shift on the rock. The memory's a turn-on. The moment passed and we staggered into the house in Upper Middlebrow, pie-eyed. Marguerite and her sister Michelle sat on the sofa blitzed out on television, also pie-eyed. Marguerite never blitzed out on TV. Through my fog of lust and scotch, I was struck by the sight of her sitting there, eyes glued to Johnny Carson. She brought us up to despise the box. I felt a tremor of pity for her; she must be upset, for all her sister's spurious protection of her, I thought, to sink so low. She and Michelle were also somewhat slurred of speech, as we said goodnight and wound our way upstairs.

'You're so drunk you're cross-eyed,' Georgia giggled.

Mike snored in his crib. We got into our respective twin beds and thrashed around a little.

'This is silly,' Georgia said plaintively.

'It is,' I concurred. It was.

'Your bed or mine?'

'Yours shares a wall with Marguerite. As it were.'

In a second she was there beside me, astounded at herself. I lay utterly still, afraid she'd shriek and flee if I so much as twitched.

'It's so nice,' she said in soft wonder. Nothing has to happen.'

Sex wasn't mandatory, she meant. I shift on my rock again, remembering. The timing's so different, time stretches endlessly, coils and curls. The only clock is the orgasm, and that becomes a series of large and small waves that go on and on until starvation or dehydration or the need to pee tear you away, take you out of the water.

29

Not that we explored such depths, that night. It was too soon. We slept, coiled together, she in her nightgown, me in a velour robe with a zip down the front. In the morning we began to burn in those soft coils, and she tugged at my zip without success, as Mike began to stir and then to whimper.

'Shit. Your zip's stuck.'

It was, and it stayed stuck, and I had to go pick Mike up or he'd wake up the household, and I wasn't even entirely sorry, though my pulses raced and thudded. An instinct told me it was better postponed, and that instinct was to prove right.

3

I'm surprised to find it isn't raining. When I came home that September, it rained and rained, an angry wind tore the trees to shreds, red and yellow leaves everywhere in soggy bundles, like letters, I kept thinking, dully, like tearing up old letters or ancient illuminated manuscripts, for the sheer destructive hell of it.

I can feel Georgia making her way towards me and I'm not sure I want her here, yet. That other time I'd been through one round, as it were, and I was resting on the ropes when she came. Though I guess I went through another round with her there.

Have I done what I needed to do, here, alone? How do I know, when I don't know what it was I needed to do?

She can't see me here, round the front. I stand, blink, take in the totality of the awnings, less like gambler's shades here than like false eyelashes, like the false eyelashes Marguerite sent me to buy for her before the funeral. Even then I knew the false thrill of moral superiority that went through me at her request was evil. My eyelashes just happened to be naturally longer than hers.

How she fought me, over the convent! Though why I should think of that now, God knows. She confiscated the pamphlets from all those hungry Superior Mothers as if they were child-corrupting obscenities. I think she thought they were. She fought from the moment she began to believe I

31

was serious, and I have to give her credit, she appreciated my seriousness far sooner than Wall did. I announced my intentions to Wall when I was fifteen, and he obligingly cried and congratulated me and tried weakly, dazedly, to dissuade me, poor ignorant Protestant that he was.

But she knew what it meant, or at least some of it. She came in and found us and yelled at the top of her lungs, even more obligingly than Wall, providing my martyrdom. But beneath the shrill screams, so familiar from earliest childhood when they had nothing whatever to do with the convent, there was a core of will, and the core was steel. She was certain she knew that whatever my 'vocation' was, it lay outside any convent walls.

'After college,' she finally said, utterly stony and resolute. 'If you still want to go in after college, I won't stop you.'

'You couldn't then anyway,' I said, hating her. 'I'll be over twenty-one.'

But the battle was won by the world, the flesh, and the devil, which she represented. Even then, I knew she'd won. I knew I'd never get through four more years and still want what I wanted; but that didn't stop me wanting it.

She took it as a personal insult, which it was, a refusal to ply her trade, which it was. White-faced, she screeched that the nuns escaped reality. They had no worries over things like food and money and –

It never occurred to me to say that she didn't, either. Anyway, she would've slapped my face for it. Instead, I contented myself by asking sweetly:

'And what is reality?'

'The clothes you put on your back and the food you put in your mouth are reality,' she screamed back, without a second's hesitation. Condemning herself, I felt, with a shudder of satisfaction much like the one I experienced over the eyelashes, to the hell of materialism and small, female, visionless existence.

Only once did she shame me. Once she'd turned all her arsenal on me and had me choking over my own contradictions, admitting that yes, Sister Gabrial was a pious fraud who believed those of us who had acne had it as God's punishment and stigma for masturbating. There were legions of similar monstrosities. She listed a few. Like sprinkling talc in the bath so you wouldn't see your own body. Like being careful when you dressed so you wouldn't commit sins with yourself. (I had told her that one, and it came from my favourite nun.) Like –

But then she closed in for the kill. The nuns, she went on, were basically irrelevant. We weren't interested in being their daughters, not really. We just wanted to marry our fathers, the only way we knew.

Wall wasn't home that night, or she wouldn't have dared. Not then. She'd put her finger on something, all right, if not what she thought; on that, too. But there was more. We Catholic girls who took the names Theresa and Joan for Confirmation and modelled ourselves on these bigger, butchier saints, no Little Flowers for us, had gone one better than Athena, or tried to. We took for our godparents JFK and John XXIII. No women need apply for the job. We denied our mothers utterly, as they had – we felt – repudiated us.

I sit on the porch steps now, in Coldwick, contemplating that night, after our last exhaustive battle over the convent. She broke me that night, and not by yelling either. I ran upstairs to my room and flung myself on the bed, too shocked by her accusation to cry, just lay there tearless in the dark. Waiting. She came up a few minutes later, and came in without knocking.

'Oh, Helena,' she sat down on the bed and stroked my head, her hand trembling. There was a long pause. 'You're a much better person than I am,' she said then, hoarsely, despairingly, into the dark.

'No I'm not,' I said automatically, a child's denial of what cannot be true without a reversal of world order, or at least not *said*. Of course it was what I'd thought all along.

She kissed me and left without saying anything else, and as I sat up and began to move around again something was fundamentally altered, some moral umbilicus cut. I wasn't at

33

all better than she was and on some level I didn't reach too often, I now knew it. I was just different, and that was far more frightening.

Funny that, of all things, should bring tears to me now. I've wanted the tears; and it's Marguerite's ghost, not Wall's, who's the provider. Typical. She was right. I foresaw a lifetime of sitting in convent parlours, talking to Wall. My hand over my mouth, I sit as stricken as I lay stretched across my bed at the age of fifteen, or whatever age I was; the old bitch, my arch-enemy and demon, dragon lady, the converse litany to Our Lady's I'd recited so many times in my mind, she was *right*. How many times in the aftermath of Wall's death, secretly, had I wept over Cordelia and Lear, God's spies, sharing the juiciest titbits of the world's gossip, sharing the juiciest titbits of love? Where else can passion, incestuous or not, be free, except in a prison or a convent? And I'd decided on a monastery; even closer to Cordelia's prison than an ordinary convent would have been.

I stand up and survey the street where Wall fell, still confused and upset but also dried, somehow, by the combat with Marguerite in my mind. Marguerite fought you and you could fight her back without fear that she'd die on you. She might kill you but she wouldn't die and leave you remorseful and resourceless.

Okay. I have to give her her due, there's more truth in her accusations than I like to admit. But she also has to give me mine. Wall and I may have been wistful old friends of the flesh, more than we knew. But we were also, and knew it, old friends of the heart, venerable friends of the soul, even though near the end the friendship had shrunken and withered, along with both our hearts and souls. Neither of us had much spirit to bring to our kinship of spirit, at the end.

The end! We drank ourselves silly, that last time. He was morose and bitter and downcast in some fundamental way I couldn't comprehend or even confront. It frightened me too much. It terrified me, I ran from it throughout my visit home, afraid to find my own discouragement mirrored in his, and, simply, afraid of his.

He'd aged. I sat one night looking at the old family album chilled and staring. Wall's young face looked out, dark-eyed intent, questioning. Marguerite's face held, improved; Wall's caved in, as the years went on, and that last summer's version, not there in the pages, was the face of a disappointed man. The face of a dying man, I felt, even then, dimly, though I meant soul-death not cell-death. I meant his and I meant my own; my own soul was in a death-throes. How could I realise his, when it echoed my own? I couldn't. I ran.

That last intimate drinking bout was the least intimate we'd ever had. He ran, too; we were both on the run, that summer. When he'd turned out the lights and carried the empty ice bucket into the kitchen we stood for a second's embrace, and he whispered to me, 'Use your head and go to bed, daughter, use your head and go to bed,' over and over in a chant, hypnotic and incomprehensible. I simply obeyed.

I shiver. Why think of that now? There's Georgia, trudging around the side of the house, looking for me, white-faced, as if she expects me to fling myself down on the road in the path of an oncoming car, in imitation of him. How can we flatter the dead, sincerely, except by dying?

I flatter Wall by imitating his unglorified bi-location, enjoyed well before death. His life was split into two irreconcilable halves, too, and he couldn't bring them together any more than I can.

Maybe it's hereditary. I remember this front stretch of lawn as the sun sparkles in the grass, lighting on odd bits of mica and broken glass. There was no broken glass here when we were little. Grandpa saw to that. We hunted the turtles who pushed their way through the grass, strange creatures strayed from another time, patient and puzzling. I used to capture them and put them under the back porch, in boxes. They always ingeniously escaped, after which I re-captured them. Serpentine heads but plodding, indomitable movements, not the gliding hypnotic dance of the serpent.

Wall lived with two versions of himself. One was the businessman who commuted to work every day, walling himself into that system with its brassy rewards and its unrelenting demands. The other Wall wanted to teach at a university, read, write, commute no more.

The business world flattered and frightened him. It was success and therefore election. In the end he hedged his bets, unable to risk that success – or was it the election he couldn't risk? Was it the Calvinistic steel girder that underpinned him and crushed him in the end, with its dictum that prosperity was merely the worldly skin of divine favour, the cloak of salvation? He flew off on Friday to teach in Texas, taught Saturday, back Sunday, on Wall Street again, elected again, on Monday. He couldn't drop out of the system to the degree needed to nudge him from office to campus. He died the second week of compromise, alone, in his Texas hotel room.

It takes guts to buck the system. Poets are asked to drink themselves silly, jump off bridges, conk out forever in taxis, slice their wrists or land in looney bins, at the very least; that's the price they're expected to pay for sidestepping the canyons of Wall Street. Even college professors have to pay something for their defection. And the price is only the outward sign of an inward damnation. That was the religion of the country. Or my reading of it, like my reading of Wall's death as a straddling of opposites which leads to exhaustion. Whatever the truth was for him, my reading holds some significance for me.

Here comes Significance, or half of it, around the corner of the house. Georgia, here, on the turf of my memories. At least I've brought her here, I've accomplished that physical fact, even if I don't know quite what purpose it serves.

'Hi.'

'Hi.'

She kisses me quickly, quietly, on the lapel. Maybe it doesn't count, since her lips hit my clothes instead of me. It counts.

'Over there, Georgia, lived one Mrs Hall,' I indicate the neighbouring house on the right of us as we walk back towards the rear of the house.

'You don't say.'

'She had a mysterious son called Alan who never appeared.

36

She talked about him all the time. Alan Hall; I used to think of him as a sort of place, in the house, like the front hall, which was dark and mysterious. People in Coldwick hardly ever use their front doors, you see.'

'I see.'

'And over there lived Mrs Cowlick.'

'Oh, come on!'

'Well, something like that. She had a husband and a son who never spoke. She talked all the time and they sort of grunted. They were both called Sam.'

'Uh huh.'

'She used to have this funny occupation – she had this machine in her basement that floodlit eggs, sort of, as they came down the conveyor belt, and she graded the eggs according to the contents, which she saw under the light, or passed them, or something. Some she'd discard.'

'Sort of a chicken abortionist.'

'I didn't think of it that way, but I guess so.'

We're in the backyard again, between the Cowlicks' barn and Grandpa's, where he kept his truck. This spot used to smell of chickens, when the Cowlicks kept them. I can hear that low, muttering choir that used to wake me with a thrill of joy, reminding me I was waking up in Coldwick.

'Helena.'

'H'm?'

'I could use a drink. Does Coldwick boast a bar?'

She looks at me plaintively. I've walked around indulging myself, wallowing and wondering and leaving her to follow at ten paces, or whatever. No wonder she's thirsty.

'It doesn't boast of one, but it has one. It's spoken of in whispers,' I whisper, linking my arm through hers. Gestures of the convent, ambiguous touching on the threshold of sex, and no further.

'A den of iniquity,' she twinkles back as we crunch down the gravel towards the road, back round the front of the house. I'm not going to drag her back across the fields and, anyway, I don't want to go back myself.

'No upright Coldwickite would be caught dead in it.'

'Oh, good. I'm not in the mood for the upright dead.'

'No,' I cast a backward look over my shoulder. 'Neither am I'.

It's past noon, well past, and the sun is slipping down towards the Pennies. The air is colder. If this were England we'd have to think of hours and Last Orders Please and all that. If this were England I'd have to think of Mike and Sam and Jonathan – but it's not and I don't.

'It's not far,' I advise Georgia as we reach the car.

'Of course it's not far. This is Coldwick!'

It is beyond grasping, to sit like a grown-up, though still a passenger, and drive down the unaltered streets of your childhood. Not quite unaltered, of course, but essentially the same early American houses and the church.

'Grandpa painted *that* church,' I instruct Georgia. 'It's probably been painted since. But he painted it, one summer when I was here, I saw him right up on the steeple. I thought he was wonderful and brave, smiling up there. And I loved the church. It was so soft. So un-Catholic.'

'Snob. Roman Catholic chauvinist.'

'You bet. You can park here. That – is Coldwick's slum.' One corner, one house conspicuously battered and blistered, children hanging round the porch in dirty clothes. One corner's worth of barrio. Everything exists here, in a microcosm. Maybe that's what made it so ideal for a child. You could see an entire span of existence in miniature.

'This isn't a den. I don't believe in the iniquity.'

'Oh, you of little faith!'

But she's right. The interior's knotty pine, pleasant in an undramatic way. Perfumed with chopped chuck and ketchup and plastic, illuminated with Budweiser signs on the bar. The waitress blinks at us laconically as we order cheeseburgers and beers. The bartender blinks at her, laconically, as he gets the beers.

'Do they really think this is iniquity?'

'Oh, yes, they do. My grandfather used to stand on tiptoe to peer into the bars when we went to Atlantic City together, him and me and Grandma. They fascinated him. The dark, and the smell of liquor.'

'Liquor. It does sound −'

'Like liquor.'

Our beers come, and we lift our glasses to each other. Licker. The alcohol buzzes through my system, meets its own kind in my bloodstream, joyous reunion. Lick her. I look across at Georgia and she looks away.

'Isn't there anybody here you want to visit?'

'There is. I've been saving that. I'll get to that in a minute.'

Our cheeseburgers come. They must throw them into a microwave oven for a brief glance and then shove them into buns. But they taste good.

'You know what happened to people like us, who wanted to join the convent and didn't?'

'What do you mean, people like us?' She bristles. 'We're just us. And it's happening, whatever it is.'

'I mean −' I mean lesbians. But I'm afraid to say it. She knows.

'All right. Go on. But watch it!' she adds aggressively. 'Don't presume too much, just because −'

'Just because we stood in the shower this morning and −'

'Shhhh −'

'You imitating the shower?'

It seems a million years ago, but we did stand in the shower, soaping each other and laughing as the inevitable and doomed-to-frustration arousal set in, despite the long night behind us. Or because of the long night behind us. But now we're slowly gaining on the long night ahead of us. I toast that salient fact with a long swig of beer.

'We joined the women's movement twenty years later. And came out.'

'*You* did. I didn't.'

'A lot of us did. A lot of us who'd taken Theresa or Joan for Confirmation.'

'Or Catherine?'

'Catherine?'

'You know, Catherine of Siena, the one who slugged the Pope.'

'What?'

'In a verbal contest. Won.'

'Oh, that Catherine. Well, I guess there were some Catherines too. If you say so.'

'I wouldn't know.'

'Well, we all wanted to be nuns to be together.'

'Oh course we did. But why, pray tell, are we discussing this now, in Coldwick, when I'm dying to know who we're going to see this afternoon? They're not nuns, are they?'

'The next best thing.'

'Which is – you know what – according to you.'

'Oh for Christ's sake, say it.'

'Which is lesbians, according to you.'

'Congratulations.'

'Thanks.' She drinks, hastily.

'We wanted each other, our fathers, and to land a good one in the solar plexus to our mothers in one fell swoop. But we didn't.'

'Thank God.'

'We decided to ditch Agape and head for Eros instead. So we got married –'

'What, all of you?'

'Some of us. The dumb ones, if you like. I don't know. The ones who decided if they weren't going to be nuns they were going to be mothers. And then they found that wasn't Eros. So they – we – joined the women's movement and found both.'

'Eros and Agape.'

'Exactly.'

She looks sceptical, and perplexed. I agree with the scepticism. It's all much, much too neat. As for the perplexity, I realise, as my body foams and brims with beer, that my dialogue makes perfect sense, provided one realises that it's a dialogue with the past. I'm picking up our conversation on Glass Mountain, that's all. Maybe if I finish one of these conversations, one day, I can move on to a new one?

'We're going to visit my aunts.'

'Go on.'

'They're my grandmother's sisters – my great-aunts. They're identical twins.'

'Another beer?'

'Sure.'

The waitress walks off somnambulistically for the beers, the bartender gets them from his invisible jet behind the bar with the same fixed expression he's worn since we came in. That's the secret of Coldwick, maybe; sleep. So why did I come here to wake up?

'My aunts. Maybe I should just let you meet them and draw your own conclusions.'

'I want a little background.'

'Okay.'

The beers come. What can I tell her? It's an act of trust, taking her to meet them.

'It's an act of trust, taking you to meet them.'

'That sounds heavy.'

'They're identical twins, pushing sixty-five, now. They've dressed alike all their lives and they still do.'

'Christ!'

'Uh huh. And they've lived in the same house ever since they were born. It's a great house.'

'I'm glad to hear it.'

'And one of them – the younger, Judy – their names are Judy and Jody –'

'Wait a minute, I thought they were twins?'

'They are. Jody came out first, as it were. Actually she didn't. But Judy –'

'I might have known.'

'Let me tell it in order, okay? Judy's the softer one, the more – open. When she was in her early twenties she used to go out with a high school principal –'

'Aren't they usually men?'

'This one was a man.' I sip. 'My great-grandmother and her sister used to cry and create, as grandma said, every time she went out the door with him. So finally they prevailed upon her to give him up.'

'Sad.'

'Then a few years ago she took up with an antique dealer from New York, who was not a man.'

'Ah.'

'And Jody threatened suicide and I don't know what all. And the antique dealer, who had come here with another woman to live – '

'Who was probably none too pleased either.'

'– went back to New York.'

'And so your aunts are living happily ever after.'

'Sort of. Jody's had a mastectomy.'

'Uh oh.'

'I don't really know how they live. Shall we go?'

She picks up the tab, as usual. She's always held the purse strings, always had more money than me. It usually doesn't bother me. It's meant to be my role as some sort of romantic poet-character (much more character than poet, these days) to be indifferent to such things. But it bothers me now, as she hands me the paid bill, as she always does, to paste in my scrapbook, a variation on the carnet that makes me uneasy. I want possibilities, not just memories. And there's something else about the gesture; it's as if she's presenting me with a whole set of bills which some day, some way, will have to be paid all over again.

Some of my thoughts've got through to her, because she hesitates beside the car and pulls something out of her wallet.

'I don't know what made me think of this, back there,' she says, 'but look. I thought you might recognise it.'

It's a much-folded-over piece of paper with a poem written on it, a poem I wrote in high school, about a little black kid we saw in Woolworth's stealing a Hallowe'en mask, which he then presented to his kid brother, who was waiting for him outside the store. It wasn't much of a poem, and the recording of the event was objectionably sentimental, but I remember the welling-up of feeling I'd had, at the time, and the sense that there was a morality beyond morality, a higher and wider thing than any I had known.

> I cried to grow into a child,
> And understand
> How such a little
> Was all, for you,
> And that all, for someone else.

That was the end of it. Not much, but a lead, a lead I'd failed to follow up, the wrinkled paper bringing a whiff of that trail I'd felt on the scent of, then, so strongly; and a scent of her love, who'd kept it all those years.

'What's that,' I ask jealously, glimpsing another paper. 'Is there another poet in your life?'

'There is, as a matter of fact,' she's grinning, teasing. 'I'll tell you about her later.'

I can wait. It's clear from her look it's nothing to worry about. I give her back her paper, and we climb into the car.

'Right here and then just keep going.'

'That it?'

'That's it.'

'What is it?'

4

What is it! A great grey ghost of a building I'd almost forgotten, beside the house. But in its own way, it's far more interesting. Now, obviously nothing, it could have been anything.

'A cider mill.' The ramshackle barnlike structure faces imminent collapse. 'It used to be a cider mill. In great-grandpa's time. It doesn't run any more.'

'Too bad.'

'I suppose.'

'You sound English when you say that.'

'But of course, you Dixiecrat.'

'Honey lamb, I'll just turn on the old y'all and the old charm for your aunts.'

But she says it like 'haunts'.

'Nobody would ever suspect anybody with an accent like that of –'

'What?' Her eyes crackle.

'Anything.' I plant a kiss on her neck.

Jody and Judy toddle out to greet us. Jody walks hunched over one side, since her mastectomy I presume, but even before there was something shambling and uncertain about their movements, a sense of lostness, an inability to manage, together or apart, like married people ingrown as painfully as toenails, eventually crippling. They have all the cumbersomeness and hopeless drowning-in each other and drowning-out each other that married couples have, and more besides.

They're eyebrow-raisers to look at, no doubt. Georgia's eyebrows stay where they are; I knew I could trust her not to make them feel their strangeness any more than they already do. Two short, stumpy sixty-odd-year-old ladies, if ladies is what girls become when they don't turn into women. Something neutered about them, in their olive-green stretch pants and sweater sets, cardigans draped around their shoulders and fastened with little clips made of seashells, designed especially for the purpose of clamping cardigans around ladies' shoulders. Shells glued either side of the chains that cross their chests, and more shells pinned to their lapels, souvenirs of long-ago winter trips to Florida. They must've decided the clips were just the thing to give them maximum ventilation with the comforting pressure of soft wool on the shoulders; another way of hedging your bets! I shake my head to clear it; I'm becoming obsessed.

They've dressed alike all their lives. Twins from the cradle to the grave (I assume), they couldn't depart from each other's wills, now, sufficiently to decide against a pin or clip or even a coat of the sultry red nail-polish they wear and have worn since I can remember. Or does Jody will their style completely, and Judy follow suit?

I don't know. They look a little bit less alike now that Jody's been sick. She's shrunken and aged, while Judy's preserved and sprightly, by comparison.

'Looks like a gay young thing, don't she,' Jody says immediately of her sister, reading my mind and inducing a sharp pinch on my backside from Georgia.

Jude's the interchangeable nickname they pass back and forth between them. When they answer the phone, they just say 'Jude', and leave it to you to work out which one is actually speaking, or not to work it out. From embarrassment, or indifference, or both, most people don't bother.

Their arms are lukewarm and thin, as if the current passes through them, but weakly, from the heart. Whether the frailty is in that generator or in the tissue of connection, I don't know. That tentativeness, that hesitancy, was always

45

there. I think it's the sense of connectedness. Coldwick's short on connectedness. We stand in front of the porch, all our smiles thin, testing, strained. An hour in Coldwick, and even Georgia's face reflects the codings of the heart less readily.

'Would you like to stay out here?' Jody asks discouragingly, obviously hoping we won't. 'You city girls might like a chance to sit out on the porch.'

'I'd love Georgia to see the house,' I answer her with a grin, and get one back, a little reluctant, a little disbelieving, but a grin.

'Come on, then. Wonder if you'll remember it, Helena,' she half-frowns over her shoulder at me, leading the way with her strange sideways walk. 'Nothing's changed much.'

Nothing's changed, period. Suddenly I'm glad the pot of ferns was gone from the dining-room window in Wall's house, glad the whole solid thing had an altered look. A house isn't a mountain, and even mountains change underneath if not visibly. This house is a dead mountain, a petrified forest.

'Beautiful,' it's new to Georgia; she's looking in open admiration at the sanded-down antique furniture.

They can work, these two. I've seen them sanding and varnishing for hours at a stretch, days, covered with grit from the wood, tireless, doggedly bringing out the grain, the finish, the original pride of a thing. It's a gift they have, or had. There's a rocker by the huge old hearth with its hanging iron pot and its spinning wheel, all rubbed and polished by them, God knows how long ago. I used to think of this house as a treasure-trove, dark and mysterious, and it is, even now, but the treasure has a cold, material gleam, the mystery's obscure, the house sunken. Was it always like this? Great-grandma used to sit in the rocker like the presiding monarch, which she was. Great-grandpa's domain was the mill, the vegetable garden, as much of the world as their world admitted. Now it seems to admit none, and the kingdom's depleted, deserted, defunct.

Georgia's making small talk, tough as rolling a stone uphill, here. It always was, with the clocks ticking away, contradicting each other by seconds, split-seconds, till you wait for each one with a certain unconscious breathlessness, in the silences that inevitably fall. Loud clocks are a Coldwick tradition. They finish the sentences that trail into nothingness, their endless...marking the pauses. That's it, that's what life in Coldwick's about, that...multiplied a million times.

I cannot keep my mind on what they're saying. I never could. Sit down on a Coldwick chair and your mind immediately takes off.

'You're way off in a fog somewhere,' grandma used to complain, right here in this room. 'You never listen to people.'

She was right then, and she's still right, though she's the one way off in a fog somewhere, now.

'Helena, this is for you,' Judy's handing me grandma's heavy gold charm bracelet, willed, evidently, to me. Georgia comes over to admire it and her hand fastens for a second on my shoulder. She points, questioningly, at Jimmy's disc hanging with the other circular discs, one for each grandchild, and in answer I point to the death date on the disc along with the birth date. Jimmy was born and died before I met Georgia. Odd to think there was life before Georgia, and death, too.

There are two lockets on the bracelet. The mirror behind me reflects an identical Helena performing the same task as I spring one open. Inside there's a miniscule picture of grandma, and one of me. Tears sprinkle the face in the mirror.

'You should've written her more,' Judy says flatly, taking her words from Jody, I realise, like a ventriloquist's dummy. How I hate her, them, for being right.

'Don't be too hard on her,' Jody murmurs in a satisfied sort of voice.

'I didn't cope with my grandparents very well, after my father died,' I say steadily, looking down at the locket. 'They all died so fast, after him,' the three remaining in the next two years, making the erosion of the past complete, it seemed. I needed them to stick around, for me, not that I intended to stick around for them, but just to be there, three thousand miles away, to go on being till I'd recovered my wind enough to get along without them. They owed it to me to stick around, when they'd had the wit, the luck, the unconsummate gall to survive Wall in the first place.

'You didn't have your father very long,' Jody sighs deferentially. 'Like us.'

They bow their heads. I should've kept my mouth shut. Their hierarchy of grief coincides with mine, they're saying. Fathers are sacred. I didn't mean that. I meant that I was too cowardly to deal with any more loss, after his, I meant that I couldn't brace myself for the next onslaught, and the next. But you can't worm out of death by pretending it isn't happening. Ignore it all you like, it doesn't go away.

The second locket doesn't open. Hard as we try, it won't open.

'Wonder what's in it,' Jody twinkles. 'Picture of your grandma's secret beau.'

She's all right now that she's seen me in tears, quite set up.

'Time for lunch,' Judy says cheerfully a moment later. Georgia and I paste expressions of abject delight and profound hunger on our well-filled faces, and follow them into the dining-room.

'You know what they say,' Jody says cheerfully as Judy serves us, 'When one twin goes, the other follows.'

'Don't believe everything you hear,' Judy winks at us. This particular exchange is a favourite of theirs, two people whose repertoire of exchanges hasn't changed in years, you can tell by the way they bring it out and display it, along with the china and silver which Georgia's admiring.

'Don't git to use it much now,' Judy sighs.

'Never did use it much,' Jody says pragmatically, 'at the best of times.'

Silence. We eat. They've gone to town on homemade baked beans rich with syrup and bacon, cucumbers from the garden in sour cream, rare roast beef on a platter, arranged carefully in layers and folds, for all the world like labia, just

48

that brown and red combination. Georgia catches me looking at it and pokes me in the ribs.

'Would y'all pass me that handsome roast beef, Helena,' she asks politely.

'Roast me coming up,' I pass it.

'Huh, huh, sounded like she said "roast me",' Judy picks it up on cue. 'Huh, huh.'

'Hush, your hearing isn't what it should be,' Jody says irritably.

'My earring isn't what it should be,' Judy says doubtfully, hilariously, fingering her own labial earlobe and bringing us all back full circle. Georgia pitchforks a piece of roast beef onto her plate.

'Helena?'

'Thank you, Georgia, I'd love some,' I accept sweetly.

We eat, for our sins. We get through seconds. When we refuse thirds Judy takes it away, while Jody crackles about our birdlike appetites and girlish figures. Georgia's eyeballs are bulging.

'Helena,' Judy puts a brown paper bag down on the table in front of me. 'Your grandma left you this, too.'

'Her costume jewellery!' Sheer delight. Grandma not only liked whipped-cream ruffles and sugar-spun lace, she had a black magic side as well, and there it is in front of me. Snake bracelets and wicked licorice jet beads, all good enough to eat or at least to lick, and all strange enough to send you shooting up or shrinking down like Alice.

'Don't know why she bought all that trash,' Jody says querulously. 'She never wore it.'

Oh I know why! She bagged it like a pet, bound it like a notebook; a parallel life of a sort. One day she'd wake up and be the woman who wore armfuls of snakes and neckfuls of licorice. Only she never did. I'd be that woman instead; I am that woman.

But I don't say that because it might be taken up and misunderstood too. 'Table'll git all green from that junk.' Jody wants me to put it away, and I do.

'I'll get all green with envy,' Georgia says, all Southern. I select a seagreen earrings and necklace set for her as I put grandma's secret life back in its bag, or closet. It's just within the margins of what she'll wear.

'Bet you'll have to show your friend the mill,' Jody suggests.

'Of course,' we stand and follow Judy out the kitchen door, past great-grandpa's vegetable plot, still faithfully tended. He died when I was about seven, come to think of it, and I registered his disappearance, all right. He once gave me a gourd in a bottle as a present. He'd stuck the thing in when it was just a sprout, and it'd grown till the yellow sides of the gourd were pressed up against the glass, a *trompe l'oeil* that wasn't. He always said he wanted to live to see my first child, which would've made me some kind of ovarian prodigy; maybe this was his way of telling me to hurry up, or trying to perform the miracle by proxy. Marguerite and Wall gave it some funny looks when I brought it home.

'Whatever happened to great-grandpa's Caddy?' I ask Judy lazily.

'Nothing happened to it,' Jody says indignantly. 'Still bring it out every Sunday, run the motor, give it a bath.'

'Who does?' Judy asks mildly, winking at me.

'Well, you do, I s'pose. With my expert supervision.'

'You just like annoying the minister across the way, doing it on Sunday,' Judy finishes what is, obviously, another of their exchanges. 'Just like Dad did.'

'Is it in there now?' I still can't quite believe great-grandpa's Caddy's behind the peeling barn door across from the mill.

'Judy, go git the keys.'

'Got 'em. They're on the string here with the mill keys.' Judy's ringing the keys like bells. 'Thar she blows,' she throws open the door and thar she blows, all right, a great white whale of a car, all festooned and begrilled with metal mottoes and crusts and furbelows of the kind they used to frost Cadillacs with.

Georgia peers, delighted. 'What a beauty!'

'Ain't she just,' Jody chuckles. 'Sister, I've got me an idea,' she turns to Judy, mysteriously quaint or quaintly mysterious or, anyway, like something out of Louisa M. Alcott.

'Great minds run in the same direction, sister, I have the same one,' Judy declares and sets out across the grass to the house.

'We'll just wait here,' Jody says comfortably. 'You two may commence admiring the car.'

'Well, commence I will,' Georgia's voice is frail with laughter and I have to, *have* to kiss her behind the great hulking thing like a fallen-over refrigerator, with all that chrome. 'Remember Moby Dick,' she asks breathlessly, pushing me away, but not before my tongue's had a chance to do a quick rout of the inside of her mouth and land in its favourite spot, in her throat; its second favourite spot, I guess.

Do I remember Moby Dick! We stand for a second saluting Melville, the car, ourselves and Cornwall, where we stayed some three years ago, the perfect moment of all our moments stretched into a perfect weekend. It's our pattern of perfection, and we only look at it when things are measuring up to that standard. That's why she brought it up now, because this is suddenly, magically, that sort of day. A Cornwall day.

When you have so little time, a poor choice of restaurant or hotel can be a killer. Every little piece has to add up, to get your puzzle together in the requisite time, and that weekend it did. The weather smiled, the hotel smiled, the sea smiled. We made more love – and more of love – than we'd either ever known was possible, and the revelation left us humble, grateful, winded and warm.

Why did something stick in my mind but refuse to come to light, like a little shadow somewhere, another ball of sadness ravelled, refusing to unravel, travelling across the sky like a dark small sun? I swipe the car with a moistened finger like the barman did this morning with his sponge on the bar, and then shake my head and lose the little cloud. It couldn't really have been there. There were no clouds in Cornwall. It was our blueprint, and it was perfect.

'Moby Dick' was a joke told to us by the captain who'd driven us round the bay on his boat, selecting us from the passengers to instruct on the ways of the place and the more

51

hidden sights of it, then accompanying us to a pub for scrumpy.

' – This feller said to 'is friend, 'e said, "Y'know Moby Dick, that book?" And 'is friend 'e said, "No, I don't like dirty books."'

He let us digest that one.

'"It's not a dirty book," 'e said, the first feller, "it's all about whales." The second feller said, "Well, I don't think much of the Welsh either!"'

Judy chases across the grass with the car keys, of course, and something else, a sort of black briefcase. She waggles the keys at Georgia.

'Fancy takin' 'er out fer a spin?'

'Oh, yes!' Georgia's eyes gleam. She gets in and we clear off to let her back the thing out. I have a moment of terrible doubt; what if it won't run? But it runs, all right, and we all clamber in, in couples of course, Georgia and me in the front and them behind us.

'Now, jest go back the way you came. We've got a little surprise fer Helena,' Jody instructs, her voice laced with suppressed excitement.

Georgia swings round the corner and up past the Bar and Grill, Jody tsking in the back.

'That place,' she says rhetorically.

'Bad?' Georgia asks innocently.

'Terrible. Well you can see it's an eyesore. There's the church.' Her voice changes. 'Helena's grandad painted the church, she tell you?'

'Yes she did,' Georgia reassures her that I have my priorities right, neglecting to mention our visit to the Bar and Grill.

The Coldwick Methodist Church is white with sapphire blue windows, an ice-cream-cone steeple, the church where I once went to a service, too young to sin at six so it was all right, but I sinned anyway, in guilty disloyalty, liking it much better than boring old Mass. You sat up in the choirloft and crayoned pictures of the Good Shepherd and they had those big Crayola boxes with colours like Burnt Sienna and Cobalt in them as well as the usual range. But I knew it wasn't real, it was a sort of children's party, all washed out water-colour and pastel, despite the Burnt Sienna, compared to the cannibalistic urgency of the Mass with its three solemn bells at the Offertory, which had grown-ups dramatically thumping their chests and prostrating themselves. Our windows were purple and red and threw bloodstains down on the plain wood floor; in the Methodist church they were blue and threw make-believe skies on the ground which was make-believe, anyway, a rich sky-blue carpet; there was something decadent and shocking about a rug on the floor of a church. All in all I loved every moment of it and felt unutterably superior with spurious Catholic superiority.

Past the house, which Jody tsks over, quite rightly, for the awnings.

'Seems like your grandma should be sittin' out there yet, Helena,' she sighs. 'We'll go see her later, if you like.'

Georgia sends me an alarmed look.

'I'd love to see her grave,' I say dutifully. Grave-spotting is the sort of national sport of Coldwick. We drive up to the corner where the Antique Barn reigns, over which we all tsk in chorus and then Jody says:

'You can stop here, Georgia.'

'Here' is a little bank, new, shiny, fake-looking as a toy. Jody almost jumps out of the car.

'C'mon, girls,' she giggles, ushering us in.

Everyone knows her in the toy bank, and they all say Good Afternoon or Hello there, Miss Willis, Miss Willis, Lo Jude, Lo Jude. Judy carries on their dialogue with the smiling teller, a relic in sweater set and pearls; then the teller disappears and comes back with a safety deposit box.

'Don't look now but I think you're about to become an heiress, kid,' Georgia mumbles.

Jody gesticulates for us to come round to the desk she's being sat in front of.

'Yer grandma left you her ring,' Jody hands me the ornate diamond, the second ring with which grandma replaced her more spartan first in times of prosperity, in the way of American wives. 'Put it on, child.'

The whole bank watches as she slips it onto my right hand; on the left ring finger I wear Jonathan's wedding ring. Otherwise we'd be engaged. What are we now, I wonder; just going steady?

'Now, you can sign the cheques when they're done,' the teller beams.

'Cheques?' I ask Jody, stupidly obvious, like someone in an old film; I'm sure I've seen this old film, the one I'm appearing in now. Black and white, wasn't it? I definitely remember the teller.

'You're a lucky young lady,' the teller says and glides away again. Is she referring to the ring, the cheques, or congratulating me on snaring Jody?

'Yer grandma left you each five hundred bucks,' Jody says, mock-Western. 'She's puttin' it into travellers' cheques. Pshaw,' she claps a hand over her mouth. 'I fergot you were married.'

How can I blame her? So did I.

'It's all right,' I tell her, 'I use my own name.'

Not for me the annexation by name and title to a man. I went through with it and then recanted. The registrar leaned over his desk and said, 'Congratulations, Mrs Levi,' and I turned around to look for Jonathan's mother, idly wondering why the man was congratulating her. Then it dawned on me that it was my mistake. About six months later, it dawned on me that it really was my mistake. At least I took my name back. At least?

'Here we are,' the teller returns with five American Express billfolds. 'Your hand'll get tired.'

'Better not,' Georgia says, barely audible.

I smile at her. 'I can take you out to dinner.'

She nods.

Dinner! I can wine and dine her, bed her and board her. I can pay. Oh, grandma, my hand shakes as I sign these, almost afraid you'll rise up in your flannel nightie and forbid me to put your money to immoral purposes. Because that's exactly the sort of purpose I intend to put it to. That and a few carnets, and a few books. This is money for me, strictly

54

for me. This is my five hundred for this year, Virginia; next year will have to take care of itself.

I've got a room of my own. Funny, I almost feel a pang, remembering it as I write. It's not much of a room. It's underground, damp and splotched with spiderwebs; to me they're tapestries. It's just a basement room with whitewashed walls, but they remind me of the scrubbed stone walls of Mediterranean dwellings, and when I go down there I'm in another country, on holiday from the house that rears above me, and all it asks me to be. I'm not a wife and mother down there. At least I'm not a wife; mother I may be, mother doesn't violate my integrity the way wife does. I can't *be* that, and down in the basement I stop trying.

I whitewashed the room and furnished it and cleaned it with money inherited, sort of, from Wall. They can't control what you do with it, the donors, any more than a blood donor can tell the person who's received the donation how to live. Wall wouldn't approve of my running away from wifehood, entertaining lesbian lovers and lesbian fantasies, there below the stairs, trying to write, failing, at least having a private space to fail in.

It's kind of a nun's white cell, too, very spare and sparse. Where I wait. For a vision? The stigmata? Reverend Mother? I'm finished.

'You know, you should write down the numbers,' the teller says, and I nod vaguely and smile. We file out in single file, a little procession, while the whole toy bank nods, smiles, the clockwork bank works. As the glass door closes behind us I peek in to see if they've all gone quiet again in their bankerly poses; they have. Frozen solid. Actually they're still smiling, no doubt gossiping away about Jody and Judy and rumours of antique dealers last seen heading for New York. But the girls are respected in Coldwick. They looked after their folks, and that's what counts.

'What a day,' I feel lightheaded as we drive down past the house again. The third time and the spell's almost broken. It almost looks like just a house instead of a museum of memories.

'This calls for a celebration,' Georgia says firmly, and when we get to the Bar and Grill she defiantly parks and gets out, and all Judes' splutters can't dissuade her.

'You stay here with them,' she admonishes me. 'No one here knows me, I haven't got a reputation to protect.'

'Well, of course she's right about that,' Judy says reasonably as Georgia disappears into the B&G.

'All right for people who can leave town when they've had their fun,' Jody says icily.

I don't dare look at them. She saw the smirks on the faces in the bank as we pulled away, she knows what they're about, and she's not about to let Judy off without a moment or two of rubbing her nose in it.

'Sufficient unto the day is the trouble thereof,' Judy, remarkably, quotes.

'Humpf!'

Georgia returns. I peek into the brown paper bag that houses her 'package goods'. Champagne.

I kiss her ladylikely on the cheek. 'You dear thing.'

'Nice to have old friends,' Jody says approvingly from the back. 'Nice.'

I can only agree with her.

We get back and set out the champagne on the linen tablecloth we lunched on, under the chandelier with its glass gobs of grape and lime and lemon and orange stones I used to think were real diamonds. Yeller diamonds, great-grandpa told me once, were the best of all, then blue, then white.

'Wish they were,' Jody sighs, looking up, and I wish I could turn them, there and then; it seems such a simple miracle, and then they wouldn't have to sell the house, as they confide over the champagne they will have to, soon, and go live down South in a trailer.

All I can think is that a trailer'll be like a coffin on wheels. At least they'll have the Caddy like six white horses to pull it for them. The Caddy's all tucked away in the barn now till Sunday, when they wash it.

'We forgot the graveyard,' Jody says suddenly, censoriously. We're all shocked. That's what visiting the Bar and Grill, even by proxy, did to them, or for them; they forgot the graveyard, for the first time in their lives.

'Next time,' I tell her gently. It seems a promise that there'll be a next time, and there probably won't be; but she accepts it with a smile and a nod.

Once when I was eight, staying here for the summer, in Coldwick that is, grandma and grandpa drove to the graveyard for a sort of window-shopping tombstone tour. It was a miserable, wet day, and eight years old though I was, by the time we got back to the house I was ready to hang myself.

They could've provided me with a great tombstone, if I had.

'We'll have to go before too long,' Georgia begins what will obviously be a difficult leavetaking.

'Have to see the mill first,' Jody says briskly. 'Would you look there,' she says a moment later, incredulously, and gets up laboriously to hang at the window. 'You come on over here!'

Coldwick's pouring out of its doors, craning out of its windows, to see the show.

'What is it?' Georgia cranes her neck.

'Some dern fool stuck in the mud,' Judy answers her, and she looks at me, incredulous.

'That ain't no mud,' Jody breaks up now, hooting with mirth. 'That's the overflow from the old cesspool. They're buildin' a new one next year. Stuck in the shit,' she crumbles in half, laughing her head off.

We stand at the window gawking like a group of carol singers in a bizzare Christmas card. Jody's all malicious mirth, Judy all compassionate laughter, Georgia and me all incredulous hilarity that the whole town's turned out to watch the dern fool climb out of the shit.

There's a very loud sucking noise, that shit has real suction on those wheels, and then the dern fool's off down the road not looking back, I imagine, till he's a safe distance from Coldwick.

'Nearly got 'im,' Jody says with regret, like something out of *Arsenic and Old Lace*.

We polish off our champagne and then it's almost time to follow his example. It'll be just as hard to detach ourselves from them, if not accompanied by quite the same sound effects.

First we head up to the bathroom, Georgia stopping to look curiously into the bedrooms. And curiosities they certainly are.

First there's the Judes' own bedroom. Twin beds with identical ruffled spreads in dotted swiss, red on white, curtains to match at two windows. One long dressing-table made of a plank with dotted swiss skirt, divided in two with identical mirrors, pots and old-fashioned dresser sets; two lamps, one with china shepherd clutching the base, one with corresponding shepherdess.

'Guess which one's the shepherd,' Georgia mutters, and makes me wait outside while she has a pee. She's against demonstrations of affection in bathrooms, is Georgia, unless we happen to be standing under the same shower, and even then she tends to be rather businesslike.

But she's waiting for me when I emerge, and she pulls me into another bedroom and begins one of her long, lovely kisses, when something, suddenly, makes her stop.

'Helena, turn around.'

Behind me there are three old-fashioned dolls' carriages, each with a tumbling pile of dolls, china-headed all, with staring baby-blue eyes. It's a grotesque little audience, and she cuts the kiss short.

'Let's get out of here. This place is starting to give me the creeps.'

There's just the mill left to see; consequently, Jody fusses and frets and spins out the time as thinly as she can, delaying the last item on our agenda, keeping us stuck as she'd like to have kept the unfortunate man in the cesspool overflow. I remember they once showed me a whole little trunk filled with sample lipsticks in little metal tubes. Maybe they captured a lipstick salesman, or castrated a whole tribe of little metal men.

I sniff hungrily inside the collapsing mill. The odour of

apples and apple pulp is still there, it saturates the old boards, sagging and splintering as they are. It was quite a procedure, the bushels of apples crated up in trucks and dumped into one huge bin, then pulped, then squeezed, then clarified, then finally distilled into Willis' Apple Cider, clear and gold and tart, the taste of Hallowe'en. Non-alcoholic, of course, though I like to think great-grandpa fermented a private stock.

Judy locks the mill respectfully. That's the real shrine. The car was a peccadillo, but the mill housed the old man's soul. The smell of pipe tobacco clings to the boards as well as apples, and the mixture is about the most benevolent mixture of perfumes I can imagine.

They seem smaller and frailer, saying goodbye. They're the ones permanently stuck in the Coldwick shit, and the fact that it's their own shit doesn't seem to make much difference somehow, or maybe it makes it worse, I don't know. Judy surprises me with a sprinkle of tears like a spray of flowers against my cheek, and Jody's voice is gruff as she hugs me.

'How're your boys?' she remembers to ask at the last moment.

'Fine, fine,' I smile, suddenly tired, susceptible, weepy. I want to stay here and live in the past, with them. I want to be able to buy the house and – what? Give it to them, so they can go on living in the past? Maybe necessity will be the Mother General of invention, maybe these two nuns in their little outpost will find or make something new, when they have to pull up roots.

I suggest this to Georgia and she grins at me.

'You're sounding very un-morbid for such an old romantic.'

'How could I compete with Coldwick for morbidness? You have to be optimistic when you leave here.'

'You're right,' she steps on the gas. 'Let's leave here.'

So in an odd way I did get something, if not exactly what I came for, whatever that was. I got a lot, actually. A diamond ring and five hundred bucks, to say nothing of junk jewellery and a gold charm bracelet. A good notion where Wall got his gallows humour, that was the other thing; and a burst of optimism in the same defiant spirit, just because everything in Coldwick was so damned terrible.

'When I realised the whole damn town was getting its jollies watching that poor bastard's wheels turn in the shit,' Georgia slams the steering wheel with her hand, 'That was when I understood Coldwick.'

'Hey, pull over.'

'Are you kidding? Not till we get out of this damned town. Hey, wave goodbye to your house.'

I wave; but it's not my house, secretive there behind its awnings. I'm glad they put up awnings, the new people. It's right that it should be different. I'm even almost glad about the Antique Barn and I'm sure as hell glad about the bank.

Out down the lonely road out of Coldwick lined with those lonely trees.

5

'Why don't you put your head in my lap, honey?'
'Timber,' I fall over with a grateful clunk. All I can see, if I look, is the sky, but why would I look? My head's emerging from her thighs much as it must've emerged from Marguerite's those thirty-five years ago, not very far from here, in the county hospital. Is this being born again?

'Wish you had a skirt on.'

'Helena, that's sexist.'

'What do you mean, sexist?'

'I mean sexist. Come on, you're the one who's in the women's movement. Surely you know what it means.'

'Sometimes there's just sex,' I defend myself, 'Isn't there? Does that have to be sexist?'

'No. Not if it's really that. But none of this ferreting around under skirts.'

'Okay.' Rebuked, I lie with my head in her lap and enjoy the fact that I can see the sky, and only the sky. It's like being in it, as if the sky was made of the stuff a child conceives it as made of, or at least I did, a sort of tent-cloth, canvas but not quite, more give to it than that, more like the material of hammocks. I used to cry quietly to myself, as a child, on the long ride home from Coldwick. It felt like leaving home, not going home, but it doesn't now; maybe that's one long-lived myth laid to rest, at last? I am, at least, at rest. At last. No sooner thought than changed, and I find myself wanting her, in a burst of love and fear that she, too, is a myth of a later stage that must be exploded too, in its time, and that time not far from now; and in gratitude, mixed with the fear, for she's the one who was with me and made the gentle, hilarious explosion of the Coldwick myth possible.

'Darling?'

She glances down. 'What?'

'Could we, please, please, pull over? If it isn't too sexist to suggest –'

'I'll have to find a place.'

'What they call a lay-by, in England.'

'Now cut that out!'

But there's joy in her voice.

'You'll have to wait,' she says, with joy in that too, cruel mistress of mine. 'Tell me a story. Tell me about your grandmother.'

'Now?'

'Oh, I see, you've had enough of that for now,' she laughs. 'Now. You can light me a cigarette too – and maybe you should have one.'

'Okay.' I sit up, resigned to the wait, not only for an appropriate shoulder in the highway but for the moment her timing decrees. 'Cigarettes. Grandmothers. Godmothers, in the sense that they make you feel like god.'

'Yours, not mine,' she insists, with something almost hard in her voice, something like a warning.

'Okay. Mine. As you could see from the locket, she was a perfect grandmother. Little smiley face atop the perfect grandmotherly build – sort of like yours, only fatter.'

'Thank you, kid.'

'It is a sort of compliment. But a funny sort, I admit. All right. Big and soft and squishy. She used to wear long cotton nighties that smelt of talc and hair nets over that thin little frizz on her head that fell out when she got old. She wore a wig then. But by then she'd changed, after grandpa died she wasn't such a grandmother any more. She was a person.'

'You sound affronted.'

'Well –' I applauded, when she fell apart and then put

herself back together, someone new, someone capable of more autonomy than ever before in her life; or ever after. 'She reverted, eventually. That's when I should've come back and been around more. She had to come back to Coldwick because she couldn't afford her lush old folks' home any more. She hated it when she came back. There was nothing here for her.'

'I'm not surprised.'

'No. But back in the old days, when she lived for grandmothering –'

'When she lived for you.'

'Yes. I guess so. She was wonderful to me, anyway. I used to visit in the summer and we'd get all dolled up, as she called it, to visit great-grandma and great-grandpa and the Jodies. She queened it over them, because she was the one who'd got married and had a home of her own and all that. That's why they took it out on her when she had to come back without – all that.'

'Poor her.'

'Yes. Her name was Helen. I was named after her, with the "A" tacked on for the sake of the saint. When I was here in the summer, once I was over seven –'

'The age of reason.'

'Yes. Though that wasn't the thinking behind it, as far as I know. I was just considered old enough to travel with her. So we'd spend a week or so here and then we'd drive down to Asbury Park, just the two of us, and spend a week at the shore.'

'Sounds terrific.'

'It *was*.' And the funny part is, I'm duplicating it right now, and have been all along, with my women lovers, without even thinking of it. I went down to the shore with another woman, once, doing this same kind of attempted return to my own country by another way – but I won't think of that right now, I'll stash it away for later, to look at. 'We had the most wonderful time. It was – intimate.' She looks at me and laughs, and I laugh back. 'It was probably the most intimate intimacy of my childhood. We lived together and slept

63

together and hugged and pigged out on junk food and candy and walked along the boardwalk and saw a whole boat-load of trashy films. That was the best part of all.'

'Didn't you swim?'

'Nope. I swam every day when I went to the shore with my family. I loved it. But with her it was different. She said she didn't want the responsibility of my swimming, but I could have persuaded her. Only I didn't because to me it was the absolute height of decadence to sit in a dark movie house on a bright summer day and watch teen trash.'

'You puritan!'

'I know. I *know*. But it was so much fun. And we'd ride in the Ferris wheel, there's a huge one in Asbury Park, with little cars that go round and round, faster than any other ones but you feel safer because you're all fenced into the little car. I loved it. I love Ferris wheels.'

'You would.'

'She'd always say that because I'd been born there, and lived the first six months of my life there, that she loved me best.'

'Must've been nice for your brothers and sisters.'

'She didn't say it to them. Only to me. Anyway, my mother wanted them, so that was all right.'

'She didn't want you?'

'Of course not. I made her have to get married, and trimmed her sails, and all that. I was unexpected.'

'You still are, kid, you still are.'

'Georgia, can we please find a place to make love, please, soon?'

She swings into a nice off-the-road place meant for broken-down cars or something. There are nice trees around us, blocking the view from us and us from it.

Her arms circle me as mine do her. Impossible to say who takes who in whose arms. It's all arms, and taking. And giving. But my hunger is keenest and uppermost, right now, we both acknowledge in that tacit way that lovers do. I manage to release her breasts from their harness and take a nipple in my mouth, more for my own pleasure than hers.

64

She has little sensation in her breasts, she thinks because men tend to fall on them, tooth and nail, as it were. One frustrated man who wanted to provoke some reaction used to attack them with an ice cube in his mouth, she once told me, possibly hinting that I should do the same, but I ignored the hint and cast out the disturbing thought of what her male lovers did to her, as I cast it out now. As she, presumably, casts out her own speculations about Jonathan. I saw her wince when she first set eyes on my marital bed, though we were soon to lie on it together – I saw it helplessly, wishing I could defend her somehow from that pain, wanting to minimise it, succeeding at least in making her forget it.

As I forget it, and him, and everything else except this hunt for the sensations that seem a reward for this long day, as they seem a reward for this long life, and a consolation prize, if any there be, for its end, and a contradiction of endings and splittings and halfway houses. Abraham Lincoln's old phrase almost makes me laugh into her thigh, where I finally have my head without the constriction of clothes. A house divided against itself cannot stand; today's Epistle to the Americans. I argue with it, as I kneel and bend to my task, those thighs; isn't there such a thing as a house divided *for* itself? Must all division be against? Then I forget laughter and controversy, too, kneeling hunched against the dashboard to worship and receive this communion on my outstretched tongue, like the old days, not the new stuff with cupped palms, not the eucharist on your fingers, though I will use my fingers, I must be inside her with them as my tongue strokes the long silky folds of her labia, returns again and again to the glistening clitoral pearl set in all that coral.

She sings for me as I love her, the soft bluesy moan and then the long high chant that ends in a gasp and a cry. Then she relaxes against the seat and I stagger up to hold her, in her newborn weakness, against me.

'I think we should go on, in a minute,' I tell her softly as her hand slips questingly, questioningly, over my shirt.

'You do?'

'Yes. I can wait.' I can, and I feel she can wait; this would be

65

polite reciprocal sex and I don't want politeness; I have no doubt of our reciprocity.

'Are you sure?'

'Yes, darling, I'm sure.' I feel a small physical shock of disappointment as she reaches for a cigarette, but it's right, all the same, to let her build her desire for me according to her will, as I built mine.

We smoke, semi-entwined, and I feel the peace in her, the not having to love me back out of some sort of conjugal justice. I laugh, and she moves, asking, why?

'Just happy.'

She nods. 'Know where we're going now?'

'No'

'I do.'

I wait.

'I'm not gonna tell you,' she sings happily. 'I'm just gonna take you there. You'll know it when we get there, I promise you.'

'You promise me?'

'Hey, one thing I do want, before we go —'

'Anything.'

'I want to see that other piece of paper in your wallet.'

She laughs, dishevelled, delighted Georgia, laughs and rifles in her bag to produce both it and a comb. 'You read it then, while I make myself respectable.'

'It's too late, Georgia.'

'It's never too late,' she says calmly, and as she sets to work, curious as I am to read what's on the slip of paper, I want to make love to her again, or do I mean something cruder, something sexist, as she accused me before? Do I simply mean I want to have her, because she's slipping away from me, from my brief possession, coalescing once more with herself? What is that desire, that need to possess, impossible except foɪ those fractional moments? Those moments of arousal and orgasm when you've done what a murderer does, driven your lover right out of herself, and paradoxically done what the murderer can never do, driven her right into the centre of herself, blasted her through all the barriers? Letting her lose

66

her life and find it and all that in one –

> I dreamed you painted me
> As a seagull (you can't
> Paint) I was so
> Happy, so
> Happy when I saw myself,
>
> Gull-clean, light as a wishbone,
> Light as a balsawood plane, coat
> Like moonlight on a sheet, I
> Smiled. What seagulls
> Have meant to us, always!
>
> At convent school, you played Nora,
> You asked me to rehearsal,
> To see you. You stepped out
> White cardigan buttoned over
> Your starched uniform blouse,
> Over your arched cuneiform breasts,
>
> On the stage in the gym, you sobbed,
> Hysterical, I
> Am a seagull –
> Years later I sent you a clipping
> 'Some seagulls appear to be lesbian,
> Scientists say'.

I look at her over the paper. She's sitting quietly, watching me, old-new love on her face. We used to fight over who'd sit on the outside, when we sat in trains together, furthest from the window, because she got to watch the other one, without seeming to.

'Aren't you afraid someone might find this?'

She laughs softly. 'If I'm in an accident, you mean? Or picked up by the police? I don't always wear clean underwear either.'

I continue looking, and she sighs.

'I guess that's a risk I just take.' She shrugs a little, and I put my arm around her to read the rest:

Last month, in Cornwall
The seagulls yelled,
Chuckled like old crones,
From the chimney pots, from the shingles,

What if the four walls fell
What if the Apocalypse dawned
While the seagulls raved like ancient mariners
Old lunatic gulls chortled and called

What if the hotel walls exploded
While we lay there, wild under the stars
In our unequivocal bed,
Would we blink, darling, would we cringe,

Wink, draw our wide knees up
In a foetal pose? Would we die
If the unceremonious end came
Of all our small, ceremonial lies,
Would we die, darling, of shame?

She'd sent me an ivory seagull to wear on a chain when I
sent her the poem, but somehow I couldn't. I kept it and
looked at it, but in some stupid, childish way I couldn't put a
chain around the neck of that seagull, where the little loop
awaited it. I couldn't wear it. Too proud to domesticate? If
the essence of it is wild? But how, then, could it live, such a
love, in the domestic world?

Maybe if the walls fall,
If they ever do, we'll turn into seagulls,
Two schoolgirls, two seagulls,

Maybe if the walls fall
If they ever do, maybe
We'll lie there, quite still
In the starlight, and smile – still,
Two women, two wills.

'It's the only poem I've written in years,' I hand it back to
her, my hand shaking.

'It's a beautiful poem. And you should write more. More –
something. I don't know if poems,' she mumbles, vaguely, as
we pull out onto the road, the poem tucked back beside the

other one in her wallet.

'I know I should.' A house divided against itself cannot write, I want to say, idiotically. Anyway, who's to say it's true? Maybe paper is the only place it comes together, besides bed. Sheets of paper, sheets of linen.

Perversely, after the revelation of the poem and her preservation of it, on her person, precarious to her foothold in the straight world, the super-straight world of the Sabine Chemical brigade, I remember what the cloud was over the riotous light of Cornwall. It was the night we got stoned.

Georgia usually carries some noxious substance about her person, much as my husband usually harbours food somewhere on his. I'm not much shyer of food than he is, but considerably shyer of stimulants than Georgia is, other than alcohol. We had a conversation about it once in which I told her that my problem was that I wasn't certain I wanted to see the demons – or even the angels – in the trees. Her laugh rang back and with it the reply, 'The difference between us, kid, is that I need the drugs to see the trees.'

On this occasion we were walking a chilly Cornwall beach, holding hands, laughing and talking, breathlessly, because of the cold. There's something breathless about all our sojourns together, something dreamlike, fearful of some rude awakening. That may be why we drink so much, when we're together – to guard against that awakening.

She's relaxing, mellow, at the wheel. She smiles at me and I smile back, but my traitorous heart's not smiling, it's remembering that strange night. She brought out her joint and we smoked together, then she went into a rap about something I couldn't make out, something 'in her', she kept saying, and she hoped I wouldn't mind, and she was stoned and I hoped whatever it was wasn't what I thought –

But it was. It was the surfacing of an inhibition, the 'something in her' was something that meant she didn't want me in her, or on her, or otherwise offending against the block that had somehow arisen out of that poisonous smoke, against our making love. Against her making love to, or with, any woman. She let me kiss her and then she fell asleep and I

69

lay there feeling forlorn and silly, high on the grass and silly in my unwilling chastity. I feel like Gandhi, I thought, quite clearly, lying here next to a nubile young woman, like Gandhi performing one of his experiments. But this one is a failure because I want her and she's just saying no, that doesn't count.

In the morning the ban was lifted, the block was gone, and she laughed in my arms when I told her about my Gandhi notion, and we made love till noon to the rasping ridiculous serenade of the gulls.

'What are you thinking about,' she asks softly.

'Cornwall.' I lie and tell the truth at the same time. She smiles, of course, connecting with the lie instead of the truth, the joy of it and not the moment of – truth? In her stoned wisdom.

This particular moment of prevarication reminds me, of all things, of the second-to-last trip to Asbury Park I ever took with grandma. I was twelve, on the brink of teenagerhood, impatiently wanting to plummet myself into it, and grandma represented everything I was desperate to cast off, she was a grown-up child, she encapsulated childhood for me, in my intolerant mind. I had my period, not my first by a long shot, while I was with her, and for some reason I hid it from her as we made our way to our old haunts, the cinemas and the restaurants. I sat silent as she chattered, and she, not as insensitive as I wanted to believe, leaned her several chins on her hand one night at dinner and said:

'Helena, sometimes you look at me as if you hate me.'

I was shamed into being somewhat less churlish, and it was decided that the following summer, my thirteenth, would be our last visit together. By then it was all right. I was established in adolescence, or so I felt, beyond anybody's ability to cast me back into childhood, and I met her with the fondness of an old lover when the wounds are healed, the breach crossed and a new life embarked upon, so that the old one can be revisited without threat.

But I'm not outgrowing Georgia! Never, never, can I imagine or wish it. Maybe outgrowing the gratuitous quality of our relationship, which leaves it subject to any which wind or whim. She feels it as a force that sweeps her away from her usual laudable life, something reckless and irresistible which will one day blow itself out, like a hurricane. I see it as the laudable factor in both our lives, something which someday will blow the other, far more gratuitous factors, out the window, and leave us in peace.

Not the kids. They'll be there in this Never-Never land, somehow, and Jonathan won't really mind, somehow, and the blowing will take place without any serious damage, like the hurricanes we used to get when I was a child, that might knock a few trees down, might make the lights go out for a few hours if a tree fell across a wire, but didn't maim or seriously hurt anyone, or anything; at least not where I lived.

'Hey, are you falling asleep?'

'No, are you?'

'No, but I feel a little drowsy. Amuse me. Another way, this time,' she laughs. 'Shit, I want to go to bed.'

'So do I. Isn't that where we're going?'

'Not exactly. But there are beds there. If we want to, we can have one.'

'What do you mean, if? And remember, whatever it is, I'm paying.'

'Good!'

It is good. My hand goes to the pocket of my jeans where I've stuffed the folded-over American Express billfolds. It's as if the money is a talisman and a prompting from grandma, from beyond the grave, a prompting from the costume-jewellery side of her, the secret snake-bracelet side that didn't get out much while she was alive. As if she'd left me that, not just money. The money was only a means; she'd made me a woman of means, to an enchanted end.

'Hey, you know who I wish we could go and see right now?' She exhales Marlboro smoke and wistfulness.

'Ummm – as an antidote to Coldwick and my aunts?'

She giggles. 'Okay. You got it. Who's the least like them of anybody you can possibly think of? Someone we both know.'

'Obviously. Um – don't tell me.'

'I won't.'

71

Guessing games and secrets are the stuff of friendship. I take a long moment because I know, with a flood-tide of joy in my mind because the magic works, I know what she's thinking, rather, whom she's thinking of. It couldn't be clearer. She's getting worried, over there.

'Give up?'

'Are you kidding? Of course I don't give up. Someone from S&M.'

'That's easy. Who, from S&M?'

S&M, otherwise known as Stella Maris Academy, is the convent school where Georgia and I met, nicknamed with affectionate obscenity. Not that we knew what the nickname implied, at the time we applied it. It was simply ingenious and blasphemous and those two qualities were enough for us.

I clear my throat and her eyebrows meet expectantly. I have to laugh at those eyebrows, and she flushes slightly, then wriggles impatiently on the seat.

'C'mon. Stop distracting me. Who is it?'

'This reminds me of catechism. Who is God?'

'God is the Supreme Being who made all things and keeps them in existence. Well?'

'Why did God make you?'

'Helena Carnet, if you don't know, say so.'

'You mean you've forgotten why God made you? Tsk, tsk Georgia, no wonder you have problems.'

'Who said I had problems?' She jumps on the seat in exasperation, her voice going falsetto, her eyebrows truly witchy. 'Who says —'

I glance out of the window. Cars speed by us, people smiling or drowsing, listening to the radio or talking. Is anyone else doing catechism questions, I wonder. What are the odds, and do I enjoy the anomaly? If so, is that somehow corrupt? Fuck this scrupulous catechism, the paralytic catechism that stops you breathing because you might inhale a microbe and so commit a murder! I stare at her, still trading places as Grand Inquisitor.

'God made me to know, love, and serve Him in this world and to be happy with Him forever in the Next. Are you satisfied?'

'I could never figure out what the Next was,' I say calmly, lighting a cigarette. 'I was afraid to ask and reveal my ignorance, because I was supposed to be smart.'

'Boy, were you dumb. Next world, stupid.'

'I got it eventually. But by then it was too late. The Next never quite took on me, somehow.'

'I'm awfully sorry about that, darling, but do you think you could –'

'What are the four cardinal virtues and why are they called that?'

'Prudence, justice, fortitude and temperance, from the Latin "cardo" meaning hinge, because all other virtues hang on them.'

'Something like that.'

'What d'you mean, "something like that",' she screeches back, 'it's letter-perfect.'

'It had to be, remember? What are the seven gifts of the Holy Ghost? Only one more after this.'

'Wisdom, understanding, counsel, fortitude, knowledge, piety, and fear of the Lord.'

'What, Georgia,' I stub my cigarette out triumphantly, knowing she'll flub this one, it was obscure even then, 'are the twelve fruits of the Holy Ghost?'

'Whaddya mean, the twelve fruits of the H. G.? You made that up, you heretic.'

'Did not.'

'The Holy Ghost is a gift-giving but not a fruit-bearing bird.'

'Oh, yes, it is.'

'How do you know it's an It?'

'Georgia, you're getting off the point.'

'*I'm* getting off the point! I'm –' Red-faced, she leans out of the car to chuck two quarters into the toll collector.

'Charity peace patience benignity long-suffering mildness faith modesty continency and chastity.'

'That's ten.' She beams at me. 'What're the other two, Thomas Aquinas?'

73

'Um –'

'And what's the answer to my question? Huh? No more fruitcakes of the Holy Ghost. Come on.'

'In the immortal words of –'

'Cut the crap –'

'Our mutual friend –'

'Which mutual friend?'

'"I have a friend" –'

She turns to me, stopped in her mental tracks, as it were, and radiant. 'You do know, you did know, all along, that it was –'

We chorus, joyously:

'Hannah!'

'Do you know where she is?' I ask Georgia through a grin that seems continuous from my mouth to hers, at the delectable thought of Hannah.

'She's in New Jersey, as a matter of fact.'

'Doing what?'

'Whaddya think?'

'All right, all right, but who with?'

'Her husband. Got you that time, didn't I? Surprised?'

'Not really. Do you remember –'

She rubs her hands. Our favourite game, 'Do you remember' – well, our second favourite, I correct myself, brightening. At least we've found something that takes precedence over our convent school days, something that surpasses them! Christ, were they really that complete, that riveting, that fine? How can we know? Only that they've been so hard to beat, so hard to live down, so hard to find a life to compete with. England is a perfect place to live when you're suffering from chronic nostalgia. You've got plenty of company. Half the people there haven't recovered from their schooldays, in one sense or another. But maybe half the people everywhere haven't. And maybe the other half pretend.

'– the friend who was on the game –'

'The one who said –'

Again we chant it in chorus, chapter and verse:

74

'"I'd fuck a zebra if I got paid enough for it!"'
'When I told my mother that –'
'You told your mother that?'
'I told my mother everything. I tried to.'
'Christ, your poor mother! Sorry, sorry –'

Hannah had friends from another world. The real world, that is. We all came from the unreal world, into the unreal world of S&M. The unreal behind us was Catholic parish life, parochial schools, not as unreal as what was to come, that is, less spectacularly ghettoised. What made S&M so spectacularised, I suddenly realise, was its crusading vision of itself, and us, while it insistently wrapped us in mist and cotton wool, thick to choking, thicker than the fog on Glass Mountain that historical night. It operated a dual consolation system: one of protection and one of exposure. It had never been so clear to me before that the place you come from determines your experience of what you see. We would travel from the grey mansion that housed S&M into the Bowery in an ordinary Short Line bus, but we would sit together with Sister Michael, greeted by stares and smiles for the Good Sister and her charges. On the way home, inevitably, an old renegade Catholic reeking of booze would crawl up and ask if he could talk to her, and we'd hear her patient voice punctuating the confession, with 'Yes's' and 'I see's'. So maybe she was, in her way, less cut off than we; but I doubt it. You can't be a tourist to suffering, though you can be a reporter. I don't know, for sure, what the difference is, but I know we never made it beyond tourism. I think it's a difference of spirit. Bernie was a reporter, I suddenly think, taking advantage of Georgia's discomfiture over her remark about my poor mother, which she thinks hit some kind of sore spot. Maybe it did. Maybe I'm taking revenge by thinking of Bernie right now. Bernadette Reilly stood out from the rest of us. She was poorer, she was bolder, she was braver. When she went to the Bowery, she talked to the people there; she knew the language and the cues. She picked up on the fact that the volunteers of the Catholic Workers' Movement were not vowed to chastity, picked up on their jokes and innuendoes, in a way the rest of us didn't dare. She understood Hannah better than we did, too, and was her friend, regarded her as another person rather than as a – zebra.

'Hey, are you mad at me?'

'Not a bit. Remember Hannah's other friend?'

'The one who had an abortion with – what was it?'

Guiltily, I know she's giving it to me, out of reparation. 'A hot bath, and mustard.'

'That's right.'

Hannah's parents sent her to S&M so she might finish high school without getting pregnant. But it wasn't even that she was experienced in ways we didn't even believe in yet, as real possibilities. It was simpler than that. She lived in a world where those possibilities existed, unequivocally, and looked at us all from an amused, lofty height. We looked back at her in awe, but simultaneously we felt we were the ones on the lofty height, and she had just plain fallen.

'I wonder if she'd be surprised by us,' Georgia asks rhetorically, and we turn to each other for a delighted shaking of our two heads.

'She probably knew all along,' I sigh luxuriously. 'Before we did.'

'Probably. Like she knew everything else before we did.'

Hannah had integrity. Bernie had integrity. Both of them knew what they knew, didn't play games of ignorance to protect themselves, didn't cling to a mental virginity till it was thin as Kleenex, full of holes, and still consider it a trophy to be proud of.

'You once said Hannah and I looked like whores,' I inform Georgia. 'Remember?'

'I do not. How could I have said anything so inflammatory, especially about you?'

'How indeed, Georgia? In that hothouse.'

She sighs, on cue. 'It was, wasn't it? Remember the Tea Dances.'

'There was never any tea.'

'There was dried-out spaghetti in the refectory, by

76

candlelight.'

The refectory by candlelight was less a romantic dining-room than a sort of makeshift chapel, with its statues of saints and the ubiquitous Blessed Virgin Marys scattered around the windowsills and mantelpieces, next to the many mirrors. S&M, being built into an already existing, donated mansion, was as full of mirrors as Versailles, and rather than remove them, the Stella Marists propped statues with their plaster backs determinedly turned to their own reflections against them, their fronts turned to us, so that we might never see our own reflections undiluted, as it were, without the plaster cast of sanctity. Consequently we moved them around like chess pieces, these foot-high plaster figures in their lurid unlikely garments, with their closed, unknowable faces, moved aside so that we could see ourselves better. They did become familiar, and with familiarity came contempt and also affection. They became our babies, as well as our chessmen; one of us, leaning to examine a pimple or freckle or suspected cavity in the mirror, to adjust a brace or tuck a spitcurl, might casually pick up little brown-and-white Joseph with his sad, off-white lily and say 'Hold him for me a minute, will you?'

'Hello, Joe,' the second might venture, cradling the little man, then straighten him up to enquire, 'Getting much lately? Guess not.'

He'd be thoughtfully returned to his perch, a pet parrot for our anxiously blasphemous ventriloquisms, a doll, a child. Sacred Hearts, Infants of Prague, BVM's, Little Flowers, all came in for the same treatment.

'Where are you now, as if I didn't know?' Georgia asks.

'You know.'

'At a tea dance? You poor thing!' She cries, to remove some of the maudlin overlay settling on us, before it sticks.

'God no.'

But I am, now. Tea Dances were held with Catholic boys' schools, of course, on Sunday evenings, maybe in the hope that temporal proximity to Mass and Communion would render them less dangerous.

'Cardinal Wily Military Academy,' I mock. 'Remember them? In uniform? Tin soldiers?'

'I remember them. It seemed unfair that we couldn't wear our uniforms when they wore theirs. An unfair advantage.'

'You're interpolating, Georgia. We didn't think that, then. We thought we were the lucky ones, and they complained.'

'Interpolating? Who called me a peenalope?'

'I got Franco's nephew once.'

'You what?'

'He was gorgeous. Tall and dark, with creamy Spanish skin – gorgeous.'

'With a schoolful of daughters of rich, fascist Latin American landowners, they gave you Franco's nephew?'

'It was a lottery, remember?'

The boys arrived in coaches. They came into the formal front hall and lined up in front of the main formal staircase with its multiple landings, the staircase only Seniors were allowed to use, except for the tea dances. We came tripping down from the dormitories; even day students like Bernie and I came early, to share in the teeth-chattering leg-shaving last-minute panic of the dorms – like a chorus line from the Ziegfield Follies, down each side of the dual staircase, to join the double line of boys and be paired off with whichever one happened to land at your feet.

Only we were the rejected Ziegfield line, most of us, between fourteen and eighteen years of female development, stunted or precocious, jutting or flat, guiltily wise or foolishly innocent. You met your invariably unequally reticent or arrogant date, quickly learned his name, and stumbled on your spike heels towards the receiving line of nuns blocking the entrance to the gym. You introduced this stranger in turn to each of the ten or fifteen members of the S&M community lined up to meet you, and him, to smile at you in your misery, to confirm to themselves that they hadn't missed anything but misery, maybe. We certainly envied them, standing there exempt from it all, or at least I did.

'Those Latin American girls were quite something,' I mention with retrospective lasciviousness; and they were.

'White Castilian skin. Soft. Peach fuzz.'

'Forget it, kid. They had arranged marriages when they were born.'

'There are such things as married lesbians.'

'I've noticed.'

Miserably, I slunk away down the staircase into the gym where a Tea Dance was in progress, if you could call it progress. Music blared, and you felt emotions welling up that were usually dealt with in chapel, and in long passionate conversations on beds in the dorms, and in dreams. Not dealt with, in other words; so how did you deal with them, then?

We watched each other. I watched the Holy Head of the School (as opposed to the Secular Head) with her frizzy blonde hair on a uniformed shoulder, her glasses turning steamy, her watery blue eyes waterier than ever. The Holy Head was going to be a nun. We were all going to be nuns, except Hannah and Bernie and the lush, voluptuous, promised Latin Americans. So what were we doing there?

'Remember Salvadora?'

'Bulldoza.'

'Of Nicaragua. In charge of Nicaragua, proud owners of Nicaragua. I wonder what happened to her afterwards?'

'Nothing much, probably.'

'Probably. Nothing much ever did happen to her, as I remember, or to any of them. They were sort of − fixed. Very excitable on the outside, birds of paradise always rushing around talking a mile a minute in Spanish, but − fixed, on the inside. Immutable. Centuries of −'

'I hate to stop you in full flood, kid,' Georgia gives me a little clerical wink, the first in a long time; it must be the conversation. 'Salvadora wasn't, in fact, part of that fixed and frozen aristocracy.'

'What do you mean? She −'

'Her family, the Bulldozas, were *nouveau riche*. She was looked down upon by the rest of them.'

'I thought that was because she was flat-chested and boyish.'

'That was merely a symptom. It takes centuries of breeding to produce those huge, creamy tits the rest of them had. Her family were arrivistes.'

'Among other things. Really, Georgia!'

'All of them were that; only not on quite such a large scale. That's why she paid someone else, a Gringo, to make her bed, till the nuns found out. Remember? None of the other Latin Americans would have done that.'

'*Noblesse oblige.*'

'Exactly. But not for her. She really lost face over that.'

'And after they found out, Sister Michael would stand over her every morning while she made it.'

'Poor kid, I always felt sort of sorry for her. She felt so humiliated by it, you could tell. Not the surveillance, the work.'

'You're a good sort of snob, Georgia. Sometimes.'

She snorts. 'So what about Franco's nephew, then?'

I groan. 'Aren't we almost there? I need a drink if I'm going to talk about him.'

'No, do it sober. C'mon. We've got another hour at least.'

'Where the hell are we going?' But I want it to be a surprise, and I have a feeling that if I think very hard, I'll realise I know. 'Okay. He was, as I said, gorgeous, especially in the skin department, and as you may remember, I was a mess in that department. Maybe that was why you thought I looked like a whore – the pox.'

She looks over, pats my thigh. 'Of course it wasn't that. I don't remember that – you'll have to remind me. After Franco's nephew.'

'All right. So I didn't exactly want his body, but I coveted his skin, if you see the difference. He took one look at me and obviously cursed his luck. Then he smiled gallantly and we settled in to argue politics all evening.'

She groans. 'Is that what you did with him?'

'I didn't know what else to do with him. I had nothing else to do with him, for Christ's sake! Thank God he was Franco's nephew, or I wouldn't have known what to do with him!'

'Cop-out.'

'Yes, it was a cop-out. You're quite right. He, meanwhile, saw Hannah –'

'They all saw Hannah.'

'And asked me about her. That was the only thing we talked about besides politics – Hannah. The next time they came to a Tea Dance, he managed to worm his way up to her in the chorus line, and that was that.'

'I remember; Sister Gabriel found her in the clock with him.'

'That's right.'

Hannah was ingenious. The huge grandfather clock in the front hall had a hollow mahogany case, like an upright coffin. The macabre nature of it didn't put her off for a moment, and Gabriel, the Mathematics Mistress and Demoness, as far as I was concerned – they amounted to the same thing, mystically and mathematically – found them, no doubt exercising some ingenuity of her own to do so.

'She must've had a pretty dirty mind to look in there,' Georgia comments.

'She had a filthy mind. She thought pimples came from masturbation.'

'Didn't they?'

'Fuck off. Masturbation could've prevented them, I bet. I wouldn't know,' I admit, regretfully. 'God, how I loathed that woman!'

'The feeling, I recall, was mutual.'

'Oh, it was. She threw me out of her class every day for one solid week because I refused to promise to say three Hail Marys a day for an increase of faith. I was an atheist at the time, so how could I?'

'You could've.'

'Of course. But I was reading Joyce.'

'Oh Christ, I remember that. You almost got expelled for *Ulysses*.'

'That's right. By Simeon.'

We sit wrapped round by the old cocoon recalled. Simeon and Michael were a couple, much as Georgia and I were.

81

S&M abounded in couples. Simeon was the practical head of the school, with Reverend Mother above her, who led the community and only occasionally involved herself in school discipline.

'Simeon called me to her office,' these are our well-loved fairy tales, and like children we delight in repetition, and we correct each other for any abridgement or inaccuracy. 'It was late afternoon, murky in her office –'

'It was always murky in her office.'

It was. The office was large-ish, with a mirror above a mantlepiece behind her desk, of course. No nun could sit facing a mirror, not even with two BVM's stuck in front of it. A chair sat ominously alongside the desk for her victim to sit in; only one chair. Interviews in her office were invariably single and singular.

She had my big red copy of *Ulysses* on her desk. Actually it belonged to some Protestant neighbours I babysat for, whose heathen cupboards, bookshelves and bedside tables I ransacked to discover such revelatory material as contraceptive foam and *Ulysses*. If I'd told her all that, she might've let me off, with a stern warning not to babysit for anyone who didn't have all the children they could possibly have.

I didn't tell her. She and I were at loggerheads, essentially, I suspect, because we tussled over Michael, with whom I was in love, who was married to Simeon, not much less than to Christ; more, in my eyes. Simeon was tall, severely slender, like a Gothic spire from behind in her peaked habit, and Michael was short and rounded, so they made a complementarily incongruous couple. Michael was athletic and butch, but emotional. Simeon was slothful, scientific and feminine.

'This is the filthiest thing I've ever read,' she said as I sat down.

I looked at her with interest. The window in front of me showed a patch of grey sky and greygreen grass; I looked at it, too, with interest, and at the high chapel windows on the side of the building, stained-glass windows I could just see, vertiginously set in the grey stucco of the house. I detected something I couldn't define, but suspected, in her statement. Something dishonest.

'The last thirty pages, I mean,' she said definitely, and thumped the book. Her hands were long and slender and cold. Michael's were stumpy and white and clammy-looking.

I looked at her with even more interest. I couldn't understand or even follow *Ulysses* very well. It fascinated and impressed me. The one part I could follow, and loved wholeheartedly, within my capacity to do so, was Molly Bloom's monologue. I didn't believe she could believe what she'd said, yet I couldn't challenge her.

'You've read your way out of the church, clearly,' she continued. 'And if you're not careful, you'll read yourself out of the school.'

I knew her priorities were peculiar, even then.

I was dismissed, under injunction to go and read no more, except Joyce Kilmer, I suppose, or C. S. Lewis, or one of the many Catholic writers we were advised to love. I could always fall back on my beloved Eliot, whom I'd discovered under Michael's tutelage.

Michael taught English. My relationship with her, I muse, sitting there next to Georgia, feeling sleepy again, was much like my relationship with Wall. There were certainly sexual overtones, undertones and vibrations, but there was strong certain friendship of the heart and soul — and mind, in this case — above and beyond, or at least threaded through, all that. She was the best and the last of my personal Superior Mothers. It took me years to get over her loss, if I have.

I sigh.

'You're thinking about Michael, aren't you?' Georgia says softly. Her hand lands on mine for a second. Then she giggles. 'Remember how she introduced us?'

'Do I remember!'

But this is her tale to tell, and after the next tollbooth she does.

'I'd just arrived, and I was putting away my clothes in those awful, narrow dormitory drawers, wondering how I'd ever fit them all – '

'Your nightgowns – '

'When in walked little butterball Michael.'

'Deceptive little butterball Michael.'

'Right. She watched me struggle for a while, smiling to herself sadistically, you know that smile they all had, the S&M's.'

'I know. The opposite of that was that martyred look Gabriel used to get when I walked into the room – or the time Hannah walked in with dyed red hair and she looked and then burst into tears.'

'That's the look. Then she said something, I forget what –'

'You forget?'

'I forget. Anyway we started talking. We talked and talked – you know what she was like to talk to.'

'I do!' God's spies again, this time in Michael's little crowded office as second-in-command to Simeon, totally unmurky, without chairs of any description. She never, ever sat, except on those buses, and once in class on a day when all the nuns had the runs. Otherwise, she stood. The two of us stood in her teeming cubbyhole of an office and talked, and talked hours away, about God and us and literature and the world and who knows what? It was wonderful. It was love.

'And at some point she said, "There's someone you must look for, tomorrow. I just know you'll love her".'

'What insight.'

'Insight, hell. One good tongue deserves another, that's what she figured.'

Our hands squeeze and we drive on in silence, with the other cars, in the semi-darkness, like schools of fish on both sides of the highway, headed imperviously in our different directions. My mind wanders, not far, to Bernie, just as she says,

'What's this about whores then?'

6

'We were all in the Junior classroom,' I remind her, seeing us, an odd foursome, 'Bernie and Hannah, and you and me.'

'Mixed doubles.'

'Mixed?'

'Hannah and me straight, you and Bernie –'

'Yes, Georgia. Anyway. We were talking about looks. About how Bernie looked Irish, and you –'

'That's not all we had in common.'

'Even then?'

'Even then, kid. Even then. But go on.'

She's flattering me to make up for her 'straight' remark; I smile to show her I've understood.

'And then you and Bernie looked at Hannah and me, and you said we looked the same, too – like you-know-whats.'

'Shit, is that what I said? Shame on me.'

'Well you could hardly have come out and said it, not then.'

'True.' She nods. 'What did you say?'

'I didn't know whether to be flattered or hurt – you know how stupid we were then. I honestly thought it might be a compliment.'

'It probably was,' she agrees, sadly.

'I know. But Hannah, who knew better, just said very quietly, "Oh, no, I don't see what you see in her at all. I think

85

she has a good face.'"

'Put me in my place.'

'She always did. Put all of us in our places, I mean.' Bernie and Hannah, Georgia and me.

Bernie kept in touch with me when all the rest faded, when I faded from them. After our intense, zealous, half-pious, half-Sapphic all-passionate friendships, we abandoned each other to the world, well, to our separate colleges, anyway. Georgia went with a group from S&M to Ladylike, otherwise known as Ladylight, of course, the Stella Marist College. I didn't, and neither did Bernie.

Bernie shone at S&M like a good deed in a naughty world, though through the perverted looking-glasses of that world we thought it was the other way round. She was always in trouble, and always for nothing. For being Bernie, for bucking the system of two-way consolations, of flowery self-delusion.

Not that she suspected the sexual foundation of our world. She was as ignorant of sex as the rest of us, though she wore her ignorance more lightly. She was unafraid of work and unafraid to work. Most of us sported, some affected, both fears.

Bernie had the good horse sense to laugh at things the rest of us stood in awe of, outdated absurdities like Cachets. At Cachets you received your monthly report card, that was all; but what a festival of repressed erotica!

'Georgia,' I yawn at her. 'Cachets.'

She yawns back. 'Bless you.'

We stood in semicircles around Reverend Mother, each class. There were one hundred of us in the entire school, made up of four grades of High School plus a small Junior Department, composed mostly of Latin Americans. Each class held twenty or under.

The twenty semicircled in alphabetical order, a militarist feat that had to be drilled for hours beforehand. Then the semicircle curtsied. Right leg behind left, both legs bent. Then you went up one by one, alphabetically, in your horrible Sunday uniforms that looked like a cross between a nurses' uniform and a waitresses', all white, spongy stuff, and curtsied again, individually, before Reverend Mother, who handed you your card, with a pithy little comment you were unlikely to forget, bad or good.

Then you curtsied again, and took your place, blindly, in the semicircle. When your class was finished, you all curtsied again and filed back, smirking, to sit down while the next class suffered.

Bernie smirked, anyway. Bernie smirked at it all, and she was right. She smirked at the chapel rank, the long lines of girls filing like soldiers in veils into the deep, cool darkness of the chapel, led by the Holy and Secular heads of the school. She giggled at the ceremony of holy water at the chapel door, when the girl on the right touched her fingertip into the fount and then held her hand out to her partner across the aisle, who slid her fingertips along her partner's proffered wet palm. Then the two made the sign of the cross simultaneously.

Georgia and I hardly ever paired up to walk into chapel together. That bit with the holy water was just too much of a risk, in our delicate condition. Ignorance was a sheet of thin ice we walked, and if we ever fell in, the water would be cold, far colder than the chapel, and much deeper.

Except that when we did fall in, the water was mild and balmy and caressive. I look across at her, caressively, and she looks sideways, for a second.

'Go back to sleep, kid.'

I go back to dream, if not to sleep. Coming out of the chapel was even trickier. You filed out the side aisles, round the front of the altar, backed up in front of the altar, alongside the front pews, and genuflected in fours. It always made me nervous, that trick.

'We all should've been ballet dancers, after that,' I murmur to Georgia, who smiles indulgently.

'Or traffic cops. Or Green Berets.'

Bernie laughed at it all and her continuous prayer was, Bring on the world! While the rest of us — except for Hannah, and maybe the Latin Americans who had prearranged marriages to look forward to – dreaded the world and clung to our rituals, our cloister, our ignorance, for dear half-life.

'Discipline,' I mutter, 'that's what it was.'

'Of course it was, Helena. Of course it was.'

'Stop humouring me.'

She grins.

Discipline. We were all much more disciplined than we ever knew. The physical drills were nothing compared to the mental ones. Custody of the eyes was nothing compared to custody of the mind. Don't notice, don't know. We didn't know. Determinedly, we didn't know. Catholicism is good for that, for learning how not to know. We'd all had plenty of training.

S&M was so filled with Sapphic emotion, with volatile female passion, it would ignite at so much as a syllable of any explicit word like 'lesbian'. It would lift off, like a helium balloon, and float away to the impossible planet where such beings lived, if such beings existed, to the brave new world where we could all come into existence and be what we weren't.

'Remember Mar,' I resurrect myself to remind Georgia, and she frowns.

Mar was the One who could be mentioned, the One from another world, the scapegoat. Without her, we couldn't have persisted in our wilful ignorance. We had to appoint an official lesbian against whom we would all compare beautifully. Then we could take a deep breath and relax, in our safely grounded balloon.

Mar had a black DA haircut. Her parents gave her a Honda for Christmas and she roared back to school on it, Senior year. Oh, she was One, all right! She kept scotch in her Listerene bottle and gin in her perfume bottle. Certainly not perfume.

That's what they were like, belted black trenchcoat and all. Every detail had to be word-perfect, just like the catechism, and if it wasn't, you weren't. It was enough if your trenchcoat didn't have a belt, if your hair was shoulder-length, if you wore it in a pageboy, if you didn't drink. If you didn't have a Honda! Of course. To qualify as One, you had to at least hanker after a Honda.

Nothing was further from my hankering. Mar was a vaccine in our midst. Even Bernie partook and was immune, for a time at least. Then twenty years later, married, a mother, I wrote to her in desperation – she was still in touch. She was my contact with the past, with myself as I was, as I wanted to be again.

I stir myself out of these particular reflections. I want to block them like the blocked mirrors at S&M, with something or someone. The last time I thought about Bernie, before today, I was on a train, in England facing the wrong way. I found an old letter of hers in my bag and read it; and left the bag, the letter, and everything else it contained, on the train. Including a copy of Freud's *Psychopathology of Everyday Life*, which I was reading at the time. I guess I believed it.

'There are two kinds of people in the world,' I inform Georgia, sleepily.

'Helena Carnet if you say straight and gay I'll scream a long, drawn-out Southern scream.'

'I wasn't gonna. Don't be so paranoid. I was going to say – well, it only works in Europe.'

'So there are two kinds of people in Europe. And how many kinds are there everywhere else?'

'It's to do with trains. American trains have seats going all one way. Facing forward. In England you can either face forward or backwards. Some people automatically sit down facing forwards, some facing backwards.'

'You can do that in some American trains, too.'

'There, you see?'

'I see.' Her hand caresses the top of my head for a moment, in a gesture at once sisterly, maternal and sexual. 'Well, we know which kind you are.'

I blank down again, this time to sleep. Her hand washing across my head like that has drawn a curtain over the present and projected onto that curtain a magic lantern show of my time with Bernie. It's that potent combination of sentiments

89

and sensations, the loves of a sister, a mother, a lover, braided into a fibre tough and tender, unlike any other. It doesn't feel like the past, however, any more than it did as I sat on the rock in Coldwick. It's a more complicated tense, past imperfect perhaps; memory works in half-generations and half-jumps and an unfinished continuum, no less than grammar. Religious language is always Perfect or even Pluperfect. Bernie came to me in a religious guise, came like a missionary across the sea. The first time I slept with her, I felt that hand on my head, like Georgia's just now, with an additional dimension in the caress, a priestly element, as if she were delivering a blessing.

The core of our confusion was right there in that gesture of blessing or transformation. Because I wouldn't in the end, be transformed to her satisfaction or my own, I wouldn't succeed, or, finally, want to succeed in sweeping whole facets of myself, bright or dark, under the carpet in order to present the pure face acceptable to her. Not that I knew that, when I first felt that hand on my head. I felt Saved.

Bernie came winging over from the U.S. to bring me out of the closet, into the light. I put myself in her (episcopal) hands, and she graciously picked me up and put me on a pedestal, from which there was no way off but down.

Maybe it's wrong. I snuggle against Georgia's shoulder, trying to dismiss what I can't make sense of, as always, and finding it won't be dismissed. So I shift back against the seat and let Bernie appear, as the apparition she was, in the beginning.

Bernie had nothing of the mere nun in her. She could only have been an Abbess or, better yet, a simple parish priest, with her practical good sense and her willingness to wink at convention. I can see her dishing out contraceptives with beautiful, watertight rationalisations or prescribing sex of whatever sort was required.

So who stood on the pedestal, I wonder uncomfortably. She fought S&M every inch of the way, while I alternately fought alongside her and went over to the enemy, never certain for long where I stood, bi-located even then.

I prop my chin on an elbow, look out the window. Town Hall, Masonic Lodge. Mercurial digits flash somewhere in the dusk, announce six-ten p.m. So in England, they're oblivious.

Are there stars? Who cares? If I do, isn't that easy and cheap. Bernie'd make short shrift of it. Shrift, as in confession. She'd have the truth. Seven summers ago, I attempted this same journey with her, and failed. Then, too, I came back alone, telling no one, trying to sneak up on the place before it could put on the mask it presented to me on my official visits. I wanted those barriers down, that gaze deflected, and Bernie, who spent her whole life knocking down barriers, seemed ideal company.

She understood what I was after. (She amplified it, interpreted it, gave it political undertones and structure; she validated it, and me.) She offered that which every terrified rebel most desires: an alternative orthodoxy. She had offered me that at seventeen, and she offered it again at twenty-seven. (Hers was the orthodoxy of revolution.) It had assuaged the pangs of faltering faith in the days of S&M. It assuaged the pangs of faltering faith again, when the consolations of marriage and motherhood were no more convincing than those of religion.

She brought me home to the movement, where the Joans, Theresas and the occasional Catherine waited to welcome and reminisce. It sounds as if we spent all our time intensively re-educating ourselves but it wasn't like that at all. If it had been, I'd have panicked much faster than I did. It was ecstatic except that the static won out over the ecstasy.

Georgia'd like that. Why haven't I told her more about Bernie? She hasn't asked. She knew the outlines, and that was enough.

We indulged a blissful femininity together. No sense of urgency or panic or making myself acceptable ever visited me when I dressed with Bernie. We gave our narcissism free rein, I suppose, and found that, freed, it receded and gave us new space when we left the boudoir and swept outside onto the street.

For me the area of feminine attractions, or lack of them, was a minefield. It was Marguerite's territory, into which I had always strayed as an invader, and a poor specimen at that. Bernie changed that; to style, not to stifle, was part of our dialogue. It's the tongue that's mightier than the sword, we might have said; it was what we enacted, in endless words and acts of love.

We spent three weeks together, that summer I came over here in secret. We went to the Jersey shore, another childhood landmark. I knew that the sound and smell (or lustre) of it (whatever it might lack of Mediterranean sheen), would bring me a real, live summer. It felt to me as if I hadn't had one in years. I'd had vacations with Jonathan, wonderful ones, enjoyed them, but hankered, guiltily, as always, for something else; something less glamorous, perhaps, but more native to me. American summer was a state of mind I wanted to reclaim. It was a symptom of simple, spoilt-child malcontentedness, I thought at my most self-damning. I should be content. There were pockets of contentment. But how do you spend your life in a pocket?

Instead of flirting and snuggling and scrapping on the long ride south, Bernie and I discussed the existence of evil. I believed in it. She didn't.

Maybe she does now. We found the house she'd rented, our wanderings as circuitous as our arguments in the little seaside town. Holden's Landing, it was called, reminding us of S&M where J. D. Salinger had been a *cause célèbre* in our second year, the year of my rebellion. We'd practically memorised the book, we quoted it and acted it out and, probably, made everyone heartily sick of it.

Holden's Landing. Our house was pink, and pink fibreglass insulation burst from the loft like sunset clouds. We had the sea to wash in and plenty of gin and tonic to drink. The pink house had a pink porch with rocking chairs and a glider. We sat in the glider like teenagers and laughed, happily caged in our screened-in porch.

Shades of grandma. *We* sat on the porch of the house in Coldwick, summer after summer, before we headed south to another section of the shore, with other drinks in our hot hands, root beer floats thick with ice cream.

Bernie and I came home from the beach, baked and drained and tired, roaringly hungry after the waves and the sun. We cooked and ate and drank, and drank. Flies bumbled up against the screen and buzzed away, tiger lilies lipped the clapboard steps.

Silences grew and pressed at us like tiger lilies, insistent, hungry silences. We couldn't, or didn't, lip-read their warning. We were afraid to slow down, let alone stop.

We went to upstate New York before heading south, of course, of course. How could I have forgotten the sequence? That was our pilgrimage. Woodstock was our Lourdes. We went there to track down our innocence, not so much lost as never possessed. We wanted to trade generations with our siblings, the real 'sixties kids who'd never known guilt. We went off to their holy place hoping their guiltlessness might rub off on us, hoping to baptise ourselves in their healing spring and be reborn; but our flowers were the ambiguous lilies, we were flower children of a different age.

You see a lot of amber in antique shops in upstate New York, a lot of fossilised flame, or neutralised fire, is that its charm? The colour of tiger lilies.

We bought water pipes and smoked dope, but by and large we stuck to booze. We were of the wet Piscean age, the age of alcohol, not part of the smoky Aquarian blur. The joke was on us. We were so intent, so serious. That was the problem. We had never learned relaxation; we would be fodder for the Growth's Movement's exercises, meditation, jogging, everything, in years to come, seeking relief from and for our burdensome selves.

Bernie snapped a picture of me in the doorway of our tent, wearing a long, rose-patterned dressing-gown I'd bought second-hand in New York. Why a dressing-gown with tucks and roses, to go camping in Woodstock? Just as a pun? Perhaps. Or an insurance policy, to leave no lingering doubt as to my femininity. I clung to the familiar with all my might, as I paid lipservice to breaking away. She stripped to the waist to fix the car, and I stood by embarrassed in my dangly earrings. For all the freeing fun-and-games playing with femininity, I couldn't play with any other aspect of myself, as she could, with her (bated breath) masculinity. I resented her for it, and I resented the challenge she presented to me, which I so much feared.

What challenge? What was it that frightened me so much? So much that the fear reared up in front of me on real legs — real, hallucinated legs, anyway. What guilt was roused by our adventure, that froze me like a fly in amber in the middle of it?

It was fear. Of that I'm sure as I sit alongside Georgia, forced upright and awake by thoughts in my head, potholes in the road. It's hard to tell them apart, as we jounce along, off the turnpike now, on back roads. There are potholes in my head, on these particular roads. When did it start, the fear that picked me up and dropped me right back in the closet I'd so arduously left, with her help?

I slide back against the seat, light another cigarette. Maybe it began the night we went to a lesbian dance in London. Bernie and I set out, carefully dressed . . . too carefully dressed. Me, not her; for all that she enjoyed our Belinda routines at the dressing table, she was basically indifferent. Not me. I dressed like an equation, for this occasion, an equation of X and Y, of butch and femme, meant to add up to something, to someone, agreeably androgynous. Nothing more or less would do. Earrings. Embroidered blouse. Jeans. Socks. Sandals. Two femme, two butch, one neutral. Perfect.

Then we hit the Rubber Baron, or whatever the pub was called. A bare, icy room with a spectrum of sexual possibilities on display. Women like cowboys and women like saloon girls. Suede and boots, feathers and satin. Women with hourglass figures, in sequins. Women with crew cuts, in suits. And in between the misty flats, the rest of us drifted, to and fro.

I was, immediately, desperately anxious and eager to escape, and equally desperately eager and anxious to hide the fact. I blinded myself to the sights of desecration and taboo, women too much like women, women too much like men, 'we' holding a careful middle ground. I couldn't look. I had taken care, had dressed in even steps; why hadn't they?

The steps led to safety, not perfection. They get so easily confused, though so utterly different. I was angry at everyone, especially Bernie, who didn't have to play safe, who could just play.

Why didn't I tell her? I smiled through the evening, danced with a few others, saw her do the same, left never to return, ran, in my mind, down the stairs, probably began my journey back to Jonathan and all the safety he represented, that very night. It's hard to be honest with an idealist, you're afraid of their disappointment. You're especially afraid when they, in turn, have idealised you. The long fall off the pedestal could be fatal, however inevitable.

I stub out my cigarette, remembering the fear, feeling it clutch as it did then. Am I still afraid? Afraid of that unknown part of me, the undeveloped side, afraid of the dark lord, as I put it, maybe to scare myself out of it? I fantasised that someone watched us from the loft. He was stern and powerful, compiled of the reserve and potential disapproval in Wall, my old ally and of my own reservoir of self-doubt and self-censorship. He, or She; for sometimes it took the shape of a faceless anonymous nun, instead of a monk. It was the self I wouldn't wear, I suppose; and so it came to scare me, up from the depths like the Loch Ness Monster. I never said a word to Bernie. She'd have had its name, rank and serial number in the damnation army. She'd have had a great bedside manner as an exorcist, I'm sure.

Meanwhile, of course, we talked loud and clear about sex-role stereotypes and all that. We went to Woodstock and tripped around putting up our tent, or I did, in my skirts, while Bernie swore and sweated in denim. When we got it up, as it were, it was inside out, as a bearded hippie came to inform us, making Bernie swear all the more.

It rained in Woodstock. We woke in a sea of mud on our air mattresses, me in my tea roses and she in her denim, both covered in muck. Cold, hungover, and mad at the world. So much for the miracle. So much for innocence, wholeness and peace. We packed up our tent and headed south towards the sea and the house and the beach. Enough of the outdoor life, we shrugged, as if that was all that had sent us away.

The sea was astringent, as always, with the good, purgative feeling I remembered, the salt-shock treatment of the Atlantic. That would send the ghosts skittering! But I hadn't even seen them yet, only felt their presence.

Joke: the drains in our little house blocked and overflowed. We waded in shit, as we cleaned up, waded literally in our own shit without for one moment applying the lesson. We scrubbed and disinfected the pink sweatbox of a house, cursing it, all pretence gone. The stuffing was coming out of it; and me, but never mind that. It was our house, all right, with our plumbing in it; but never mind that. We drove to the beach and threw ourselves onto the all-absolving surf.

Confession came after Absolution, that day. Bernie wanted a confession out of me. I wanted one out of myself! But I didn't know what I had to confess.

We lay roasting ourselves after a plunge in the sea. Sunwashed and seawashed. She took off her bikini top. Not a radical action; but it depends how it's done. She did it, to my eyes, in aggressive challenge, throwing down a gauntlet as she heaved it unto the sand, eyeing me.

I sat up unhappily and yanked my own top off, even more unhappily. She leaned over and kissed my left nipple. I groaned. She misinterpreted the groan, and kissed the right one. Then she ran, topless, down to the edge of the waves and stood toeing the surf that washed up, brown as leftover snow, till I plodded after her reluctantly. Her breasts were big as watermelons and green, it seemed to me, in the sealight. Mine were conical, white absurd islands in my tanned flesh.

She leapt into the sea with a liberated whoop. I clambered in, sullenly, after her. Why push me, I was screaming silently. Why not just leave me alone. I was often screaming at her, silently; in bed for instance, when she never seemed satisfied with the heights or excesses of my ecstasies. These, once so real, such a source of closeness and joy, were crumbling around me, within me. I felt pursued, cornered in my own head, and I hid there, panting, letting her mistake my pantings for lust, as she had my groan.

'Hey,' another whoop, and she was waving her bikini bottom over her head like a flag.

'Look, Bernie.' A man, a repulsive redneck, craning in our direction, stood some distance away, with field glasses, having a field day. She gave him the finger and waved her bikini bottom in triumph.

I would not, could not, take off my pants. I was so bound up in my inability to do so that it never occurred to me I might not want to, and had in fact a perfect right to keep them on if I wished. I just felt hungup and guilty and clothed.

Bernie walked out of the sea, naked, casually dangling her bikini, her long hair soaked and streaming, her heavy body slick and magnificent. She walked slowly towards the man who was rooted to the spot, though he'd let the field glasses drop. She went on walking towards him, menacingly. He stood.

Some guilty, rednecked fiend in me stood there with him, rooted and guilty, and some gay revolutionary nut case in me walked slowly, deliberately with her. So where was I? Nowhere.

Halfway to him, she dropped her bikini and began turning one hand and squinting, bending over in unmistakable mime, as if she had a film camera. I never quite knew from the way she talked when she was referring to films she'd made or was making, and when to films she would make or might make, someday. If I confused past and present, she mingled present and future; more positive, anyway. She was the most positive person I ever knew. The redneck stood as she proceeded towards him, cranking all the time, then turned tail and literally ran down the beach.

She collapsed in triumphant laughter on the sand. I came out of the sheltering sea to congratulate her, and she turned her imaginary camera on me, as I walked up the margin of wet sand to her. Every doubt, fear, outright heresy must be clear to the camera's x-ray lens. I still slept with Jonathan. I hadn't expected to want to, but I did. Sometimes, even during those three weeks, I'd wanted him. Often during those three weeks, now coming to an end, I'd not wanted her.

She must've seen through me, seen where the weak points were. Later she probed them with the overwhelming question:

'Do you think you'll be gay all your life?'

She asked it as we walked up the beach towards the car.

'Oh,' I said airily, but surprised enough to tell a truth, if not *the* truth, which I didn't know, which was unknowable, 'I suppose I'll always *sleep* with men, now and then.' Implying there was nothing else you could do with them, certainly not love them, or even probably like them very much. But as sex objects they'd do, when the batteries on the vibrator fizzled out.

That's all I meant to say. My tone must've given more away, or maybe that was enough, because she clammed up after that, the tiger-lily silence became a silent smoking volcano which occasionally let off a few sparks, like the lightening bugs gathering just then in the twilight air of the beach.

The night before I left for England, we made a last attempt to break through to each other. We were alone in Bernie's sister's New York apartment, no sea to clean us, alone, gritty, sweaty and irritable with New York heat. We got stoned, and drunk, turned on the radio, took off our clothes – this time I shed them wishing I could shed the skin and bones underneath them, take it all off, I was so covered in lies and half-truths, so obscured by my own ignorance and fear – and danced. Danced and danced and danced the night through, shedding tension with sweat, the only way left to shake loose of all that shit, finally danced locked and rubbing together, loud and shouting till we came at the same instant, for me the first orgasm for the entire lost week of our time together. We shouted our triumph, collapsed in a shuddering, juddering heap and slept where we fell, till plane time the next day.

I cried all the way across the Atlantic. Six hours, shorter coming towards England, is that why I always cry coming that way, instead of the other? I knew that whatever happened and however long it took, it was over. I had been asked something, and I had given the wrong answer.

Bernadette Reilly. Her laughter boomed out of her. She freed my laugh. It never shrivelled up again into the pathetic little tinkle it had been, before her time. That's what she left me; it isn't only the dead who bequeath things. I only hope she still has it. It should work that way, with the bequests of the living. Her laugh was infectious, that's all, and I caught some of it.

She was tender and passionate, rakishly charming and funny. I had come to her in my confusion and incompletion and said, like the rich young man to Christ, what shall I do to be perfect?

She had looked at me, like Christ at the young man, with great love, and said, go, sell everything you've got, leave it all to the impoverished, come on, follow me!

Like the young man, I'd gone away sad, for like him I had huge possessions, motherhood even wifehood, holes I knew how to fill, much-despised but well-worn and comfortable. Generations before me had trod, cursing and crying, but they'd worn a path. It was familiar.

The description is apt, that the young man 'went away sad'. I was sad, and would stay sad for years. I had saddened myself unutterably by my own refusal. Convention and safety had won. Fear had decided. Perfection slipped out of sight and away, and if you're not on the trail of perfection, what trail are you on?

7

'Helena, we're here.'

I fell asleep. Not only that, but I fell asleep in a blur of Bernie. I wake guiltily. Could I not watch beside her one hour, or something like that? While she drove me to the Mill Wheel Inn, of course. I grab her, but she ducks away, saying, 'Let's pretend it's back then.'

'What? Back when? At S&M? You want I should curtsy?'

'No. Back then, the last time we were here, before it all —'

'Came out?'

She laughs. 'Want to?' she asks, curling her tongue into her cheek in a way that makes my pores spring a cold sudden sweat.

'You just want another night of initiation, don't you? You —'

She puts her hand over my lips. 'Not yet. I don't know yet, remember?' Laughing, she climbs out of the car.

Puzzled, I follow her. It makes me uneasy, as if I'm making a bad bargain with her. What are we burying under these layers of pretence? Tension strains her too-determined laughter and mine as it chimes in obedient echo.

Places like the Mill Wheel Inn never change, and it hasn't. Before we step inside, I examine it, a big old mansion turned restaurant, and it strikes me that it resembles S&M.

Georgia looks at me over her shoulder. 'I know.'

She leads me inside and as the headwaitress defers to her, I

100

realise there's one aspect of the game I do want changed. Once we're alone, I inform her of the fact.

'I'll play, Georgia, except for one thing.'

'What one thing?'

'This one thing, I'm paying and I want the privileges that go with it. You know. Wine-tasting. Giving the order. All those things you usually do.'

'Okay,' she grins. 'Go ahead, kid. Only you'll have to remind me. I'm a natural leader.'

Maybe she's trying to deal with a public situation which would otherwise pose the awkward question of letting it all hang out or tucking it all comfortably in. It's easy enough, as the waitress comes and I order champagne, to imagine we're in the past, except for my means.

'Champagne?' The waitress smiles prettily. 'Is it a special occasion?'

'Yes,' Georgia says wickedly, 'My friend here's engaged. Show her your ring, Helena.'

I have no choice but to show her my ring.

'It's lovely, honey. Set the date yet?'

I shake my head.

'Well, don't wait too long. Get him while he's hot,' she dashes away. 'I'll get your champagne, anyway,' she twinkles over her shoulder.

'While she's hot,' I say thoughtfully, whirling the ring on my finger. 'Wonder when that was?'

'This is your stag party, Helena.'

'I thought we were going into a Time Machine? It wasn't my stag party then.'

'No. It was mine.'

I'd love to take her hand, but I don't and that tells me why she's doing this. Apart from possible duplicitous social or political motives, which may well be lurking somewhere in the background, it's sexual. She's just building the blaze into a bonfire, rewarding me for my patience, rewarding herself for hers.

'What did we talk about, Georgia? I mean, first?'

I hadn't seen her in ten years. There was an S&M reunion

at Ladylike while I was spending the summer in the U.S. A classmate called me out of the blue to ask if I wanted to come. I left Sam and Mike – three months old at the time, Wall had two months to go – parked with Marguerite without a second thought, and went, having asked casually who'd be there, to be given a list with 'Georgia Manion' at the bottom. We drove to Ladylight chatting casually, mostly about my marriage and her lack of one, our parents' various nefarious problems, childbirth, abortion and suicide, the usual things. Then we pulled into the Ladylike driveway and there was Georgia in a straw-coloured pants suit, much like the outfit she has on today, in cotton, as tailored and classical, reading the Sunday *New York Times*, hunched on the grass.

She climbed into the front with a cool backward 'Hi' to me. I bided my time. When we landed at another classmate's house for the pre-reunion drink we felt we required, I waited till she'd gone to the kitchen for the vodka, followed her, went up to her as she stood at the sink filling the ice bucket, turned her around and kissed her. On the cheek, of course; but it was a kiss, not a peck, nonetheless.

'Hello,' I said, and made her look at me.

'Hello,' she blinked like Rip Van Winkle, recalling who I was.

The waitress comes back, blonde and smiling, with the champagne. She pops the cork and it overflows ritually into the glass.

'That's good luck,' she recites. 'Means you'll have lots of beautiful babies.'

Georgia chokes on air.

'If you want them,' the waitress says, hastily. 'You enjoy it, now.'

'Why don't you have a glass?' I invite her, determined to show Georgia that I, too, can run the show.

'Oh, I – ' she resists minimally and gets the glass. I pour, and we lift our glasses.

'Congratulations,' Georgia says solemnly. 'May you live happily ever after.'

'You too,' I mouth through my teeth at her as the waitress

seconds her supposed emotion. Then she takes her glass and goes back to work, still smiling, and Georgia and I hold our laughter the requisite forty seconds before we, genteelly, explode.

'You're so childish,' I stage-whisper.

'I'm so childish! What about you, getting engaged to your aunt? That's not only childish, it's illegal.'

We're off again.

Jonathan stayed in England that summer. We'd given each other our blessings and said to go forth and fuck whomever we pleased, while we were apart. It was some kind of admission that we hadn't exactly settled down into bliss, once Bernie was off the horizon. I didn't take advantage of our arrangement, at least not technically. I just happened to see Georgia again, at an innocent reunion. That was the only sort of innocence I understood. Half-conscious denial, wilful ignorance, I was alone with her, on that first Sunday, for approximately fifteen minutes. Just long enough to tell her about Bernie and me, and plant certain notions in her head. By the time I left that evening, she'd invited me to lunch the following week, at the Mill Wheel Inn.

'Last time we went round the back first, to look at the mill wheel,' I remind her. 'Remember?'

'A detail,' she says dismissively. 'We can look at it after.'

'What time is it?'

'Seven-twenty.'

'You sit there and remember what we talked about. I'll be right back.'

She looks at me enquiringly, but doesn't insist that I explain. I glide, champagne-fuelled, lust-lubricated, out of the restaurant and into the lobby of the inn, and there, for the first time in the course of my five-year relationship with Georgia, I reserve a room for the two of us, in my name.

My name! In that name, with that backing, I ask for a double room as firmly as I dare, hoping he won't question it and he doesn't, why should he? He imagines I'm with a man, of course, or maybe that I'm alone and a restless, wealthy sleeper. Or maybe he couldn't care less, most likely of all.

103

He goes about his finicky business as I stand there in the glare of another memory, one I hope this moment contradicts. Once in a London pub, on a Sunday, with Bernie, in Soho, I went to the bar to get drinks and the bartender looked at me cheerily.

'How's tricks,' he said, and I smiled.

'Fine,' a little surprised, at the expression and the friendliness. Then I looked a little to one side, out the window on the opposite wall, into the face of a strip club, and realised he'd taken me for one of the girls; one of the strippers, one of the whores. But the reason I turned away from the window, in front of which Bernie sat, smiling fondly in my direction, was not that I was ashamed for feminist reasons, or not the obvious ones, that I'd colluded with him in his untoward friendliness. What went through me like a knife as I stood there, was a sudden image of myself in his eyes, buying drinks with some man's money. Jonathan's money.

Oh, shit, I think, standing here, and the thought's a prayer, addressed, I suppose, to my grandmother, the one I never knew; the one she never knew. Not the lady who never wrote a cheque in her life till her husband died, to the woman of the gypsy bracelets. If you're a mother, your husband pays if you've got one. If you're a nun, the church pays, sort of alimony for your husband. Either way, he who pays the piper, calls the tune.

I walk away with my room key in my hand, imagining Grandma Carnet nodding away up there in the clouds. Today, at least, I pay the piper and call the tune.

I dangle the key at Georgia.

She blushes. 'Don't let the waitress see you with that. You'll confuse her.'

I shrug, sitting down. 'Well? Thought of what we –'

'Blessed Seldom.'

'Blessed Seldom,' I pour out more champagne, 'We'll have to have another bottle, you know. At least one. I'll drink to the dear old fruitcake.'

We clink glasses.

'Maybe she's Saint Seldom,' Georgia speculates.

I shake my head. 'If there ever was anybody doomed to be Blessed forever, it was her.'

'Why?'

'Because it's easier for a camel to pass through the eye of a needle than for a non-virgin to enter heaven, Georgia.'

'I guess you have a point, as it were.'

We groan, and drink.

'Especially when, as in her case, the facts on record are somewhat, uh, murky.'

'Murky as Simeon's office, any day of the week.'

I pour the last of our champagne.

'Once upon a time. There was a lady. Was she beautiful? I've forgotten.'

'They never said.'

'Must've been ugly, then. There was an ugly lady. Who married a lord. Ugly?'

'Who married Lord Ugly. In England, where people are often ugly lords and ladies.'

'How would you know?' I ask her, and signal loftily for the waitress.

'Wait a second, honey,' Georgia whispers, the waitress having signalled Wait a second, honey. 'I don't think I want more champagne − at least not before I eat. Why don't we order?'

'I was about to order,' I inform her, sternly, making my displeasure plain.

'You were? Without consulting me?'

'Just like you did, remember? Without consulting me?'

'I did, you're right. I did. *Mea culpa.*'

'That's all right, Georgia. I'm going to order the same, if that suits you?'

She nods, still doing her humble bit. 'That'll do fine, kid.'

The waitress arrives, and smiles when I order our lobsters and another bottle of champagne.

'My, you ladies sure are celebrating. I hope your fiancé can keep you in the style to which you're accustomed, honey,' she says as she whisks away, giving Georgia another choking fit.

'Well, you never know,' she manages from behind her

napkin. 'She might acquire a taste for champagne. Your fiancée, that is.'

'Georgia. My mind was on higher things.'

'I'm so sorry. Well, one day, Lord Seldom went out somewhere. A thing he seldom did, like other things. He seldom did anything as far as I could tell.'

'You're taking this narrative far too lightly.'

'You're right. I'll sober up. Lord Seldom drifted off to the pub and there he remained, or somewhere, for the next seventeen years. Meanwhile Lady Seldom married Our Lord and founded the Stella Marists.'

'And then. The good part!'

'Helena. I'm surprised at you.'

The waitress returns with our bottle and we press another glass of champagne on her, which she as graciously accepts.

'Then Lord Seldom returns,' I continue. 'And sues the Foundress of the Stella Marists for his conjugal rights.'

'Well. He couldn't very well sue Our Lord.'

'Seldom vs. Seldom.'

'Rights which he'd enjoyed, so the story goes —'

'Blessed Seldom.'

We clink glasses.

'But of course he loses,' I finish happily, 'And Blessed Seldom lives happily ever after with Our Lord and lots more ladies.'

'Lots more.'

'And Lord Seldom — what does he do?'

'They were always a little unclear on that point. I think he went away sad,' she repeats the end of my tale of Bernie aloud, which sounds strange to my ears.

Everything sounds a bit strange to my ears, through the haze of champagne.

'He must've had them pretty often,' she says thoughtfully. 'Before he went off and got lost. They never say what he was up to, all those years . . . I mean, they had lots of kids.'

'That doesn't take so much.'

'I wouldn't know.'

I look over quickly, the haze dissipated by her bitterness.

'Oh God,' she sighs. 'Helena, it's not your fault I don't have kids. At least it's not your fault yet. I mean it's not your fault I don't have any now.'

She's alarming me, rather than reassuring me.

'What's this not yet, not now?' I growl.

'This isn't the time —'

'Or the place? Why not? Let's be in the present, for a minute.'

'Let's not. Please, let's not.'

'You have to explain.'

'Up till now, it's been a choice, more or less,' she says tiredly. 'Now, I'm reviewing the situation, in the back of my mind. When it gets to the front of my mind, when I have something to tell you, I'll tell you. Okay?'

'Can't I help with the reviewing?'

'No.'

'But Georgia —'

'Gimme a break, will you?' she begs as the lobsters arrive. 'I'll be right back,' she gets up and wavers her way towards the Ladies'.

I sit in front of my lobster, which is soon splashed with a stray tear. Now where did that come from? From the confusion and kept-in emotion of the day. From the fear that her tale, when she tells it, will be the sound and fury of an end, for us. From the fear that I'm being utterly selfish even wanting anything else. Where would that wanting leave her, if she followed it? Childless. I hadn't paid that price. Why should she? How could she?

But even now, while she's away, I can't concentrate on that question, can't or won't stay in the present and deal with that dilemma. I have to jump on my horse and ride away, back to a bleak point in the past, but still safer than I would be if I stayed here.

I was visiting Georgia in New York at the time. Sleeping in the study, so the mythology went, if it needed to go, but she'd told everyone she was away on business so we didn't need to use it. I'd managed to save up my own fare from the part-time teaching I was doing, but that was strictly It as far as my

107

funds went. We'd dined out and I'd made minimal contributions to each huge bill. We travelled in style, as always, and on this particular evening I'd almost reached rock bottom, stony broke.

I know why I'm thinking of that time. Because that afternoon she'd said something about children, about wanting them, maybe, someday. I hadn't said anything. What could I say? But the very idea, or my silence, or my helplessness, had made her angry. The anger had stayed there all day.

That night she started getting dressed to go out, and my heart sank. She was getting dressed up, as we loved to do, dolled up like grandma and me, like Bernie and me, flattering each other and ourselves, making a beautiful, beautiful couple. Except that that meant an expensive restaurant, and I was broke.

We'd been in bed all day, making love, or making something, making it well, from a technical point of view. Making it superbly, but heartlessly. Or so it felt, to me. As if she was taking her revenge that way.

'Georgia,' I ventured as she stood in front of the mirror combing her hair, scowling, 'Could we eat somewhere – not too – I mean, could we just have a cheap hamburger, or something?' I finished crudely. 'I'm stony.'

She turned, shaking with rage. 'You're stony, so I have to eat a cheap hamburger to save your pride, is that it? All right. You'll get your cheap hamburger. Come on, kid.'

She had me in the car in two minutes. She roared out the driveway. The atmosphere in the car was sub-zero. It was my second-to-last day and I had about ten bucks left. If I lived on hamburgers, or if we ate in, which I hadn't dared suggest, I could just about do it.

I was expecting McDonald's but she went one better, she pulled up in front of Roy Rogers. At R.R. the staff wore cowboy uniforms, that is the men wore cowboy, the women cowgirl, outfits, à la Roy Rogers and Dale Evans.

She stomped in; I shuffled in. We went to the counter and ordered. She plopped down at a plastic booth and looked at her cheeseburger in disgust. It did look pretty disgusting.

I drew up behind her, sat down and picked up one of those plastic tomatoes with ketchup in them. I squirted it on and it made that farting noise they make when they're almost empty. She stared straight ahead of her with a poker face. I lifted the thing to my mouth, staring at the cowboys and cowgirls, holsters at their hips.

'Oh my God,' suddenly, miraculously, better than the miracle at Cana any day, she was shaking with laughter, and wolfing her hamburger. 'This tastes wonderful,' she shrieked with laughter as she ate. 'Wonderful. What a great idea you had there, kid.'

'Happy trails, Georgia,' I toasted her with my polystyrene cup.

She's back, with a chastened after-tearfall look to her face.

'Sorry I took so long, kid.'

She sits down.

'Your lobster's cold.'

'There's nothing wrong with cold lobster,' she says stoically, sticking a piece of it into the congealed butter.

I begin taking my lobster apart, then look at her across the table. 'Georgia —'

'Don't do it to me, Helena. Not today. C'mon,' she pleads. 'You're not playing!'

'But Georgia, it's escape. I came all the way over here to stop escaping.'

'Did you?' she asks in an expressionless voice, picking up her lobster claw.

'Well if I didn't, I meant to. And if I didn't mean to, I should have.'

Silence.

'Remember,' she says softly, breathlessly, 'the Vocation Rally?'

I look across my lobster at her. Red it is and happy-looking as a toy. We're playing like two witless kids here, and she's asking me to stay witless with her, for one more round. She has the right to ask that, after what I've asked her. What can I offer her, anyway, if we get into her childlessness? She's not the AID type, and I'm not in the least sure I can criticise her for that. Neither was, am, I. If I have nothing to offer, hadn't I better shut up and play?

I pour more champagne.

'Of course I remember the Vocation Rally,' I tell her gently, loving her face in its weariness. It brightens.

We lift our glasses.

'To – ' she hesitates 'which order?'

'Maryknolls.'

She shakes her head. 'You just liked their habits. I know you.'

'Of course I just liked their habits. That seemed as good a basis to choose on as any.'

'You're so vain. And so beautiful,' she adds, taking my breath away. If this is my reward for conspiring with her to avoid certain facts, how can I not play it? What kind of Virgin and Martyr would I need to become, to have that sort of integrity?

We went in a chartered coach like the ones the military academy boys came to us in. One busload of girls wanting to be nuns. One busload of girls wanting to be wanted, willing to give up a lot to be wanted, as I'm willing now.

They set up stalls to solicit us, the Superior Mothers, and stood at them smiling alluringly, passing out leaflets. The atmosphere was bizarrely festive, bizarrely competitive. Georgia and I did extremely well. We had endless offers. We'd pause and ask questions at the stalls just to watch them salivate at the prospective catch. Our school had prestige and then, of course, we had those voluble tongues of ours to impress them with.

'We were shameless, Georgia. Shameless.'

'We were.'

'Plus which, we were obviously eligible. With your size, and my pimples, what could we possibly do but Enter the Convent?'

'Helena,' Georgia says, ruffled, 'they saw through our outward blemishes, to our inward qualities.'

'If they'd done that, Georgia, they'd have thrown us right

110

out of the place.'

We eat our lobster for a few seconds in silence. The champagne is raising me again, from the depths into which it and it alone, well almost alone, I decide, had sunk me. After all, there are ways around everything. With this vague sentiment firmly in mind I turn to the past again.

On the bus home we allowed ourselves one of those moments, those rare moments of clarity, probably allowable as much because of the howling inappropriateness of the circumstances as anything else. We had our arms full of bumph from the nuns, which we promptly deposited under the seat. It was late, and dark, and in ten minutes we had our arms full of each other.

Discreetly, of course, but it was dark, and who was to notice her arm around me and my head in the small, flat, fertile crescent between her large breasts?

But we noticed. We noticed especially, a certain buildup of radiant heat. And we couldn't help but notice the radiator(s) from which it proceeded. Until I had to move, or melt.

'Georgia,' I moved, and pulled her ear down to the level of my mouth. 'Georgia, I love you – so much.'

'I know,' she groaned into my ear, and we sat rigid for the rest of the trip, only our hands clasped as tightly as we could clasp them.

They clasp tight, again, now, under the table. Oddly enough, it's the nuns at the Vocation Rally I'm thinking of, and of what they were really saying, to us, or at least to me. They were offering us something forbidden by the canon of the Mothers, tempting us to something like adultery. I'll bet your mother doesn't understand you, they were twinkling flirtatiously at us. She's a bitch, isn't she? Is that what you want to be? I'm a witch. Come and be apprenticed to me.

We unclasp our butterslick fingers and smile, as the waitress comes over to make sure Everything's All Right.

'Everything's splendid,' Georgia says in her hearty, characteristic way.

Overstated, I always think, calculated to shut people up. If you ask someone how she is and she says 'Splendid', there

111

isn't much room to ask further. It's a good technique, for avoiding questions.

Hush my mouth, as her ancestors would say. Enough. We're here. Rather, we're there. We're not here. I'm drunk.

'I'm finished,' she's said to the waitress, after announcing her splendiferousness, and I concur, stuffed with soft lobster and cold butter, not bad once you get used to it. It's somehow richer than warm butter, more like icing on the lobster. The thought makes my stomach heave, now that it's over.

I order coffee and Sambucca.

Georgia shakes her head at me, but she orders the same.

A silence falls. No clocks tick. Voices murmur, people move around us, but that isn't the difference between this and Coldwick. The difference is anticipation.

'Think we'll make it upstairs?'

'We'll make it, upstairs.'

We sit without even needing to clasp hands, clasped together in a warmth richer than butter and lobster and champagne and Sambucca and – truth?

'You know what comes next,' she says teasingly.

'What? Graduation. That's no fun.'

'Not Graduation, stupid. Sand.'

'Sand! I'd almost forgotten.'

'Almost forgotten.' She snorts derisively. 'Don't give me that. If it weren't for Sand, we probably wouldn't be here.'

'I wonder if that's true?'

'It wasn't the cut of the habit that made you decide on an Order to join, in the end. It was Sand.'

'You're right,' I stand up, swaying. 'I have to find the –'

'Over there.'

I remember. And oddly enough, or not, it was at this juncture in the epic that I left the last time, too, just before I produced my trump card, unaware that Georgia had one to produce as well, to clinch the case I was building, that we'd been in love with each other when we were sixteen.

Alone in my cubicle in the Ladies', I sit and think of Sand, who lives in a cell in a Carmelite monastery not all that different from this little lavatorial cell. I stifle my laugh with a quick hand over my mouth, for the sake of the woman in the next cubicle. Sand, or Sister Blaise of the Most Holy Passion, would hardly appreciate or agree with the analogy.

When I met her she was twenty, and in love with God. She was also stunning. Tall, archangel-like, she wore 'thirties suits with nipped waists and padded shoulders and she looked a little bit like Lauren Bacall.

I worshipped the sand she walked on. Everyone did. She was followed around by a whole procession of women who hung on her every, frequent word. She talked a lot. How does she cope with the silence? She was silent a lot, too. Auburn hair, brown eyes. I leave my cubicle.

Outside, I'm still alone. I sit at the dressing-table after I've washed my hands, thinking: Sand. She was an archangel, to me. Bringing me an Annunciation of something. At the time I thought it was a vocation to the monastery. It was more original than the convent, more melodramatic, something no one could utterly approve of or even comprehend. Nothing as immediately and evidently useful as a nursing or a teaching order, an enclosed, contemplative order was a law unto itself.

Sandra Johnson. A very straight name for the daughter of a very straight, wealthy Episcopalian family who'd made the mistake of sending their artistic, impressionable daughter to Rome to study art. Too bad they didn't send her somewhere else; anywhere else. But then, as Georgia said, I might not be here.

She ran into Padre Pio, in Rome, the priest with the bleeding palms, and was converted to Catholicism. By the time she got home a year later, she'd decided Uncle God wanted her, in the monastery.

I'm sure He did. I would.

What do I mean, I would? I crayon my eyes, shakily. I did! I wanted to *be* her. She was everything I wanted to be and wasn't, mostly herself. That was the vision, that was the Annunciation.

I take the mascara wand. Nostalgia sweeps over me like snow; I could die in it, numb and blank, but content. They were all ageless, and lovely, even old harpies like Gabriel with their weird beliefs and prejudices. They were a breed apart, a breed who stayed young forever, in their whispery, esoteric clothes with an essential perfume to them, like musk; yes, definitely musk, I decide with a sad smile at my reflection, taking the little bottle of musk from my makeup case and dabbing behind the ears. Rosaries hung from their waists and pealed softly when they walked; they threw back graceful little capes to consult smug little watch-faces on ribbons and in doing so revealed the carefully contained profile of a breast just swelling the bodice underneath. They taught us songs and silly catechism answers, they schooled us in love even while they denied its expression, and they fed our incipient dreams to be something other than our mothers, as they were something other. No wonder Georgia and I, walking around the Vocation Rally, in love with each other, were also in love with our crazy little world, no wonder, no wonder!

I waft out to Georgia, my spirits lifted by all that retrospective love. She smiles.

'You look mellow.'

'I am.' The coffee bean in my Sambucca's gone out. The waitress comes rushing over to relight it, smiling. The evening stretches again, far from over.

'Do you think they would have accepted us,' I ask curiously, as we sip, 'if we'd gone so far as to apply?'

'Of course. They'd have jumped at the chance,' she says indignantly.

'I wonder. They had tests, you know. Psychological tests.'

'We're sane.'

'They're not just about sanity. They're about – I dunno. I remember Sand saying that the psychiatrist who interviewed her asked her what was the worst thing she'd ever done in her life, and what was the best. I asked her what she'd said and she told me her worst was being terribly intolerant of her parents, after she'd come back from Rome and told them about her conversion and her vocation and they fought her so hard.'

'What was her best?'

'She didn't say.'

'No, I guess she wouldn't, being holy,' she says, rather snidely.

'You're not still jealous. I worshipped her from afar, Georgia. Far afar.'

'Maybe I'm jealous of that. Not really,' she says hastily, taking my hand, not bothering to go under the table this time. Let the waitress think what she likes! I'm engaged.

'You could've gone off to a monastery to get away from me.'

'That's just about all I could've done too,' she says moodily. 'It's my turn now, to want a return to our game.

'I'm not sure we would've gotten in. To the convent,' I insist. 'They might have sensed something.'

'There was nothing to sense!'

'Georgia! Do I have to persuade you all over again?'

'Well, you could,' she says archly.

The test was tantalising, back then. It was like a pregnancy test, to determine whether you were in the appropriate condition, whether you Had a Vocation. There was always the chance that you didn't. God's ways were mysterious. Maybe he, like Franco's nephew, preferred Hannah's type. Maybe he liked those like Bernie, who stayed away from Vocation Rallies, who played hard to get.

Like Georgia, right now. Leaving me the same task I had that afternoon five years ago, to rewrite history, to convince her of the facts beneath the facts. I contemplate the circle for a silent moment. Where did it all start, really start? In the womb, where it ended? Was that the full circle?

The mothers didn't want us, but they wanted us to share their fate. 'Wait till you have kids of your own,' they said, threateningly, gleefully, cursing you, grimly anticipating the downfall of all your illusions, of all your aspirations. Wait till you're just as tired and trapped as we are. But we wouldn't be! We were going to be different.

'The dear sisters', the mothers said, patronisingly, indicating that the dear sisters were out to lunch. Come to me and I'll make you fishers of daughters, Christ had said to them, and they'd gone fishing all right, the mothers indicated, gone fishing forever, on permanent vacation from kitchens and bedrooms and delivery rooms, where the real business of femininity went on. Not that they told us very much about what went on there. That knowledge belonged to a sorority like the nuns', a sisterhood you had to go through parturition to join.

Meanwhile, the nuns did their own one-up number. 'Your poor mothers,' they'd say, sweetly insinuating that pregnancy did something to the brain cells, as well as swelling the ankles and dropping the arches. Poor cows, they might as well have said, out to grass, if we're out to lunch; now which sounds tastier?

What a choice!

Georgia's looking at me incredulously across the table.

'Helena,' she says in an awed whisper, 'You look like you're *thinking*. I've always had the greatest respect for your intelligence, but is it humanly possible that after the amount of alcohol we've consumed today, you can still think?'

'Oh yes,' I nod casually, 'I'm having another. You?'

'I need one,' she says meekly. 'Maybe you are Thomas Aquinas reincarnated.'

'I will be if I go on,' I survey my droopy belly unhappily. 'You know he was so fat they had to cut out a section of the refectory table for him so he could eat?'

'Only you could tell me that,' she laughs joyously. 'Shall we continue? We were on Sand, I believe. Stuck on Sand, hung up on Sand, you could say.'

'It was a schoolgirl crush. An archetypal schoolgirl crush.'

'She was eminently crushable, I have to admit.'

I'd gone down to Ladylike to visit another old friend, a former S&M graduate, and get an idea what the place was like, when I met her. Sand had gone to live there then, to get away from her parents.

'What did her family do?' Georgia asked curiously. She's back on my wavelength again.

'They sent her to a psychiatrist. Before the Order did.'

'And?'

116

'He said she *knew her mind*. I liked that.'

'I can see why.'

'So can I.' I can, too, I still like it for the same reason; I still don't know mine, that's why. 'She took us to a Mid-Eastern restaurant, with bellydancers, the first time I met her, and she ordered all this wonderful food.'

'No wonder you fell for her. You're like a dog, you love anybody who'll feed you.'

'You're just jealous. She was in great form that night.' She was having her fling, before she Went In, and loving every moment of it. It was like a Mardi Gras. She was a nun and a mother, for that brief period, uniting the opposites sublimely. The nuns were seductive, the mothers destructive; somehow, you have to be both. She was on the turn, neither a compulsory breeder nor a compulsory virgin, all possibilities intact. Not vowed, not yet, not fixed, not dead to the world; to any world.

'Well?' Georgia leans across our new Sambuccas. 'Are you ready to tell me what happened at her Clothing Day?'

'Shouldn't we do Graduation first?'

She sighs a long sigh and lights a cigarette. 'I guess we should.'

We all looked forward to Graduation, in theory. Panic feels like excitement, and I felt panic and called it excitement. Michael and Georgia, Bernie and God, all lost at the same moment. God couldn't survive without the rest. S&M was His life-support system. And mine.

I would have to become someone else. I couldn't survive, not as I was. But I couldn't look that in the face, either. So I went on dreaming about entering the monastery, dreams that never got further than arriving, changing into the costume and kneeling in front of a statue praying while my family drove away.

'You know those calling cards we got at Graduation,' I recall suddenly.

'The things we never figured out what to do with?'

'That's right.'

'My mother still had mine, till recently. I told her to throw

117

them out.'

'Remember how we had to choose the shape – a fat rectangle or a thin one, one kind of print or another?'

She nods, owlishly sleepy.

'Bernie and I both chose a thin rectangle with a nubbly surface, nice to touch. When they all came, ours said on the boxes they were for boys.'

'It figures.'

We practised endlessly, the slow, bridal walk into the gym to the tune of a tinkly piano rendition of *Pomp and Circumstance*. We wore long white dresses and carried red roses on arms white-gloved past the elbow. The dresses had short cap sleeves, unbecoming to almost everyone. Even as the bottom dropped out of my life, I managed to memorise the inch or two of Georgia's forearm that showed between sleeve and dress, as we sat listening to speeches. Bernie's face glowed with delight, not tears. She was Getting Out.

The smell of our roses was heavy in the gym, in the hot June air. Wall had chest pains and had to leave during the ceremony. I didn't notice. The waves of parents and relatives in folding chairs were a nauseous sea I avoided looking at.

Georgia catches my eye. In a long look, we recall the desperation of those long looks, when it was all ending. Neither of us would be nuns. We'd struggle fitfully with the idea, but we both knew it then. But that wasn't the worst of it. While we'd had each other around for five days a week, we hadn't had to think what we felt. We just felt it. Now we were losing those five days a week, losing everything, and the feelings screamed for recognition. Georgia reacted typically, by avoiding me. I reacted typically, by becoming depressed.

The floodlit nightmare of Graduation came to an end. We hoisted our stiff skirts over our arms and scrambled upstairs to the chapel for Benediction. The last holy water handshake, through white gloves. Eyes filled and emptied under long white Sunday veils, worn for the last time. Some of us sobbed out loud, almost drowned out the singing. The incense on the altar might as well have been tear gas.

Out. Into the world. The what?

118

Into the predatory smiles of our proud families. No Superior Mothers to protect us now. We sensed that a romance was over, even if we were headed for Catholic colleges, to be taught by more nuns. Faithless, adulterous as we had been to our biological mothers, we sensed that 'My mother doesn't understand me' was running low on credibility. We wanted to leave our roses on the BVM's altar, superstitiously, to leave something of ourselves. Our relatives made us keep them, for photographs. They were in charge, not us, not the BVM; they were the authority. More than two sets of parents had found themselves with a Vocation on their hands, and nipped it in the bud.

Georgia and I, kneeling next to each other in chapel, for once, couldn't meet each other's eyes. Our fingers grasp each other's now, at the memory. We made our way out in the usual file, and as she took holy water from my gloved fingers, we looked, and then we ran. Up the stairs, to the roof.

She laughs softly, now. 'Are you on the roof yet?'

'Just.'

'Good. Me, too.'

Georgia had always spent a lot of time in the infirmary. For all her bulk, she was really quite delicate. Whereas I, skinny then, was strong as a horse. The infirmary was right near the flat, railed-in roof. When I came to see her, we couldn't stay in the little infirmary room, furnished only with a bed, with her in it and me on it. It was much too dangerous. We didn't know we were fleeing our surroundings. We just thought we preferred the roof.

'It was ideal,' I speak into our reflections, certain they're mutual. Such certainty, in a perilous world, is precious. 'The roof was open, so that any dark desires could be dissipated in the air, and it was private, too.'

She nods. 'Except that last time, it was different.'

'Sure. We had nothing to lose.'

Our voices are soft, disembodied, the voices of ghosts. There was a death that day. We would both become other people, and it would be a long time, there would be more deaths in the meantime, before we would become two people who could meet. Up on the roof, we were safe for one last moment, as we left safety behind for good.

Safe enough to lunge for each other's arms, to take that risk. It was to be the first, last and only time. We were ending, so we could begin. There was nothing equivocal about that embrace. Two would-be brides of Christ in full regalia were consummating their love, not for the Bridegroom of the Canticle, but for each other.

We had read the Canticle, on the roof, in trembling voices.

My body drank in every detail of hers. I memorised bones like a medical student. I could have drawn her skeleton, if I could have drawn. We wrenched apart, in silence, and left the roof, she by the infirmary, I by the choirloft. I paused and looked down at the altar on my way, in a whirl of conflicting emotion. Another romance was ending. My Vocation had been to set up housekeeping with Georgia, in the only setting I could imagine. Who was Christ, except maybe our Best Man?

I couldn't move or make a gesture. What would the gesture have been? Blow a kiss, or spit in that all-seeing Eye? I felt betrayed and betraying. It was the end of Mardi Gras, the end of a masquerade. I walked downstairs shaken and drained, more like a bride of Dracula than of Christ.

The present asserts itself. We look up. We're not, pinch those older, flabbier forearms, saying goodbye at S&M or anywhere, not limited to a quick flick of damp gloves, or fingertips. I'm not in England longing for her, guiltily, I'm here, longing for her, guiltily, but I'll pay the price, in guilt, for my bride.

'I've got to go to the Ladies' again,' she stands up. 'One more Sambucca and we'll be done.'

'Okay.'

She goes; I order. The waitress smiles at someone she thinks I am, as I do at someone I think she is; we smile at bit parts in our own dramas, kindly, incuriously.

We graduated in 'sixty-four, after a manic-depressive four years. JFK elected. JFK killed. Things fall apart. I fall apart. Bernie would've had no tears left at Graduation even if she'd been sad. She cried them all for JFK.

It was a good thing I had a never-ending supply. Or maybe tears re-cycle, evaporate in from the skin and become new tears the next time, so that the more you cry, the more you cry? Wall sat on the Hudson tube coming back from a day in the Wall Street salt mines, or canyons, no tear ducts offloading anything for miles around, and felt something behind his eyes, behind his mind, something like a wave of blood rolling over him. The next thing he knew he was in a hospital in Hoboken waking up from a coronary. Hobroken, I heard it with childish distortion, the first time I went there to see him.

Georgia's back, and she's insistent.

'Helena, it's midnight. We're crazy. Let's leave all this. There's plenty of time to reminisce. I want to go to bed. With you, now. Now.' She picks up her glass like a candle, the coffee bean burning with a blue flame. Now.

I pick mine up. Bless her, *bless* her. Saved. Wall, I'll have to leave you in the hospital in Hobroken, for now. It's better than where I found you, anyway.

We walk out of the restaurant processionally, with our blue vigil lights in our fluted little glasses, careful not to jolt them into the liquor. The alcohol might burn off, I suppose, but who cares? I stop to inform the waitress, like a priest giving instructions to an acolyte, of our room number, so that she can put the tab on the bill, and we walk across the lobby, the coffee beans out by now, still holding our glasses ceremonially, not that there's anyone to look. Into the elevator, where we stare at each other, relieved and appalled.

'You're a real junky with this stuff, you know?' Georgia steps out into the hall. 'Not this,' gesturing with her glass. 'That. The past.'

'I guess I am.'

'Well watch out, you know, it's like junk — the more you take, the more you need. And it's expensive.'

'Drunken wisdom.' I open the door of our room.

121

8

'Not another moment, not another word, not another memory, damnit,' her hands are on my buttons. Usually we undress ourselves. Only sometimes it's nice to lie and be undressed. You feel your own body in a different way, as each bit hits the air. You have time to concentrate on the sensation of it, since you aren't busy doing anything.

I guess it means you're the daughter. She's the mother, taking my arms out of my sleeves, trying not to break them in the process, like a mother with a baby, also like a little girl with a doll, half-smiling, biting her lip. It's nice to change around, being mother and daughter. It's the primitive trinity of Demeter, Persephone and Hades who make the most sense to me, physically. Maybe spiritually, too. I don't credit myself with much spiritual insight these days, these years. But I can find those three repeated and repeated in myself, and in my bed. The dark, ambiguous lord always sneaks up.

But now it's spring and I'm out of his grasp and in hers, and she's saying my name with the same lips she's glueing to my neck and my earlobe:

'Helena –'

'Georgia –'

She takes off the rest of my clothes and my name's gone, now, too. Everything, everything, take it all. Take all the pieces and give them back whole. Take my name and my face and my breasts and my cunt, take my sex and my race.

First noname grips noname's hand in a sisterly grip, almost a handshake, a grip that says, it's still me without my name, loving you without yours, or any of the rest of that luggage you carry, I carry around.

'It's like opening a flower,' she says wonderingly, as she does it.

'Just like lobster again, I bet,' I answer her and she decides I'm getting off too lightly if I'm still in my voice and my reason, there are times for light humour and this is not one. So she takes me right out of the realm of lobsters and conversation and comparisons, right out, on her tongue, magic carpet and then with her fingers inside me too until they split into light and I emerge.

Again. To throb against her fingers. Thinking she's finished. But she's waited a long time and she's not to be easily satisfied, she's coming up first to kiss and give me a taste of my taste and then to climb on top of me, jiggling and jerking her hips to find the place, the pieces of the puzzle fitted together perfectly, two dry sticks, no, better yet, two wet clits rubbed together to make fire.

She discovered that way. I paged through the dictionary, years before, when I was about to sleep with Bernie for the first time, to find out what that word meant that I'd come across in Germaine Greer and other places: tribadism.

'Unnatural vice between women,' said Webster's unhelp-fully. I didn't really find out till Georgia did it to me, doing, as she said, what comes unnaturally. I'd known in theory, but held back from it as too masculine, for the top party (who somehow in my mind was always me), and too aping of heterosexual intercourse. It might be all right as a sort of horsing-around technique, I figured. But it could hardly count as real sex.

But it counts. As real sex. The trick is to find the spot. Sometimes you have to wait for her – not tonight. The two hollow cunts have their parts to play, in fanning the flames, producing a sort of bellows effect.

Bellows. I bellow, holler, stop, don't stop. Rhythm. To do

123

this to her. To have her do it to me. Right there, *right* there, groan rhythm lost, groan rhythm found, lost and found, found, lost-lost, drowned.

'Wow.'

'Don't talk yet,' I reach for her, trembling. Don't go back yet, into that place they call the world. It'll get you in the end, I know, but not yet.

'Okay,' her voice quakes and she's going down, again, to excavate the ruins, to hunt the last fractional wave with her fingers and tongue. There is no last, only fraction on fraction, breaking like glass, but soft stained glass. Then a fracture again, huge, I am laid beside her on the beach, what's the kiss of life?

'Tribadism,' she murmurs as if in answer, lighting me a Gitane. 'I wonder where they ever got that name?' I was shocked, the first time she ever did it to me, shocked by her need to have me. I'd only known my own hunger, before. Hers was as intense, as fierce. It matched mine. For the first time, I was certain of that, and I swallowed the certainty hungrily. She put her mouth to my ear as I lay underneath her, as if she felt that need for certainty rise up from me, and said, in a voice that boomed in my eardrum like the voice of an Old Testament prophet:

'Not only do I love you, Helena, but I want you. Want you with a deep, carnal passion.'

With every syllable came a gnashing of her hips on mine, until I was blubbering, yes, back at her, outdoing Molly Bloom. Then we were silent, as we're silent now.

'Can *I* have a cigarette now?'

'Okay.'

'Thanks.'

She lights her cigarette and we lie smoking in the dark.

'Hey, you know what?'

'What?'

'We never brought our luggage in from the car.'

'So what?'

'So.' She puffs and shrugs in a characteristic sequence. 'It looks cheap.'

124

'Oh for Christ's sake, Georgia. The guy at the desk didn't ask about the luggage. I think he just assumed I was that sort of client.'

'He hadn't seen me.'

'True. Do you want me to jump out the window, to knot some sheets together and let myself down, get some luggage and haul it back up so we can walk out respectably?'

'Yeah,' she blows smoke at me, lets herself laugh. 'That's what I want.'

'Tough.'

'Maybe I don't care what he thinks,' she says finally.

'The guy at the desk, you mean.' I'm thinking of my bedside spook.

'Yeah.'

'Maybe you're losing your inhibitions.'

'I hope not,' she says soberly. 'I need them.'

She needs hers as I needed mine and for the same reason, to meet the same fears. She squashes her Marlboro out and lies, dense with sleep, against me. What a sad, lonely sweep of understanding; we meet in our fears, mine past, hers present. True, or false?

I lean to kiss her. Her breath never falters in its rhythmic pattern. She's driven a long way today. Under normal conditions she'd have had the hassle of organising the room, too, and the burden of paying for it. What a lot of burdens I've let her carry. No, my fear is far from past. If it were, I'd have learned before this to carry them myself, at least to try. I'd have tested that water, of independence and autonomy; and loneliness, maybe. She knows it, she lives in it.

This is a rehearsal, a chance to practise skills I might make my own, sometime. I must make them my own, sometime. There's a kick to it. I must remember that, when the fear bites. There's a kick to writing your own name on the register, to signing the bar bill, to handing over the cash, to tasting the wine. No wonder men like it. No wonder they crave it and live for it, even when it gives them ulcers and hardens their arteries and decorates their hearts with fat like paper doilies around valentines. This is what it's about, that sacrifice I could never understand, this feeling of power and prowess, this sense of being able to move in the world, of being alive.

It brings me back round to Wall, of course, but also to Jonathan. Waiting at home, denying to himself that he's waiting but waiting, nonetheless.

You always wait, when someone goes away, even if you tell yourself you're not waiting, you are. God knows, I've waited for him often enough.

Georgia sleeps on. Something not sleep is stealing over my eyeballs under my eyelids. I can't believe I can be awake but I am. This must be the longest day of my life, for better or for worse. Amen.

It's Wall, in the oxygen tent in the hospital, where I left him, struggling back into view, no doubt wanting to get out of there. He woke up to see a cop reading a comic in a chair near his bed. Then his eye went to the window, which looked out on the morgue. He could see two orderlies struggling across the gritty little path from the hospital, with a stiff.

If he'd been superstitious, he probably would've had another heart attack right then and there. But as he was blessed with a profound sense of gallows humour, he laughed. That made the cop look at him with interest, thinking he was some kind of nut, like the rest of them in there, and they struck up a conversation on that basis.

Wall soon felt he couldn't compete for lunacy, or black comedy. The cop was guarding the guy in the next bed, who was wounded while witnessing a gangland killing, and might be wounded again, if left unguarded. He was also keeping an eye on the guy in the next bed, whose girlfriend had slashed his face and might also strike again. No one knew what he had witnessed, or failed to witness. And he was also glancing now and then at the luckless old guy in the next bed, who'd failed to kill himself quite dead enough, on his third attempt, to make it to the grey building across the path.

Wall liked them all. He was in his element, really there, for once. I think the failed suicide was his favourite; maybe he had a secret identification. Charlie's friends brought him

126

pizzas, beers, meatball sandwiches, none of them on his diet. He'd given himself a very sore gut. The exasperated and rather humourless doctor he shared with Wall would come in, find the remnants Charlie didn't bother to hide, and demand, 'What're you trying to do, kill yourself?' Charlie would just look at him, mournfully. The rest of the ward would laugh.

Wall's heart attack was a reprieve. It took him out of the salt mines. It hit him like a snowstorm hits a schoolboy; it closed the school. First he borrowed the cop's comics and read them. Then they moved him from Hoboken to a Catholic hospital next door to Stella Maris, in Cryon, upstate New York. It was clean and neat and gentrified, and it bored him. He needed something a little stronger to read. So he read the Bible, that highly advanced comic.

It was an opportunity to take his life by the scruff of the neck and shake it, as it had shaken him. And he tried. He did what I'm doing now, in a way. He went back to his own adolescence and asked all the questions they let you ask then and never let you ask again.

My eyes burn, overflowing in the dark. How could he, how can I, what happened in the twelve years between that opportunity and his death? Not enough? What business is it of mine?

I visited him every day. Oh, we were God's spies in the hospital, reading the Bible, discussing the nurses, the flowers, the doctors, the cards. We took on us the mystery of things every day, when I came to his room after Mass in the hospital chapel, every afternoon when I hurried there after school.

'How,' Marguerite raged, 'can a man with six children say his life is meaningless?'

I knew the answer then, and now, a woman with two children, I still know it, and I know she knew it, too. I also know why the question hurt and why it felt like an attack and threw her into such a rage.

Poor Wall! He had a mother on one side and a nun on the other, and we pulled. She berated him for rejecting her meaning, or even questioning it, and I strained to persuade him to mine, and between us we took away the small breathing space he'd bought himself at so high a price.

If only we'd left him alone, she in her way and I in mine. He needed space. He got it in Hoboken, with the cop and the stiffs in the yard. That was a monastery to meditate in! He converted to Catholicism, afterwards, and lapsed almost immediately. He gave up smoking and began drinking. That's a sort of space, I guess. I should know by now. We didn't know anything, Marguerite and I. How could we? You can only be what you are. She was a fanatical mother. I was a fanatical nun. The mysterious hidden life of silence and prayer was the ultimate call, the supreme vocation. To live in a world as blank as a sea, its blankness broken only by regular waves of Gregorian chant rolling out into the dry, sore world, healing, making good. Starting with Wall, of course.

Aha, of course, Marguerite would say. A textbook case. Starting with your father, to make up for wanting him, Sister Electra.

Oh, maybe, old lady. Go away. Your vision is limited. It may be right as far as it goes, who knows? But it's limited, limited, limited.

Mine, on the other hand . . . I settle against Georgia's warm unconscious back. Mine, on the other hand, is non-existent. Better to believe even in Freud, than in nothing. I suppose.

My mind unfurls the past, now, of its own accord. I can't stop these cameras, or projectors; once you set it in motion it goes on and on, and where it stops nobody knows. The summer after Graduation Wall gave me three weeks in California with Marguerite's youngest sister, my Aunt Michele. Michele almost made up for the loss of Michael. Nothing made up for the loss of Georgia and I couldn't even locate the loss, it was a loss that dared not speak its name and so would bruise for years, until it spoke, and was answered, five years ago.

Michele drove us down the coast from San Francisco to Santa Barbara, winding through breathless Kerouac country, and I watched the Pacific and thought of my brief flirtation with the Beats, discussed it with her, a bit of history independent of Georgia, almost unbelievable. There was no place for women in Beatnikland, we agreed, despite the long dangly earrings and white lipstick and fishnets. I told her, as we drove, about being a New Jersey girl whose idea of really living was to take the bus to New York and stroll in the Village and take home some of those earrings, as a sort of charm against the suburbs, where you knew all along you didn't belong.

'To which *we* all aspired,' she laughed. 'From the Bronx.'

I skirted the dangerous areas, telling her about hearing *Howl* read – on T.V. of course, where else in New Jersey? – and being shocked by the lines using menstrual blood as an image. I told her about the Haiku I wrote Michael: The only light/In the world/Is the ashen tip/Of my cigarette/ and how she advised me to study the Haiku form and read the Surgeon General's Report.

I didn't tell her that when I finally got my long, lank Beat hair cut, to everyone's relief, I did it for Georgia, because I knew she'd prefer it shoulder-length and respectable. I didn't tell her I'd given up Ginsberg for Georgia when I heard what she thought of *Howl*. It was only later that I decided I thought roughly the same.

One day as I was sitting next to Michele in the front seat of the car, trying to stay awake as we wound through the hills, we passed something I saw only peripherally. On one side of us was the Pacific, on the other side were mountains. This was on the mountain side. A little brown adobe building with a modest sign. Carmelite Monastery, it said.

We were in Carmel; of course. I'd never thought of that connection. Carmel, California was Kerouac's country not God's. Heavy-handed, literal-minded as I was, I thought it was a Sign, which it may well have been, or at least a signal. But I thought it could only mean one thing. That I really was meant to be a monastic, inside those walls or walls like them. I knew I never would. So I just felt guiltier, and more lost, though I hugged to myself the vision of that simple adobe building.

Maybe it meant something else. It looked like a painting of

Georgia O'Keefe's, of a church in New Mexico. Maybe it meant that the monastery was everywhere, more definitely and more radically than I had ever begun to believe? What if that little building in California that summer was giving back something I'd lost with relief, in the end? Something I'd left untouched, like the window I left unbroken in the house in Coldwick.

Sand had her Clothing while I was in my first year at Aquinas College for women. I'd wanted to be bricked away, to escape. But I also wanted to be part of that powerhouse, to live in that white heat. It seemed the furthest you could go, the most you could live.

But I had my trial by fire, instead. Trial by ash, it felt like. I had to lose Georgia, S&M, everything, everyone. To live among nuns, strangers who'd never replace the nuns who'd mothered me. I'd vowed not to love another nun. By the time I got to Sand's Clothing, there was nothing left of me as I had been, and nothing new. Nothing. I mourned Georgia without knowing I mourned her, without knowing I needed to mourn her, alongside the other girls mourning their boyfriends at home.

Sand's Clothing would restore me, I decided. It would work a miracle. I would come away refreshed and restored, my vocation in place again like a hymen lost carelessly, not even passionately. I hadn't lost it passionately; it had just gone, along with Georgia.

I look at Georgia, asleep, and think again of her fear; and mine. Then and now. How could we have been so ignorant? What in the world is there to hide? Why should this be held to blight a life, why?

There's no answer to that, in the night with the katydids debating away. I remember them from all my Coldwick summers:

> Ka-ty did
> Ka-ty didn't.

Stubborn and insistent as ever. 'Critters', Wall called them, one of his backwoods words. What would he make of all

130

this? Not much. When I'd told him, when I told him and Marguerite, that I'd slept with a woman, bragging that I could love anyone, anywhere, now (actually there were about fifteen people in the State of New Jersey, approximately), he'd blinked in his owlish way, standing behind the bar, of course, sipped his drink and smiled at me, his dark eyes fond and considering.

'You're the same old idealist,' he'd said.

I should've taken him up on that, made it more than abstract, but I was grateful and flattered and left it at that. Marguerite said very little, just looked thoughtful.

Georgia was among the missing, then. She was somewhere in another world, in the wide world I knew would claim her, once S&M was over . . . in the wide world I know will claim her, once this is over.

I roomed with her, at Ladylike, for the weekend of Sand's Clothing. Georgia invited me and then regretted it, and resented both the invitation and the regret; and me. She couldn't resist inviting me, or help regretting it, and what response was there to such double helplessness, but resentment?

Nor, of course, could I refuse. She ordered a cot which was duly placed in her room, at an angle to her chaste single bed, so that my head was at her feet. Oh, such Euclidian clarity in that angle. The room was empty when I got there, except for those two fatuous beds, and a note. I went to the dining hall, as instructed. She waved, vaguely, and I had dinner with another old classmate of ours, someone who'd prospered less conspicuously at Ladylight and had less to lose by association with me. Georgia was a big shot at Ladylight, and I was an embarrassment.

I went to bed early. What else was there to do? I read the Chaucer I'd carted with me from Aquinas, my first Freshman English assignment. Nothing's more depressing than Chaucerian bravado and bonhomie when you've got the twentieth century blues. I read the story of the Prioress with her little lapdog and her ring flashing *Amor Vincit Omnia*, and tears ran down my face.

Very much later, I heard Georgia come in. Heavy sigh at finding me there, a skeleton emerged from her closet, a ghost made flesh. She must've hoped I'd evaporate, bed and all. Take up your cot and walk! If only I had. Rustly undressing noises, and then a sense of radiant heat where there was none. A condition of the blood. A quality of the glorified body. Radiance. Spreading fast, alarmingly.

Georgia, the source of it, nudging my supposedly sound-asleep head with her feet, but gently, steam-shovelling it till it lay across her calves. Ladling it upwards to just above the knees. Then she stopped. Radiance; and fear.

'I don't mind your head there, Helena,' her voice came out of the darkness, unmistakably husky. I would pay for that huskiness, I would pay for not mistaking it. I'd better mistake it, before it was too late. I kept on, barely moving, making for the safe ground of the cot.

'I really don't mind, you know,' she repeated, irritably this time. 'You can put your head back there,' she all but ordered.

I put it back, trying to keep the rest of me separate as I presumed the rest of her was separate from her calves, twitch though they did in a most suspicious − and auspicious − way. I had no wish to read the sexual auguries. I was protecting myself from her, her from me, me from me, her from her. Single-handed, I felt.

Actually, there was no danger. She would never have undertaken an act from which there was no recovery, no forgetfulness. But I didn't know that. That furtive embrace of head against calves opened channels that led to channels that led to ruin. The night was sheer torture, dangerous, delicious, and long.

I must've fallen asleep at some point. I remember being scared, above all, that she might hear my heart, alternately pounding and cymbal-clashing; how could she not hear it? Then there were my pulses, visible as they throbbed, or leapt. Then worst of all there were my continual excited swallowings; if they didn't signal excitement, what did? They sounded loud and graceless as gulps.

Percussive heart, neon pulsations, bassoon tonsils; then it

was the grey dawn, from which I shielded my eyes, and she was gone. There was a crisp client-to-prostitute note to the effect that I could have the room on her; ten bucks' worth.

The Clothing itself lay ahead of me. Groupies all, we stood, her fan club, waiting for Sand to materialise behind the grille at Carmel. Carmel was a chamber of horrors. I assume they're all alike, like Roy Rogers'. A chain of monasteries, with religious art that could've been manufactured with the help of a farting red plastic tomato. Blood dripped off those plaster saints and crucifixes like a red Niagara. Once when I'd left the place after a visit with Sand, I found I'd got my period while inside; in sympathy, no doubt.

When Sand did, finally, materialise, she was chopped into little squares by the bars, which went both down and across like a tic-tac-toe grid, so that she was a sort of completed jigsaw of a bride with a wax taper in her hand. She looked very beautiful and very silly. A few people giggled, nervously. I may have been one of them; I never could remember that moment, when she first appeared, probably because at that moment I felt my heart flop over like a bug and then it was helpless, I was helpless. I righted it, and in that instant I had my revelation, sort of. I knew I'd loved this woman, with no mere spiritual love, I'd loved her nipped waist and her long auburn hair and her laugh and her appetite for Mid-Eastern food, which was the only appetite of hers I knew about, specifically. But of course I stopped knowing immediately, and went blank and numb and stayed that way, for years.

There was a smell of soup, or glue, and cleaning fluid, or embalming fluid.

'What's it like?' someone asked her. It was like nothing so much as a Funeral Home, actually, and there was a distinct resemblance between her in her white regalia and Wall all made up in his coffin. The thoughts you can have, in the dark!

Sand smiled. Not her old smile. The new version was much more patronising. 'You have to be very docile,' she said, lisping it playfully, so it came out 'dothile'. 'Almost sthupid.'

I could've puked. 'Do you still paint?' I asked her.

'Helena,' she said sweetly, extending that smile again, and a

133

gloved finger with it, through the bars.

There should be a sign, I thought savagely, as I touched her glove: Please Do Not Feed the Postulants.

'I paint little pastel holy cards,' she said, and a ripple of criticism went through the room. Holy cards!

She smiled a cryptic smile, and withdrew her glove. 'I don't really have time to paint,' she said simply. 'It's a very full life.'

'Full of what,' someone asked, flatly, and she smiled a more direct smile.

'Full of love,' she said. She, who had always talked on and on, entertaining us, dazzling us, seemed to find talking a strain. Her Superior came then to lead her away and she seemed grateful for the intrusion of a gorgon with a death's-head, face invisible under a black veil. Strangely like the apparition I saw in the little house with Bernie. That's what that figure in black looked like, exactly – like Sand's superior, that nun all in black with her face covered. But she couldn't have been all in black. They wear brown.

But I remembered her in black. And the face, the death's-head without a visible face, just a suggestion under black cloth, that was the same. It was like black armour, the black habit she was wearing, she or he, standing there summoning me. Not reproaching me for being in bed with Bernie, as I'd thought for all those years. Summoning me to recover, to replace what belonged, to me.

The second revelation I had that day at Sand's Clothing was that I would never be a Carmelite. We went into the chapel and sang the Mass. The nuns were invisible to us, in their cloister chapel behind the altar. I threw myself desperately into the beloved Latin. The Gloria. The Creed. The Kyrie. Nothing. Agnus Dei. Panis Angelicus! When you don't feel anything while singing the Panis Angelicus, you've had it.

I willed myself to feel God. God had always been a feeling, and it had always been accessible, with an effort of will. Not any more. There was no feeling. There was no God.

I don't remember when the Clothing took place. After the Mass, I presume. Sand was led away, stripped and shorn, as I imagined it in my no doubt lewd imaginings. She came back in the Carmelite novice's outfit, lay down on the floor and was covered with a black cloth while the nuns chanted the De Profundis in Latin and I made myself say it, pray it, in English. Out of the depths I cry to thee O Lord. Lord hear my voice. Oh let thine ears be attentive to the voice of my pleading. If thou oh Lord should mark our guilt, who would survive? But with thee is found forgiveness, and fullness of redemption. I wait, and in his word do I hope. My soul doth wait upon the Lord more than the watchman for dawn. More than the watchman for dawn, my soul doth wait upon the Lord.

I had always loved that repetition, that emphasis. My needle stuck there and I just went on praying it, blankly. My soul doth wait upon the Lord more than the watchman for dawn, my soul doth wait upon the Lord more than the watchman for dawn, my soul doth . . .

Like those people who use repetition to get their hearts synchronised with the music of the spheres, or something. But my heart was stone. I was just a broken record. I feel more now, saying those words, than I felt then.

More now — and something has been restored. Because if that was the Novice Mistress beside our bed there, at the New Jersey shore, then it wasn't, after all, such a bad sign. It meant I was picking up the pieces — I just didn't always recognise them when I saw them.

That's why I wanted that whitewashed cell in the basement, all right. I almost feel a twinge of wanting to be there now, in the damp and the dark, alone. But there's a way of erasing that particular twinge, alone of all the twinges to which I'm subject. The thought comes with a wave of sleep. That cell isn't important, not the walls or the whitewash or the furniture or anything else. It's only important in that it allows me a space. That's what I needed with Bernie and couldn't get, because I had to conform to her pattern. I'd only had half the revelation, after all, that far-off day of Sand's Clothing. The other half stood there beside the bed in New Jersey, demanding recognition.

I had known in the monastery that day that I would never be a nun, and I was right. But that was only half of it. The other half was, that I could never become a nun because I already was one.

It feels better now, 'it' being the sum total of sins and guilts, especially the recent, present, ubiquitous one, taking time out from Jonathan and the kids to be here. I'm here, at least, at last, in one place, for one moment, all alone, in my skin. That's the Carmel that matters, the only hermitage. And not even that lasts forever.

I move against Georgia. Not made to be a celibate for all that, not me! There's enough space, enough dizzying loneliness, in simply living out the life of that clay building, flesh and blood. Quite enough, without going looking for it. Oh, relieve it when you can and be glad! I drift away lying flat against her back, like a raft.

9

' Hey, lazybones.'
Waking up with Georgia is a miracle. Waking up
at home is –
Why can't I wake up with Georgia? Forever, or at least right
now?

Things most themselves bring a flavour of return, not of
strangeness. Waking at home is always strange. The planet is
strange. Everything. This is home. Unfolding into home the
way a child does. Greeting things again. Hello. Oh, Jonathan,
with your endless cups of coffee you know I don't want, go
away. Why can't I say goodbye to you, once and for all?

'Hey. Who're you calling lazybones?'

'You. What're you gonna do about it?'

For an answer I spring on her and she's on her back
underneath me. Funny how paradoxically powerful someone
feels when you're on top of them, how gathered and spruce, as
well as vulnerable.

'Am I crushing you?'

'No, but feel free.'

Oh, I do, just for one moment, feel free. My own heat
overflows, this bed is a pool again, dripping with us. She
groans, discouraged, taking too long, but I groan back in some
language she's just invented that it doesn't matter in the least,
she can take forever, and as if in answer she speeds up, all of a
sudden she's shouting and urgent, it's like running

137

a race with yourself or yourselves, four hips, all hands on deck, like crossing the Sargasso sea, with her hair tangling in my teeth then up again like something – someone – who'd bust the dam and live in the wash. That the something or someone is two-faced doesn't matter. Both faces are hell-bent on release at any price.

Then I'm a diver, touching the hem of the sea like the hem of the healing garment, going under, touching and tonguing and finding and losing her pearl of great price.

'Hey,' she speaks from her own wash, in the lazy aftermath, little ripples still passing through her. I lie with my head on her belly and feel them, small currents tugging her outwards even as she settles back, still releasing her. 'I had a dream last night.'

'Yeah?'

'I only ever remember my dreams when I'm with you. I can't see you but I can feel you smiling, a great big, smug smile. Stop it!'

She's right. But it's my vindication, what she's said, how can I not smile?

'What was your dream about?'

'We were going to a tea dance, you and me –'

'Together?'

'It seemed like it. I was a wee bit perturbed –'

'Yes.'

'But you said it'd be all right, only I should put my glasses on, so I could see the receiving line.'

'And did you?'

'Yes. And they all gave us little conventual pecks as you introduced us, and sort of winked, you know that flirtatious clerical wink?'

'Know it well.'

'As if to say they *knew* but they'd go along with us. Then we went inside the gym, and danced.'

'Who was leading? I notice you put yourself in the role of the visiting male.'

'Well – you did the introductions, if that's what you mean. But nobody led, Helena, Christ you're competitive! And there were no visiting males. We were all dressed up, dancing with each other, and the nuns were watching and smiling.'

'I'll bet they were. What a great dream.'

'It did leave me feeling rather − set up.'

'I'm hungry.'

'You usually are,' she regards me tolerantly. 'Breakfast?'

'Then what?'

'It's your party.'

'I can cry if I want to.'

'I thought you already had.'

'Wonder if they have Room Service?' I pick up the bedside phone. 'Makes me feel like I should speak French, should be in Paris.'

'Why should you be in Paris?'

'Everybody should be in Paris. Hello? I'd like to order breakfast in my room? Yes? Scrambled eggs, sausage, toast − muffins, yes, blueberry muffins, and coffee. Yes, please. Thank you.'

'Sure you ordered enough?'

'Don't you want that much?'

'If I don't you'll eat it.'

'Are you insinuating that I eat too much?'

'Not insinuating.'

'What the hell. Georgia, I just had an idea. But you don't have to go along with it. Only if you're not gonna, I want to know now, so I can compensate by eating too much for breakfast.'

'You'd like to drive out to California maybe? Something calling you towards the Pacific? Now that you've gone where you've been, you want to go where you haven't been? To round out the mystic circle or something?'

'Don't you like me?'

'No. I only drive halfway round the country, watch lunatics watching other lunatics pulling their cars up out of the shit, hold up banks −'

'Who do you think you are, Butch Cassidy?'

'Sure, Sundance.'

'I've got to pee.'

'Before you tell me your idea?' she wails. 'I have to pee, too.'

'*Tant pis.*'

'You want to go visit another relative. *Tante pis.* I might have known. A good follow up –'

'Very good, Georgia. While I'm in here I think I'll take a shower.' Sunny tiles, that brash early American cheerfulness, even in here.

'Goddamn,' she comes in and plops down on the john while I'm in the shower. 'Can't get any privacy around here.'

'I was here first.'

Alone, sealed off in the shower, with her out there brushing her teeth, now, the centre of all those circular paradoxes, at last, being with someone for real is being returned to yourself, this is the return of the native I looked for, found, and yet, and yet – there's the time bomb of guilt ticking away, too, clocking up the different hours. Are they awake yet? To an absence that chains them away from themselves, those two little boys, while I, absent, bask in the presence that releases me? How can I ever draw the two together? How can I go on keeping them apart? Risking that damage, that –

Out of the shower. Escaping the tick of the time bomb to breakfast, tipping the bringer of breakfast, exchanging good mornings.

'I haven't said no yet. You don't have to compensate.'

Oh, Georgia, I'm compensating for the hunger I'm inflicting, elsewhere.

'All right. Here's my idea. Instead of going straight back to New York, to your apartment, we go on to New Jersey –'

'We're in New Jersey.'

'I know we are, Georgia. But we go on into New Jersey –'

'New Jersey never seemed so damned big before,' she complains, pouring coffee. 'Ummm, it smells good.'

'Ummm, so do these sausages. Sausages in England are horrible. They're full of some sort of filler – something yucky. Not meat.'

'How can you live there? I mean, seriously.'

'I guess I like it. Not necessarily my life there, but it. I like the freedom of it.'

'Whaddya mean, the freedom,' she asks indignantly. 'How can you be freer there? When the sausages are full of lint? I've tasted them, and that's what it is.'

'Belly-button lint. And toe-cheese. I'm sure of it.'

'Definitely not,' she shakes her head. 'That'd be saltier.'

We're silent, chewing.

'I know this is the land of the free and the home of the brave.'

'Damned right.'

'But somehow I never felt very free or very brave here,' I lift my coffee cup gratefully. 'The coffee's better. The money's better. The weather's better. But – maybe it's personal. When I left the U.S. for the first time, it was like getting out of prison. Whether it was just leaving my family, I don't know – that was part of it. It's just somehow very provincial here, very cut-off, very – I dunno,' I'm left shrugging. 'I could argue the case against what I'm saying just as well as you could.'

'At least you're not saying it's more civilised over there,' she growls.

'It isn't. Only people do conform less.'

'Of all the grotesque generalisations.'

'True. But it's true. No. I conform less.'

'But if you'd stayed here you would've found people like yourself.' She groans at the thought.

'Sure.'

There's another eating silence. American food, the sheer abundance of it, is awesome after Europe. The bulk of it. No wonder Americans are energetic. We fuel ourselves so well.

'I was thinking of your sailing,' she says softly. 'That was my contribution, last time we were here, to the revelations – remember?'

'As if I could forget! It hit me between the eyeballs. I've never been so surprised in my life.' Sailing away on a Greek liner for the indispensable year abroad, in this case second year, not third. After a miserable meek first, to inherit the earth.

She lights a cigarette, sitting naked in an Early American

141

rocker with American Eagle-patterned cushions on the seat and at the back.

We exchange expectant grins, no more or less than lovers retelling our favourite myths. Jonathan and I hide from our mythologies, the ones we created together, they're cruel and terrible. Maybe that's why we had children together, to try magically to transform them – but it doesn't work, of course. You have something else, but you still have what you had to start with.

'It was a hot, sweaty New York evening –'

'Georgia. It was a flamingo-pink simmering New York evening. Everything glowed.'

'Like the inside of a blast furnace. Who's telling this?'

'All right, but it was – gorgeous.'

'To you, languishing no doubt by the swimming pool in Upper Middlebrow. I was working. In summer stock. My big break,' she laughs disparagingly. 'The start of a great career in the theatre. Dear God, I was young.'

'Georgia.'

'Yes?'

'Two things.'

'Yes.'

'One. I was not languishing anywhere. I was a soda jerkette at one Shoppers' Paradise Store Cafeteria in New York State. Got that?'

'Check.' She chuckles unrepentantly. 'I love the thought of you as a soda jerkette.'

'Thank you. Two. It's never too late –'

'Just cram it,' she says softly, steadily. 'All right?'

'Check.' Georgia's visits to London, during which we went to Cornwall, among other places, were also full of half-frenzied visits to the theatre. Half-frenzied because she tenses, in her seat, with a sort of vertigo. She wants to be out there on the stage so badly, there are times when I've been certain she's going to plummet herself into the play and see what happens. To me she's still Nora in *The Sea Gull*, spellbinding on the stage in the gym, just as to her I'm still the poet, if no longer in residence. If she's finally given up on herself as an

142

actress, really given up, as that steel in her voice seems to imply, then how can I feed her dreams as she feeds mine? But I do feed her dreams! She remembers them when she's with me.

'Okay. Sorry about the swimming pool.' There's a tremor in her voice, despite the harshness. She's silent a minute.

'The mass of men lead lives of quiet desperation,' she says unexpectedly. 'Maybe I'm just coming to terms with that.'

'Joining the quiet mass? The silent majority?'

'Maybe,' I venture, frightened of her tone, 'Maybe that's why I left the U.S. Not that I've beaten them yet. The ones inside.'

'Helena, you make everything so complicated. Maybe you make everything too simple. I don't know.'

'Maybe,' I surprise myself and her, my own voice shaking in turn, 'We're just different.'

Her eyes narrow, and harden, and soften, become unreadable. She exhales with the sound of a sigh. 'Maybe we are.'

'Do you want to be a partner with Sabine Chem?'

'I don't know any more. I want the money, the expense account, the power, the –' she shrugs. 'It's what I am. You have to be something. A lot of people would give their eyeteeth to be –'

'But you've given yours. Whatever they are.'

'Can I tell the fucking story?'

'Georgia – it's just that you're free, I mean you don't have kids or anything. You could be anything, or nothing.'

'You think that makes so much difference?' She's angry now. 'You think just because you've got those kids to hide behind, like most people have, by the way, and do, you don't have choices?'

Is that what I think? I open my mouth and close it again.

'We're both hedging our bets, my dear. You in your way and I in mine.'

Why does that phrase strike such a melodramatic chord, a loud phantom-of-the-opera chord? Maybe I make everything too complicated. 'You seem to mistake the complicated for

143

the profound,' said some boorish nun at Aquinas. Wall died hedging his bets, and from that hedging, more than from his death, came my inability to let him rest. Do I want to die hedging mine? His death threw down the gauntlet, and I've let it lie. With what right do I throw it at her?

Confusion. I can't even lay out the terms of it. Maybe he couldn't either. I've lain them out all wrong, making it a choice between Georgia and Jonathan. But then, what is the choice?

'Now.' She lights another cigarette, pours more coffee, and turns to me. 'I'm the Ancient Mariner and you're the wedding guest, right? And you have to shut up and listen to me.'

'It was a hot sweaty night in New York.'

'Dashiell Hammett.'

'Shut up, Lilian.' But she's grateful for it, just the same, and she adopts that shady, nasal tone. 'I had rehearsals all day. I was grooming myself for the big time, living in fairyland. It was a good place to live, that hot New York summer. Only sometimes in the cool of the small hours would come a chill moment, when we'd all finished drinking and talking and pulling the play and ourselves and the world to bits, sometimes I'd sit there in the ruins and laugh a chilly little laugh at myself, and hate the sound of that laugh.'

'Christ.'

'This particular night, though, there would be no partying after rehearsal with the rest of the cast, failed suicides, failed homosexuals, against whom and to whom I represented the rock of Gibraltar, a sort of pillar of normality −'

'Corinthian −'

'This particular night I was going to see an old friend off on a Greek ship. I was glad she was leaving, and I wasn't sure why. I was sorry she was leaving, and that was easy enough to understand. She was an old friend, had been my best friend, maybe she still was in some inactive way, if there was such a thing. But why was I so glad? Why was I so damned relieved, as I drove too fast, too late, from Long Island where the summer theatre was, to the docks?'

144

'It was a beautiful night for a sailing. I almost envied her, almost wished I was going with her. Then I clutched with terror, at the very thought – going with her?'

'Then I laughed and drove even faster. I was seeing her off. Relief swept through me again. She'd be three thousand miles away for a year and when she came back, I'd be safe.'

'Safe from what?'

'I was desperately late. Almost had sixteen accidents. Roared up to the dock, parked illegally. Raced to the ship. It hadn't sailed. A Greek ship, just her style. Nothing American for her.'

'Ooh, she was suspect and scurrilous.'

'You're jumping the gun. And using too many syllables. Will you shut up?' She settles herself in the rocker and continues.

'I landed in First Class. In case I haven't mentioned it, I'd found or made time to gulp down a few vodka and tonics before I left Long Island. Quite a few. She wasn't in First Class, of course, she wouldn't be, on a bet. Tourist. I came round the corner and there she was, bent over backwards in the arm of some beefy hunk of an adolescent wearing a cravat, for Christ's sake –'

'He must've thought I was going to Greece on a yacht. His.'

'She didn't see me. I backed up, not out of delicacy, not because I wanted to spare the feelings of the enraptured couple. I wanted to spare my own damn feelings, damnit. I wanted to spare my own damned self those own damned feelings.'

'Damnit.'

'Damn right, damnit. Is the style okay?'

'A little heavy on the damnits.'

'Shut up, damnit. When I want your opinion I won't ask for it. I could've dived over the side to cool off, only I couldn't. That would've been too obvious. Or something. So I turned tail and fled, back through First Class, down the gangplank, to the car. I put my foot down and drove home faster than I'd ever driven in my life. My mother took one look at me and said, "You look like you've seen a ghost." '

145

'Good old mom.'

'I smiled weakly and –'

'Went to languish round the swimming pool.'

'Check.'

'If only I'd known.'

'If only I'd known. Helena, we didn't know a damned thing.'

'No, we didn't. Another friend of mine was at that sailing. She was pregnant – a Protestant friend, of course. She'd been trying to tell me all week, and I hadn't heard.'

'You heard, it just didn't compute.'

'That's right.'

'I didn't figure out that sailing until I told you about it all those years after.'

'You weren't ready to make the connections till then.'

'I guess. I could've gone my whole life, if you hadn't come back –'

Yes and the poisonous question lies between us, would that have been better?

'It's better to know,' she says softly. 'It's always better to know.' Then, briskly, 'And where are we off to, today?'

'Oh, raising a few more ghosts.'

'Darling, we are the ghosts.'

She's an irresistible spectre, in the rocking chair, a nubile grandmother. I'd never tell her. It's long been a fantasy of mine to put my head in her lap as she sits in a chair and then keep going. The fact that she is naked, seated in a rocking chair, embellishes the fantasy. The reality's better, the edge of the seat to give me better leverage, and she grips the arm rests, her breath beginning to come in hard gusts. Oh, but I want them harder and gustier, and I strafe her thighs with a sore, protesting tongue. I want it to be that tongue alone that brings her chair to a halt. It's rocking, more jerking now, back and forth with the sweeps of my tongue so she's not my grandmother rocking me in her lap, she is my child. I'm rocking her electrically awake and the chair halts as she falls in a heap in the seat and sobs, as she sometimes does. I brush her thighs with my head, for comfort, and she slides down

146

into my arms.

'Whew.' She lies back sweating and I get a robe to cover her with.

'Don't want you to catch cold.'

'Thanks, mom. I think I catch hot a lot more than I catch cold.'

'Good.'

We lie under the robe together, cocooned, not even smoking; content.

'Know what I need?'

'What?'

'A shower. You coming?'

'What, now?'

I join her there. It's a tropical rainstorm. It's liquid manna from heaven we take on our tongues. My hangover's taken a religious turn this morning. Wonder if it'll last? Hangover from dream as much as from booze.

'Time to dry out. I mean off.'

'Freudian slip.'

We dry each other and ourselves.

'Where to now?' she asks me.

'Do you want me to tell you? Where I'd like to go?'

'If it's not California.'

'Funny you should say that. No, it's New Jersey.'

'We're in New Jersey. As I said.'

'More New Jersey? Could you stand it? Are you tired of driving? Are you tired of me?'

Teasing, she half-shrugs, considering. Then she frightens me. She looks around the Early American room with its rocker, and her eyes land on the bed with a strange, yearning expression, as if they want to rest there forever.

'Georgia? Want to stay here another night? We could go for a long walk today, and have an afternoon nap –'

I still have five whole days left in the U.S.

She looks at me with a little smile. 'This is gonna sound awfully funny coming from me, kid. But you've got me hooked on this odyssey thing of yours. It'd all be left undone if we stayed here now. I feel like I've got to hassle you on, if

147

your own will is fading.'

It does sound awfully funny coming from her. As if she's as driven, now, as I am. As I *was*. I've done it. I've been to Coldwick. What more can the gods require? Apart from having her chauffeur me to the graveyard to exhume Wall's casket and stare at his bones, slime, whatever remains after five years, at best a black liquid, as that cheery soul, Albert Camus, put it, what more can I possibly do, to come to terms? Whose terms, anyway? She's talking as if it were a mission. She's taking it seriously. Much, much too seriously. Taking me. Much too seriously. As long as she kept herself ever so slightly aloof and ironic, I was safe. What now?

'Georgia,' be funny ha-ha, not funny peculiar, I want to say, indulge me but don't believe me or we'll both sink into – what? Madness? *Pursuit.* Of what, for Christ's sake, of what?

She's dressing. I turn to assemble my own scrambled clothes, lucky jeans and t-shirts don't show the lust, I'm about to say, when I know where I want her to take me.

'Well?' She asks it into the mirror where she's settling her eyebrows.

'Okay. Got it.'

She nods, satisfied. Not even 'It better be good' – or 'It better be bad'.

We trudge down into the lobby and I have the joys of billpaying to explore. There's a deference about the person who accepts your money. I always envied her before, as she received it as her due. Now that it's mine I find it isn't that big a deal. It's more businesslike than anything else. Of course it would be. What fools we nuns and mothers are! Letting ourselves live in abject humiliation and embarrassment over transactions we imagine we never could master – and all the time they're so simple. Poverty, chastity and obedience, nuns and mothers have those three in common.

Out to the car. If I believe my own inner configuration, if instead of Father, Son and Holy Ghost I find Mother, Daughter and Dark Lord or Lady, then today we're en route to the latter's domain. By whose definition? I thought I'd decided to own my own underworld?

148

'We're looking for Route 202,' I pick up the map, and there it is, five miles from here there's an exit to 202. Of course, there is. Hades can't be far.

Resist! Both the morbidity and the spurious theology. I'm determined. We light cigarettes.

'I'll just drive, kid, till you tell me to stop, okay?'

'Aren't you tired?'

'I love driving,' she answers. 'I never get tired of it.'

She loves driving, I love being driven. What compatibility.

'I might try to give you some background.'

'Oh, good.'

The unacknowledged sun shines through the windshield at us.

'Hey, it's a beautiful day!'

'It is. I'm waiting for the background.'

'Okay, okay. I'm trying to figure out where to start. First stop is the Assumption.'

'What Assumption? How can you visit an assumption?'

'Do you want background, or not?'

'Sorry.' She subsides, my crumbled darling. Field of threshed wheat, this morning.

But she's still too serious. She's treating this like some sort of task from the Major Arcana – well, I'm treating it like that. But she's not supposed to ask me for intensity, she's supposed to relieve me of it.

'Can I ask you something? Before you go into your – uh – background?'

'Sure.'

'Why did you marry Jonathan?'

'Because of Mr Joy's Theology 101A,' I answer promptly.

'Oh, I see. This was at Aquinas?'

'I met him my second year there – only it wasn't there, it was in England. As you know. The sailing and all that.'

'Right – the sailing and all that. Let's stick to chronological order. You went to Oxford and then –'

'Then I met Jonathan. Outside Blackwell's in Oxford next to a map, reading a map. We were both lost.' We still are.

'And he said?'

149

'He said, "What a super sunset." '

'Ah, yes. I see. The old sunset ploy.'

'The day I surrendered to him the precious flower of my virginity, by then nineteen years in its vase and beginning to go brown at the edges –'

'Yes –'

'A prophetic thing happened.'

'Oh, yes.'

'I was walking down the Woodstock Road towards his college, to meet him, when a man came out of the shrubbery and exposed himself. Not prophetic in the crude sense, though you could take it that way. But in another sense. A misleading sense.'

'Yes? What did this prophet have to say?'

'It was Indian summer. That in itself was misleading. It doesn't happen in England. Much. Like self-exposure. In fact that was the first, last and only act of self-exposure I was to witness in England for – years. And years.'

'And he was probably a foreigner.'

She's dry and ironic again, I've drawn her back in, we're going to be all right. The relentless note is gone from her voice, the pushy Virgil to my Dante, or some damn thing. Damn!

'Hey, remember Virgil?'

' "Sunt lacrimae rerum –

' "Et mentem mortalia tangunt".'

'Wish I hadn't thought of it.'

'Wish Virgil hadn't thought of it, kid.'

That was the best thing of all, our last year at S&M. I had her to myself, almost, in a class of four. Fourth Year Latin wasn't very popular.

'All right, so you got to his room and he exposed himself.'

'All right. It all happened on the floor. I thought in my foolishness that if I stayed away from the little alcove where the bed was, I'd be all right. I was wrong.'

She sighs.

'Well, Georgia, you know the rest. Spreadeagled like a frog on a dissecting table, wanting to laugh at the absurd position

150

you find yourself in, which you somehow had never imagined. Then he was giving me a smelly old sweater of his to wear home and back I walked along the Woodstock Road with the wind howling up where no wind had ever howled before.'

'I remember that wind. Cold. But how come he didn't walk you home?'

'He was like that.'

'No men in the bushes this time.'

'No prophecies. Only, I got back to the convent hostel where we lived in Oxford and ran straight upstairs to have a bath, of course. Will all great Neptune's ocean wash this blood back between my legs and all that. And as I was getting out of the bath, I saw it.'

'It?'

'A little pink thing like a wad of Kleenex with a faint pink stain. Down the drain it went.'

'So you lost your virginity in a convent, after all. Congratulations. Bathos. Go on.'

'Go on – to what? Guilt, fear, paranoia –'

'That can be an assumption. What happened next?'

'Don't you like this road?'

'It's great, kid, great. Go on.'

'I had to go back. I wrote and he didn't. But all along I knew I'd get back to him eventually, because Mr Joy had said so. In Theology 101A, in my first year. He said it was okay to fuck if you were commited. He said it in a roundabout sort of way, but that was the gist of it. So I was committed. Married, in short.'

'And that's it?'

'That's it, Georgia.'

'That's a great little stand-up comedy routine you've got there. Or sit-down,' her eye flashes over me sternly as I sit like Simeon in her office. 'Only I asked a question. I want to know why you married Jonathan.'

'Well?'

This is as bad as Bernie's inquisition. Worse. Why? It's an easier question. It has to do with the past, my speciality. A

151

question to answer with hindsight, the only sort of vision I seem to achieve.

Bathos.

'I can wait,' she says determinedly. 'If you're thinking.'

'I'm thinking, I'm thinking!' Distractedly, thinking of slinking around that convent hostel with my guilty secret, my guilty pain, wincing when I peed, wondering how easy it was to get pregnant, wondering if it didn't happen automatically, an exchange, swap that pink plug for a baby.

'Children, our bodies are temples of the Holy Ghost,' the nuns had said down through the years and I always thought it was plausible, it must be cool and quiet in there, like a church. But what now? Was the temple a nursery? Didn't it have to be one or the other?

'You know, this is a nice road,' she says conversationally.

'So glad you like it.'

'Is it really such a tough question?'

'Yes. It is. I'm stuck. I don't know.'

'Okay. I'll accept that. But wouldn't it be an idea to try and figure it out?'

She's doing to me what I did to her this morning. Do you want to be a partner of Sabine Chem? Do you want to be Jonathan's partner?

'I'll try. I won't think. Ask me again.'

'Why did you marry Jonathan?'

10

'I can't say, like Everest, because he was there,' I recognise a familiar weakness in my voice, but I go on anyway. Why not try? 'Because he wasn't. I had to pursue him across the ocean and then chase him all over London –'

'So we've eliminated that one,' she says pleasantly, my interrogator. 'Could it be that you loved him?'

Could it? I want, suddenly, to plot our course like a general plotting a war, to plant pins with coloured heads on the important battle sites. 'I think I wanted him – sexually – right away. Only I didn't recognise the feeling.'

'Being a virgin.'

'Being a virgin.' I'd wanted her, first, and not recognised that feeling either. Being a virgin. The dangling participles around here are getting to me. But I feel I must go blindly plunging on, not backtrack. 'I went on wanting him, but it changed. The wanting. Less about wanting to incorporate something in him I recognised as my birthright, but thought I couldn't have, or was too cowardly to go and get for myself –'

'Like ambition and energy –'

'Like ambition and energy – it changed into just wanting him. Wanting him to give himself to me. Because –' I want to describe him, as he stood by that map, but I can't. Silvery-black, curly hair stuck out around his face like a sort of Jewish Afro, only there were no Afros yet. The same

153

Christmas-tree stuff bubbled up on his chest where his red wool shirt was open. His eyes were elusive grey-green chameleon, like hers. Would that make it better for her, or worse?

'Because he was the most beautiful man I'd ever seen. He answered some hunger in me, the way certain landscapes answered me the first time I saw them. The landscapes were – are – rocky and harsh and sunburnt. Greece and Spain. I'd give all the green leafy foliage in the world for a parched, scorched, threadbare landscape. I didn't know that till I went there. Like with him. Is that love?' I shrug. 'I fell in love with what I thought was him. What I thought his landscape meant. I made it up and called it Jonathan, that meaning. I've never found him. I know less about him than about people I've known for half an hour. I've never had him, either.'

'What?'

'I mean – he likes games with sex. Teasing is his speciality.'

'There's a lot to be said for teasing,' she says, teasingly.

'Sure there is. It's very exciting. Very heating. But it isn't enough. Once in a while, when we make love in the much-maligned missionary position, I have the feeling he – almost – gives himself. But he draws back from the brink.' Oh, shit. There's a lump in my throat the size of a baseball. 'But I get confused about what's him and what's – men. He's been the only one, really. He cuts me off all the time and I don't know,' a weird convulsive sound punctuates that sentence, shocking us both. 'I don't know if that's just the nature of the beast, or him. He just cuts me off. Talking, making love. Being together. I feel he gets his bit, as much as he wants – or needs – and then it's all over, and I'm still in the middle, or even at the beginning. Even if I've come, as far as sex goes. You know?'

She nods.

'And I do come. Almost infallibly. But I make it happen, I sit on top of him and make it happen. Sometimes I hate it like that, I feel like I'm using him – but he doesn't mind. He prefers it, I think; he doesn't have to do much. It never seems to occur to him that I might want more than just any old

154

orgasm. His tenderness is locked down deep, and it's so rare it seems rich when he produces it, but I've come to the conclusion it only seems rich because of its rarity. And I think he values it that way. He's afraid, God, he's afraid! He's afraid that if he let it be common currency it'd be devalued, somehow. He thinks it has to be special or it's – unworthy.'

'So,' she clears her throat. 'He devalues yours, assuming you show it rather more often.'

'I used to.' I smile. 'He used to do what I did when you first asked me that question. He entertained me instead of answering me. Now he doesn't bother. It's hardly surprising, given – everything.'

Meaning, her.

'What're you waiting for?'

'He just deflects me, nowadays. I guess I'm waiting till the deflection becomes rejection. Then I can, as they say, go in peace.'

'But –'

'I know, I know. But I can't seem to give up. I try. I should. He holds me back. He ties me in knots. He gives me just enough rope to hang myself and I do, every time. But I can't help thinking it'll all change.'

'Ah.'

'Yes. I keep thinking the next time I turn round, he'll *be* there. Then he is, and it's great – for ten minutes. Then I feel like shit.'

'Ten minutes?'

'The first ten minutes, or hour, or whatever. Then he starts to think about when he has to go, or he has to go, and it all collapses, he isn't really there at all. And when he goes it feels like an amputation. Of me. So I go around feeling amputated, then I recover, and by then he's back and it starts all over again. And that, Georgia, is the clearest way I can describe our relationship.'

'I'm sorry I asked.'

I shrug. For all my infidelities, all my desertions – Bernie, and now Georgia – Jonathan is a pursuit all its own, a royal hunt of the sun that's long since become a royal pain in the ass. And still, somehow, I don't give up. It's just stubbornness, or inability to switch courses, to change tacks, tracks or anything, for that matter. An inability to change.

'Tell me about Mr Joy,' her hand covers my knee for a second.

'He looked a little bit like Frankie Avalon. A very little bit.'

'Who the hell is Frankie Avalon?'

'Georgia Manion. I was in love with Frankie Avalon. Remember Fabian?'

'Of course I remember Fabian,' she says indignantly. 'I, too, aspired to normality, once upon a time.'

'I thought you still did?'

'So did I,' she says thoughtfully. 'Anyway. Frankie Avalon?'

She's given me hope. 'Frankie Avalon was around the same time as Fabian, when we were thirteen or so. Just coming up to S&M.'

'Hang on, this Theology teacher, this Mr Joy, did he wear tight pants and sing, while encouraging you all to find the nearest floor and –'

'He did none of those things, Georgia. He was dark and shy and intense. That's all. I saw him on the Dick Clark show.'

'What was Mr Joy doing on the Dick Clark show? Preaching free love? No wonder Dick Clark got into trouble.'

'He didn't preach free love. He read D. H. Lawrence to us and said, "Love God and do what thou wilt", only Be Committed. That was the whole point about him. Have you got that now, Georgia?'

'I think so,' she says meekly.

'I saw Frankie Avalon on the Dick Clark show. I had my moments of normality. I almost fainted dead away into the arms of my best friend –'

'Girlfriend, of course.'

'Of course, I was thirteen and –'

'Normal. So you said.'

'You know what I mean. Didn't you want desperately to pass for WASP?'

'What?'

156

'You know, Georgia, WASP. White Anglo-Saxon Protestant. All of us kids from the Assumption wanted to be it, or as close to it as we could get. Didn't you even watch the Dick Clark show?'

'You mean American Bandstand? The show where they all danced? How could you go to that with another girl? They'd throw you off.'

'That was a different show, Georgia. There were two.'

'Okay, kid, you're right. It all comes back to me now. Only they didn't rate, in the south.'

'What a cultural backwater. How's this for a diagnostic map of the U.S.? The East Coast's manic-depressive, the West Coast's schizophrenic, the Mid-West's catatonic, the South's paranoiac?'

'Not bad for the spur of the moment. That show you went on, was it the Friday night one, with the -IFIC buttons, for TERRIFIC?'

'I kept my -IFIC button for years.'

'You mean you don't still have it?'

'It was wonderful. The show, I mean. It was Paul Anka, not Frankie Avalon. I only wished it was Frankie Avalon. Paul Anka, and he sang "Lonely Boy" and the lights flashed telling us when to shut up and when to applaud. It was just like being back at the Assumption, with lights instead of nuns. And I was there with my blood sister, we'd done the whole bit with the razor blade on the finger and all that.'

'You started young.'

'Much younger than that.'

'You never asked me to come on the Dick Clark show with you.'

'Want to?'

'There is no more Dick Clark show.'

'I'll be your blood sister if you want.'

'I suspect you already are. What was her name?'

'Lorraine.'

'I used to visit my cousins up north and they watched all that crap,' she says after a second's silence. 'Every afternoon they watched American Bandstand. All these juvenile

157

delinquent-looking kids dancing –'

'Hoody-looking, we said then. Yes. And there were favourite couples everyone adored. Especially Bob and Justine. Justine looked like a Barbie doll and Bob looked just like a Ken doll.'

'Better equipped, I hope.'

'I wouldn't know about that. Justine had a long blonde pageboy, perfect, it never moved as she danced, and a perfect face that never moved either.'

'So you spent your afternoons lusting after this Prom Queen.'

'Maybe I did,' I agree sadly. 'I certainly adored her. I wonder what ever happened to Justine and Bob?'

'Do we have to go look for them, too?'

'No. On to the Assumption. Once we had a basketball team, once while we were trying to scramble out of the ghetto and be normal.'

'You played basketball?'

'No. Worse than that. I was in love with Pat O'Rourke, who was captain of the team. And I was –'

'Don't tell me. Captainette of the cheerleading squad.'

'No,' I regard the wavy hills round us with sorrow. 'That might have made all the difference. The road not taken. Captainette of the cheerleading squad. Might have normalised me forever. Turned me into a Barbie doll. With Pat O'Rourke as my very own Ken. All would've been well.'

'In the best of all possible worlds.' She shudders at the wheel.

'I lacked the prime American characteristic required – co-ordination. But I did cheer, in the back row somewhere. I could stay with everyone else for the words or the actions, not for both.'

'So you chose the words.'

'Well. But my own individual failings were nothing compared with what was to come. First there were the cheers. Cheers are made for nice short WASP names, you know? Names of places, like "Cryon". That must make a great cheer name.'

158

'It must.'

'But Assumption. "Give me an A – give me an S – give me another S" – the other team would give up trying to spell it after that.'

'Don't blame them. That was enough.'

'Especially since our principal, Sister Gloria, had ordered the uniforms. In her unforgivable innocence, she ordered the shirts for which we'd sold cakes and babysat and generally hauled ass, shirts for the boys and shirts for the girls, with those first three letters on them in big, gold, fancy all-American print. A – S – S. With big gold dots in between.'

'Oh, no!'

'Oh, yes. And we couldn't even tell her what was wrong. She would've hit us all on the palms with her steel ruler. It was like Queen Victoria and lesbians. There were no such things as asses, to her. So we wore them. Once or twice. Then the basketball team died a quiet death.'

'Tell me about Pat O'Rourke.'

'He lasted a long time.'

'Then what happened to him?'

'I mean for me, he lasted a long time. From the age of seven to the age of fifteen, when I met you. With a few –'

'A few blood sisters in between, h'm? To say nothing of the other kind?'

'Something like that. My problem with Pat O'Rourke was, I never learned to play hard to get.'

'You're right.'

'From the very first I was shameless.'

'Relentless, Helena. Relentless.'

'You know what I did when I was seven?'

'Raped a nun.'

'No – but Ricky Wilson did. Not raped her, just pulled off her veil when she leaned over his desk. She was a very short nun. Sister Dolores. Of the seven veils.'

'Nope.'

'Sister Dolores, anyway. He reached up and yanked it off and there she stood with this short funny hairdo. Not a "do" – just hair. Looking ridiculous. With her wimple round her

159

face like a picture frame. The veils were only pinned on.'

'What did she do?'

'First she just stood there. Then she bent down very, very slowly, and picked up her veil. He cowered, thinking she was gonna kill him. It was sacrilege, we all knew that. The word hung in the air: sacrilege. She pinned her veil back on, very efficiently, in seconds, over her short grey unexceptional hair. We told all the other kids in the school that she was bald as an egg.'

'Of course you did. Go on.'

'She said, "Ricky Wilson, go sit in the wastebasket." '

'What?'

'She had to say it twice. Then he did. I guess it was the first thing she could think of. He slouched up and plonked his seven-year-old arse down in the wastebasket, which will have a large part to play in the story I started out to tell, Georgia — it was a First Friday, so we'd had to bring our breakfasts for after Mass. Remember fasting?'

'I remember. A sort of metallic taste in your mouth. Empty stomach. White cloth on the Communion rail, very white. Not so white when we stopped having to fast from midnight.'

'Right. So there were eggshells and grapefruit halves in the wastebasket. The next thing that happened was, Dolores forgot all about him till lunchtime, and when she told him to get up, he couldn't. She had to get Pat O'Rourke to prise him loose and for a while it looked like he couldn't. She was scared.'

'Of course she was. It was her arse on the line.'

'She really lost face then. That, on top of the picture frame.'

'She had quite a day.'

'It wasn't over. Pat O'Rourke got Ricky out and then she asked him to take the wastebasket round for our scraps. We'd been doing art or something. When he got to my desk he bent over to pick something up and I —'

'Pulled his veil off!'

'Kissed him. He marched right up to Dolores, wastebasket and all, and said to her, " 'Ster, Helena Carnet just

160

kissed me." '

'What a little creep.'

'I know. I should have known right then and there.'

'Did she make you sit in the wastebasket? Is that the tragic secret of your life? "A case of arrested development – eight years in the wastebasket?" '

'She just said, "Who kissed you?" And he said, "Helena Carnet, 'Ster." And she said, "Oh, no." And that was all.'

'I like that.'

'Then another time in dancing class, which we all went to at the local public school, in another doomed attempt at normality, I raced across the room so fast in a Sadie Hawkins dance, to collar Pat O'Rourke, that I fell and broke my leg.'

'Sure, and they shot you. You did not.'

'Well, I fell. And the shame. I wanted to be a knight on a charger, not a horse.'

'You weren't supposed to be either.'

'I know. Till now. Can I be your knight on a charger?' I squeeze her thigh. 'Please?'

'What's involved? Do I have to be a princess in a tower,' she squints at me.

'No. You have to be – what you are.'

'I have a feeling that's some sort of statement,' she growls. 'I'm hungry.'

'Me, too. Hey, we're in Mountain Vista, the ugliest place in New Jersey.'

'In the world.'

Right out of somewhere, comes this hiatus in natural beauty, this nowhere, this dump. Squalid, ugly, brazen as Coldwick's one-corner slum.

'We'll be out of it in a minute. Then we come to a delicatessen. I'll buy lunch.'

'Why? I dunno. I don't want to feel like a kept woman.'

'Why not?'

'Why not?' She laughs. 'Why not? Okay. You buy lunch. I'll be a kept woman.'

'Forever?'

'On five hundred bucks, kid?' She shakes her head.

'Well. When my ship comes in.'

'Oh, then. Sure, I'll just say goodbye to my life, my family, my — I can just hear my mother. "Mom, I'm going away forever to be a kept woman." "Georgia, that's terrible. But — okay. Who's the lucky guy? Is the bastard married?" '

'Sorry, darling,' she says a moment later.

'I don't see why you should be sorry.'

'Well neither should you be,' she snaps. 'If it weren't for your husband and children, I wouldn't be here. You must know that. It'd be far too risky. Not,' she adds with a laugh, 'that it isn't far too risky anyway.'

'You know something, Georgia? I can't imagine your life. The one you'd say goodbye to.'

'No, I don't imagine you can.'

'What's it like?'

'Expensive.'

'What else?'

'Very crowded. You know me, I like crowds. Dinner parties. All that. I give them and I go to them. Every once in a while I get sick of them. I break the rules.'

'What're the rules?'

'Oh, telling dirty jokes with extreme delicacy in a thick southern accent. Staying with the women, when it's indicated. Only sometimes, like the last dinner party I went to, I don't. I'd just had enough. So I stayed with the men and the brandy instead of drifting across the room with the women, to the sherry —'

'Sherry? After dinner?'

'Awful, isn't it? I wasn't having any. The women were all watching me. The men smoked these big, fat cigars, and they offered one to me just to make the point that I didn't belong. So I took it, and I slid it in and out of my mouth, and I nibbled it and gobbled at it and commented on it, and I had them all sitting there hard as rocks when they were supposed to be hard as nails. And the women were furious, because it was as if I was sucking them all off, collectively, and also giving them all the finger, including them. I won't be invited there again, but I will be remembered.'

'Georgia. What a performance.'

'Oh, I know, I know,' she wails. 'One day I'll go too far.'

'You know what I think?'

'You think I'm cruisin' for a bruisin' on purpose. You think I want to get fired so I can go off and be a great tragic actress, don't you?'

'I knew someone once –'

'What, someone else?'

'She was bitter because she'd had this daughter who married a brain surgeon and gave up a career, as a tragic actress, when she married him. And got leukemia. Her mother always thought she'd acted out a tragic role in her life because she'd not done so on the stage.'

'I get it. So you think I've given up a career as a comedienne and so I have to act the clown at clients' dinner parties.'

'Something like that.'

'You're too smart for your own good, you know that?'

'Unfortunately, only about other people's lives, not my own. A sort of Cassandra syndrome.'

'Do I detect a note of self-pity?'

'Perhaps. Not being a great tragic writer, I suffer a lot from pity and fear, or self-pity and fear, in my life.'

'I diagnose that you want to be a real poet like that bloody Greek woman who shall be nameless, and so you play a Cassandra role in your life instead.'

'Thanks, Doc.'

'That'll be a hundred bucks. This isn't England, you know.'

'No. No National Health. Good thing I've just come into a small fortune.'

'If it's small, you'll get well fast or not at all.'

'I'll try.'

'Which one?'

'I love you.'

'Is that in lieu of the hundred?' Georgia sniffs. 'What's that smell?'

'Hey, slow down, that's Boontoon!'

'Known for its smell. It's horrible.'

163

'It's carbon.'

'Dear old carbon. The stuff of life. Too bad it stinks.'

'This is the halfway point between Middlebrow and Coldwick. We used to meet here, behind the carbon factory, when I came in the summer. To Coldwick. And home.'

'I see. Memories of a carbon factory. Olfactory memories of a carbon factory.'

The smell disappears, but the landscape turns grimy as if the carbon had settled on it.

'Look at this place, Georgia. Isn't it horrible? It's worse than Mountain Vista.'

'Why is it called Mountain Vista? Was it named by pathological liars?'

'This is the ugliest place in the state –'

'No, Mountain Vista's the ugliest place in the state. *This* is the ugliest place in the world.'

'Delicatessen, my delicatessen!'

'I hope you're not referring to me.'

'To it, Georgia, right there. Even the ugliest place in the world has something. But I could call you "Deli" – like Delilah. Shall I compare thee to a delicatessen? Thou art more lovely and more smelly – than the average Jewish deli –'

'Oh, God. That poor Greek woman is turning in her grave.'

'Or maybe make it a verb, a synonym for love. I delicatessen you, Georgia.'

'Sounds cannibalistic.'

'Of course. Why are all the best things taboo? Like incest and cannibalism?'

'Beats me. Well, here we are at the Love Store.' Stopped, we look at each other. Tired but titillated, you might say.

'Well, kid? Let's go get that pot of chopped liver at the end of the rainbow.'

'Italian salami. Sliced tin.'

'What?'

'Sliced tin,' our car doors slam and we stand in the truly anaemic street of wherever-we-are, NJ; I'd have called it

Delicatessen, NJ, but I doubt that the person who named it had such vision. 'That's what my grandmother used to say. My other grandmother, in her French accent, at the delicatessen. Ah, transubstantiation is nothing compared with the marvels they perform at a good delicatessen.'

'Mr Joy might not agree.'

'He'd say only if they were committed.'

'Sounds to me like he should've been committed.'

The delicatessen's run by a satisfyingly large lady with an even more satisfying accent, thick and mysterious.

'You looked at her with your tongue hanging out.'

'Jealous?'

'Of the Venus of Willendorf? Are you kidding?'

'But think of her dowry!'

'Marrying for money is one thing, Helena. Marrying for food is another.'

We carry our packages to the village green, or the village grey, where we sit in a little pool of sunlight, shallow and faint and evaporating fast as we eat.

'Mama used to come and see us every weekend in New Jersey, carrying CARE packages from the local Italian deli. She didn't believe people in the country could eat decently.'

'She was probably right. Fuck the farms.'

'Before we moved to Jersey, we lived next door to Mama and Pom, in an apartment building they owned. The rents put Marguerite's sisters through college. Would've put her through, except for me.'

'What've you got against higher education?'

'It was heaven, living there.'

'In the Bronx? I thought heaven was a delicatessen. You didn't live in one, did you?'

'Not quite. But Mama always had stuff around, French bread and salami and cheese.' Just like grandma always had salted cashew nuts, root beer and ice cream. But the taste was the same: love.

'There was a little connecting door between our apartments, just big enough for me. Made for me, I thought. I used to go in first thing in the morning and have breakfast with Mama and Pom. Then in the afternoon, Michele, my mother's youngest sister, would come back from CCNY with pockets full of Necco wafers and Hershey bars.

'I think I expected Communion to taste like Necco wafers. A new, hitherto unknown flavour of Necco wafers, a very stinging pure peppermint, or maybe aniseed. But of course it didn't.'

'More like chewing gum that lost its flavour on the bedpost overnight.'

'I'd like to be four again. Before we moved from New York.'

'I might have trouble arranging it. You keep on going backwards, kid, you know where you'll end up?'

'Given my recent excursions, it's not a bad place.'

The sun's given up the ghost, just disappeared. Melted into a pile of ash in the sky. No, there it is, phoenix-like from an ashen cloud. It rises in my solar plexus, too, and I can see it in Georgia's eyes. In England you can go for months without it. Are they going without it, on that little island, as I sit here on this one stuffing myself in the recurrent sun? And what are they eating? Between the booze which the Michelob in my hot fist is reviving in my bloodstream, and the fatigue that lodges in all my bones, I want to put my head down somewhere and surrender. I want to say okay, I give up. But how can you say that, and who can you say it to, to make it official?

'Speaking of poets. I once read something about Anna Akhmatova. It said "She was unable to cope with the exigencies of everyday life" or something like that. I always wondered how she managed it.'

'What?'

'Being unable to cope with the exigencies of everyday life. So that someone would come along and say that. And make it okay.'

'It's only okay because she's dead, dodo.'

'I guess. And doesn't have to cope with the exigencies of everyday life. That's one good thing about death. Who was your first corpse?'

She jumps. 'Jesus, Helena.'

166

'Was that a vision, and if so I must say it's a rather morbid one?'

'Oh, shut up. I guess it was one of those endless birds that didn't make it. You know.'

'Eyedroppers full of water and warm milk. And they always died anyway.'

'And you had great funerals.'

'The best. And you got to be a priest.'

'At last. After failing as a witch doctor. But you believed they'd live the first few times.'

'At least they were more fun than dolls.'

'I hate to tell you this, Georgia, but I loved dolls.'

'Oh, *no*.'

'Yes. I know, it's pretty bad. I was the only one in my women's group who'd admit to it. But I loved them, all kinds, the kind you played with and the kind you just looked at. I had four of those. Show dolls. There was a nun, a Spanish dancer, a bride, and a chimney sweep. I used to tell my friends I was Queen of the Dolls and they'd talk to me, at night, in a secret language only I could understand, out of all humans.'

'Of course. Always the same old egotistical yo-yo.'

'Then one summer I went to the shore with a friend –'

'You've spent most of your life running off to the seaside with various women! And I thought I was unique!'

'Only then our families came, too.'

'Yours still does, kid.'

'We both had these rubber dolls, baby dolls, the kind that leaked all over the place, that you could pretend were crying or peeing or dribbling –'

'The incontinent dolls. I remember them.'

'Anyway, all summer long we had this fantasy that our dolls were turning real. We kept finding evidence, like we'd leave them on their backs and they'd turn onto their stomachs, stuff like that.'

'Guess you were fated for motherhood.'

There's a note of bitterness in her voice. Fated for what sort of motherhood? Are they still only real to me sometimes, only animated when it's convenient? When I can spare the time, from reverie and prophecy and plain old fantasy? I miss them. I miss them less drastically than I missed Sam while I was with Bernie, because I'm happier; but I still miss them. They give me an ache of longing in my stomach somewhere, maternal hunger the salami and hard roll don't do much about. Maybe this time it'll work and I'll go back and know – what? Maybe this time, whatever it is, I'll find out and then go home, wherever that is. No. I'll make myself at home.

'Time to go,' Georgia says flatly.

Garbage considerately placed in the bin on the green, we climb back into the car and Georgia starts up. She smiles her pained smile, the one I see, have always seen, with love and dread.

'Go on, tell me about your first stiff. I dare you.'

'It was my great-grandfather, on my mother's side. A Frenchman. He'd come to New York after his daughters, with my great-grandmother, to live in the Bronx, where he had mistresses –'

'Nobody in the Bronx has mistresses.'

'Don't be such a snob. He did, and he grew vegetables.'

'In the Bronx. Mistresses and vegetables. Well, he was French.'

'That's all there is, anywhere. Lovers and aubergines.'

'Lovers and tomatoes. And lettuces.'

'Maybe a little Camembert.'

'How come you never talk about your great-grandmothers?'

'It was a bad year for great-grandmothers. Bad. Vintage. They had rotten lives and they were sour old ladies.'

'I see. Go on.'

'When he first came over, they took him to Coney Island –'

'Ellis. Island.'

'No, Coney. They didn't come from mainland France, they came from a tiny island off Newfoundland called Saint Pierre. Tiny and cold. He'd been sent there to be chief of police.'

'Was that some sort of punishment? One too many mistresses or something?'

'I don't know. But they took him on a roller coaster at

168

Coney Island and he stood up and tried to grab an overhead rafter to get off –'

'Christ –'

'And then died in his sleep at ninety-six. That was when I saw him.'

It was hard to remember that Mama, his daughter, had been that brave. To come from Saint Pierre and get a job teaching French in a girls' academy, probably not unlike S&M. It was as if that one leap exhausted her. It hadn't exhausted her faith in any apparent sense, and yet she was afraid to move very much, afterwards. She'd never lost her French accent, just like I've never lost my American one.

'I used to speak English with a French accent. When I was little. From talking to Mama. So they tell me. Funny, that's the only accent I've ever picked up.'

Who was she? Brave enough to cross the sea, and after that almost afraid to cross the street. Only the church and the delicatessen persuaded her out; and visits to our house, at weekends. She'd haunted me almost as much as Wall did, after her death, with a similar sense of waste, of unfulfilment.

'I inherited her tickle spot. Right here.' I touch the side of my neck, and Georgia grins.

'Her what spot?'

'You know, the ones who haunt you are the ones that don't seem to – *do* – their lives. To live them out. You know?'

She doesn't speak and when I look over, she's reaching for a cigarette, tight-lipped, a little pale.

'Georgia?'

She shakes her head.

Is she wondering, as I am, whether she'll be one of the restless dead, the unsatisfied ones? Will we dodge our lives? Hedge our bets? I don't want Sam and Mike to feel about me what I feel about Wall. I don't want them to mourn me the way I've mourned him, with that stricken, bottomless mourning, a useless mourning for what never was. But unless they're living on the sidelines of their own lives, they won't. It'll be up to them, whatever I do. But also up to me. That's what I'm here for.

'Is that all about your great-grandfather?'

She sounds weary. How could she not be, after a day among the dead; at least we lived our night. I remember another teacher at Aquinas talking about Romeo and Juliet, about love that only blossomed at night and couldn't face the light. It was something in the nature of that form of passion, she said, a flaw there in the centre of it, not anything that came from outside. Not family feuds or prejudices; or social strictures, I think, now, with a sinking heart. Surely it applies to us, too! Not the ocean itself, that separates me from Georgia, Georgia from me. But a flaw at the centre of our long passion, a flaw that renders it destructive.

If I let Mr Joy determine my marriage to Jonathan, I need not let Mrs Grey determine the course of my marriage to Georgia. I felt it to be one. I never exactly felt unfaithful to Jonathan, with Georgia; I felt bigamous.

It was that first time she came over, the spring after Wall's death, that I married her. In Oxford; the site of both my marriages. But this one took place outside, in the Magdalen deer park, as we strolled and she took my hand, swearing about how she hated being unconventional but she couldn't help it, the hell with it. Then she was silent, and then she went to pick me some crocuses that were ruffling the grass under an enormous plane tree. I watched her pick them, my heart fluttery but ordered, somehow, like the flowers, perfect for all their pleats and their fragile opacity.

I watched her and thought, now, yes, here, I'm yours. She brought me a flower and the second thought came: And you're mine. I gave her a flower. We walked out from under the canopy of the tree, into the sun, into the light; so there, Mrs Grey, my silent, sceptical matron of honour! We exist in the day.

Georgia's looking over, quizzically. She's back in the Bronx with old grandpère.

'Oh, my godmother took me up to see him. It felt like the stairs went on forever, that day, as if we were climbing to heaven, though I'd been up them before. Maybe I felt it was an effort. We went in and there he was, on the big bed, in his blue suit. It seemed very strange. I asked her why he wasn't talking, and she said, "The talking part's gone up to God."'

'So you figure as long as you keep talking you'll be all right.'

'Sort of, I guess. I didn't feel scared, I remember. I had a feeling of – majesty.'

She nods.

The road's starting to look really familiar. We can't be more than ten miles from Assumption. It's a good thing, too, because that dark feeling, I won't personify it by giving it a name and a title, putting it into a habit – is coming over us again. Georgia looks tired. I feel tired. I close my eyes and see, of all the superfluous unnecessary sights, another dead man in a suit, another mute, this one not in a bed but a box, in what they have the gall – or is it gallows humour, once again – to call a Funeral Home. Home. A word more misused than love, or at least as much . . . I light a cigarette, disgusted by the quicksand in my mind, the sickly sentimentality of my thoughts, only meant to distract and dissuade from the fact of that Home . . . what would it matter if they called it an ice-house? If they called it Limbo? It would be as cold, as nowhere, as it was under that warm, wry word: home.

There were plastic flowers, in the convent-type parlour; did that make anything worse? Would beautiful live wires stemming out of brimming bowls with bright heads flaring like torches in a cave, in the underworld, would they have helped? Probably, yes. Real flowers arranged in a recollected frame of mind by some informal nun. What am I thinking of? The Home was run by someone and son, two ghouls who had pictures of themselves on the wall, standing smiling with shy pride in front of their first, black, polished hearse. That made us grin like skulls, sipping cognac from a paper cup in that plastic parlour.

Inside the other room, the adjoining room, Wall lay in his box cosmeticised beyond description or belief into someone's perverse idea of life-in-death. There's no such thing, and that's what he looked like; something that isn't.

Or was it something else? I dreamed him like that, before it

171

ever happened, years before. Dreamed him embalmed, only in the dream he wasn't dead, but alive, not quite, he was an understudy, or overstudy, for an actor in a film, shoved onstage by my own processes of association or information at a strange time; I was pregnant. That was the strangeness stirring internal waters, producing dense, free-floating images. This one sat on a beach with a black cloth over its head and its make-up ran down its face. It combined two nightmare images in one. One was the image at the end of *Death in Venice*, which I'd seen with Jonathan at our little local Rialto just a few days before, of a man on a beach painted and parcelled and perfumed and primed for, he thinks, a flirtation with an angelic blonde child; actually, for the plague, for death. The other I hadn't identified until now and it makes me laugh a harsh crow's-caw of a laugh that makes Georgia look over, appalled.

'Just thinking of the Assumption,' I lie weakly, unable, unwilling to impose my horrors on her. 'People being *assumed* into heaven.'

'Only one,' she says, somewhat stonily. 'Only her.'

It was a detail in the autobiography of St Thérèse of Lisieux, the Little Flower, which I read obsessively despite my preference for her bolder sister, Theresa of Avila. It's an obsessive book, full of coyness like a constant barrage of those nauseating clerical winks, infantile, cloying; but also astoundingly readable and real, precisely because it dwells on the minutiae of experience as precisely as a child does.

The bit that was served up disguised in my dream was a vision Thérèse had of her own father, some years before his death. She saw him, head bowed and covered with a black cloth, face sorrowful and lost.

And so with Wall, lost in a different sense, make-up or mask like the moon in the man, shining when the man was gone, not before. A full moon! But what of the full man?

'Wall used to call me Sam,' I comment, hardly aware of speaking aloud.

'Like your son,' Georgia says, startled.

Like my son; with whom I was pregnant when I had the

dream. Here we are; it's crept up on me, after all, the Church of the Assumption.

'It's pretty,' Georgia says, surprised, parking in the lot I remember being cleared and tarred, in front of the rectory I remember being built. So what? The church is, as she says, pretty in a classic country church way, built of heavy stones set in concrete, with tall, satisfying cedars, not stunted Coldwick ones, flanking it in neat lines.

'I remember a Christmas night here,' I step out into the parking lot and get a whiff of pine and of that night, 'clear as clear, stars and snow.'

'I love you.'

Clear as clear.

Round the side of the church we walk, I almost push her in my eagerness, or curiosity, or sense that we're nearing the end of the road, at last.

'First grade first.'

'Of course,' she says steadily, smiling again.

What if they lock the place?

They don't. I march her down the hall and turn into Dolores' First Grade classroom. It smells the same: rubber boots and bananas.

11

'**R**emember how the day began, in First Grade?'
She stands solemnly beside a Lilliputian desk, and
makes the Sign of the Cross.

> 'Angel of God, my guardian dear,
> To whom God's love commits me here,
> Ever this day be at my side
> To light and guard, to rule and guide,
>   Amen.'

'Right from the start, commitment was a theme. Only in
those unenlightened times, the shoe was on the other foot. It
was God who was committed.'

She looks around. 'God! What a dump.'

'All right. It was more of a dump then. This is all fixed up.'

She shakes her head. Then she straightens. 'Hey, we forgot
what comes next.'

> 'I pledge allegiance to the flag
> Of the United States of America
> And to the republic
> For which it stands
> One nation, under God, indivisible,
> With liberty and justice for all.'

'I don't remember,' I squinch up my eyes in an attempt,
'when they put in the "under God". It wasn't there when I
first learned it.'

She shrugs. 'I don't remember either.'

It's a luxury to have so many memories available that some, like 'under God' in the pledge of allegiance, like the parking lot and the rectory outside, feel dispensable, as if I might finally begin to discard some of the myriad memos and keep the important ones; as if I might, someday begin to know the difference.

'Good morning, Sister, I salute your Guardian Angel.'

'The girls curtsied.'

'And the boys bowed.' I bow solemnly, from the waist, the way they did. 'If we were bad we had to write, "I must obey" one hundred times. It was called a Punish Lesson. They loved those words: punish, obey.'

'Were you bad?'

'Never.'

'That's bad.'

'I know. Then there was the Punish Chair.'

'What the hell was that?'

'A sort of equivalent Electric Chair, to six-year-olds. Who weren't even capable of sin, in the eyes of the Church – but Dolores' eyes were different. You sat on it sizzling with shame and then you wet your pants, usually, which made you sizzle even more. Fried in piss, that was the idea.'

'Charming.'

'Dolores would pounce when she saw the puddle under the chair, gleefully calling everyone's attention to it, and everyone would snicker, a sort of collective sigh of relief really, that snicker, everyone just glad it wasn't them.'

'Then Dolores would order the fried child to go downstairs and get some paper towels from the janitor, to clean it up with. She had some Kleenex in her desk, but they were for good noses, not bad puddles. The janitor's name was something Hungarian and unpronounceable and he glared and mumbled. Rumour had it he was to be seen, after school, stirring buckets of blood in his room.'

'Buckets of Bloody Marys, probably, poor man.'

'Probably. He hated to be disturbed by a damp child looking for paper towels. There were never any in the dispensers in the lavatories. Catholic schools! There were rats in the basement, where we sold ice cream in the spring . . . anyway. It was all quite medieval.' Lucky we didn't wake the sleeping microbes and send the Plague out into the shiny New Jersey streets. 'Then you came upstairs and went to work on the puddle under the Punish Chair, and of course coarse brown paper towels aren't at all absorbent, so you had a miserable time scrubbing and spreading it. Then you had to go back downstairs and hand the fistful of smelly towels to the janitor for incineration. He was even less pleased, this time, to be disturbed by a kid with a bunch of reeking paper towels. He'd open the door to the incinerator and motion for you to throw them in. The door was metal, and big, like the door to a vault, and inside the flames were orange and white like creamsicles, only hot, and very orange, and wild. He'd be standing behind you and you'd be sure he was going to push you in.'

'How often did this happen to you?'

'It never happened to me. Just to the bad kids. Only once, I got sent to the Punish Chair. I'd thought I was immune, but I went and sat there, trying to pretend I didn't care, trying not to feel as if I was sitting on the john in front of everyone, that was the feeling of it – and suddenly I didn't care, it was just an old folding chair and I had my uniform modestly over my knees and I didn't have to do any work. I looked at Dolores up there, coolly, and she looked back at me and told me to go sit back in my seat. I think she saw what was happening.'

'They didn't usually bother much about girls.'

'No. She didn't, for the most part. It was boys who got sent to the Punish Chair. Except for Orianna.'

'Who was Orianna?'

'She sat –' Where the devil did she sit? I can't remember. I can't remember what I want to remember and I'm starting to remember what I don't. Once you start the music of the past, it plays on like a player piano. But whose feet are pumping the thing?

'Hey, remember First Communion,' I start babbling again,

to drown out the swell. 'Remember that story they tell you, about how Napoleon said it was the most important day of his life, the day he made his First Holy Communion?'

'I remember. Why Napoleon, I wonder?'

'I wonder too.'

We perch on desks. The room seems less menacing now. I begin to remember a few other things.

'Sophie Maggiori sat there, where you are,' I sigh. 'Oh, Sophie!'

'What happened to Orianna?'

'That was different. Sophie was blonde and when I made my first Communion, my godmother gave me a book about this saint called Imelda who died of joy when she made hers. I just remembered that. I wonder if she was suggesting something?'

She seems to go a shade paler.

'Imelda was a nun at ten. She even beat the Little Flower. Anyway. I used to leave anonymous notes in Sophie's desk. I had this idea she was a princess in disguise.'

'Uh oh.'

'She wore this blue ring, that was what did it. I'd write, "Dear Royal Princess of the Nile, I won't reveal your secret, ancient as the peeramids" – spelt p-e-e-r-a-m-i-d-s. I was very disappointed when I saw how they were really spelled.'

'I'll bet you were. How did Sophie react to all this?'

'She had this confused look all the time.'

'I'll bet she did!'

'And then, I have to admit, she was dumb. One of the dumbest. Well, you know, Georgia, those pharaohs. Inbreeding. Incest. All that. I forgave her. My poor princess. Not playing with a full deck.'

'And then?'

'And then – she was left back. There were two grades in one room, in here, Dolores had sixty-odd kids to contend with.'

'Sixty very odd kids, by the sound of it.'

'And I had to leave, to go across the hall to Francesca's classroom. Leaving her. I wrote her a last tragic note: "Dear

177

Royal Princess of the Nile, I shall think of you immorally" – I thought it meant –'

'Go on, go on –'

'"And shed infinitesimal tears." I thought that meant – in finite.'

'And then?'

'I consoled myself by falling madly in love with Francesca.'

'Aha!'

'She played the organ. She had long, slender, tapering fingers. Only she liked tomboys, which I wasn't. So I got a sidekick who was. Who was called Skipper.'

'Aha!'

'Yes. I once had a dream that I killed her, and buried her body in a river. Once a year the river would overflow, and then her body would float up to the top and everybody would know.'

'That you'd killed her. Back to the Nile, I see.'

'That I *was* her. Sort of. That she was part of me. The androgynous part. It was that sort of dream.'

'I see. Sort of.'

'Francesca discovered me. She found a poem on my desk, and she liked it so much she took me, and it, to the principal.'

'Go on, kid.'

'I can't.'

Silence.

> 'If the good Lord chose to be selfish
> We would never be
> But the Lord did not choose to be selfish
> So He made you and me.'

'If I could just make one comment, kid.'

'Go on. Remember, I was eight.'

'Yes. If I were you I'd change the first line, just a little. "If the good Lord –" "– chose to be shellfish –"'

'Thanks, Georgia. I'll work on that.'

'Let me know what evolves, kid. Now I think I'll take a little walk back to the car, smoke a cigarette, no doubt Dolores or whoever's here now doesn't allow smoking in her classroom, and take a nap while you continue your – thing.'

'Okay.'

I kiss her on her nose as she moves away. She waves to me sleepily from the doorway, descending into the semi-darkness outside. Leaving me to the semi-darkness inside.

I can't call or, almost, even wish her back. I should've stayed in Coldwick or the Bronx, back where love was. Back with the two Venuses of Willendorf, my two grandmothers, cradling and feeding, why couldn't I have crouched, shrunken and small, in their land, in their care, instead of coming here? Or clung to the nuns' habits, smooth as tablecloths, that served love later? Instead of this.

School, and before that a new home – home! – out of the warmth and Mama and Pom's warm kitchen in the mornings, out of the daily anticipation of Michele's Necco wafers. Away from them all, during the week, except Marguerite, mother now not only of me, but of him, my brother Wally, whose coming disrupted my world completely.

I stand looking out at the pine trees, the neat rows like good children. Although full-skirted and tall, unlike the Coldwick trees, they still don't touch. Their green cedar skirts just miss; like good children.

Life was good in the Bronx. Lunch with Marguerite was intimate and sweet and always hot, or so it seems, always soft and buttery and hot, egg pastina or something; love. One day we walked, after lunch, driven by some need of hers I felt without fear, only with interest. She was heavy and hungry, too, then; I didn't know why. That day she wanted something else, something she couldn't afford to buy, couldn't even find, in that part of the flower-starved city. Even the expensive stalls were uptown or further down, in the Village. Not in the Bronx.

The Bronx had vacant lots. They were places of singular urban magic, as different from the rural form as delicatessens are from farms. People pulled and pushed and carried their old fridges and retired furniture and stoves and radiators to the lots. There nature took over and used the discarded articles as best she could. Springs popped out of sofas and flowers grew up through the springs, the petals perched on shredded cushions and nodded as the breezes blew. An exotic brew of wilderness and domesticity steeped in those lots, like houses you see in the midst of their wrecking, one wall still up, and windows, with nothing behind them but sky, with geometric shapes on the wallpaper where pictures hung. The illusion of the vast city, the frailty of its hallucinatory dream, stood exposed right there, in the outdoor living rooms with the occasional rude white porcelain fixture, standing pathetically bare, not closed away behind wooden doors like the Coldwick outhouses. It was all picked clean, slowly and surely, all the furniture that stood from season to season, picked clean of one set of stuffing, cushions, and lined with another. The bareness was like the clean-picked chicken bone that always hung in Mama and Pom's kitchen, slung over one corner of a picture of the Sacred Heart, becoming something else as it dried: a wishbone.

There in that vacant lot that hot afternoon, we picked Queen Anne's Lace. We harvested that carroty-smelling weed, bushels of it, or so it seemed, and carried it home. I imagined the only magic to follow and complete would be the arranging in bowls and bottles, that basically it was a reversal of the lot's own brand of magic, a transplanting of the wilderness indoors, which in turn would transform; but I was wrong.

It wasn't just that rooms could frame flowers inside just as furniture framed them in the vacant lot, or that flowers could make over rooms. Marguerite took down a box with little glass bottles inside, bottles I'd never seen before, like inks, but in colours I'd never seen written, orange and yellow and red as well as green and blue. She emptied each little bottle into a saucer and then we dipped the heads of the flowers into them, the chantilly heads of the Queen Anne's Lace, and sat them on sheets of newspaper to dry.

Then we put them in whatever we had, various bowls and jugs, arranged them and placed them around the immaculate apartment. They were more than flowers then, a magical blend of wild and tame. If I was her satellite, I was happy to be; the signals that came to me from her were rich and complete.

Till they no longer came to me, but to him. Son and sun. I was dispossessed, I might as well have lived in the vacant lot. I went there to play and dreamed of that secondhand wilderness, smelling the clean smell of Queen Anne's Lace. She had real florist's flowers for his Christening, white Baby's Breath and yellow roses.

I stuck pins in his soft baby's flesh, behind her back, I tickled him till he gasped and when she told me to stop I said: 'He's laughing, he likes it.' We moved to the suburbs of New Jersey, and exile was complete, mine and hers, too, to her confusion. Lost from her own mother, lonely, afraid, listless, angry, she had 'everything' she 'wanted'; what could be wrong? Her eye fell on the one thing she had that she hadn't wanted, me; all she had on which to take out that strange hunger she couldn't answer by dyeing flowers from a parched city lot, not any more.

Angry and empty, accumulating furniture and clothes and carpets, in a house. Accumulating more children; a girl baby came, golden and laughing, to gladden the house, and the weight began to lift. But that was later.

Only Wall was loyal, in that family starved of sons, surfeited with daughters. She screamed and raged, while the baby slept, in the grip of a passion she couldn't understand or control. I went rigid as stone, the statue of the daughter, archaic smile frozen on the Kore's face. To lie sobbing in bed when the storm was past, fully dressed like the old man in his suit, made of stone, too; maybe he, too, just had no one to talk to. Maybe that was why people died.

I didn't come back for this, but it's coming back for me, right out of these walls, out of this classroom, because here I went through the looking-glass and saw myself in the guise of another little girl, whose life at school was the mirror-image of my secret, non-happening life at home. It never happened, no one heard, saw or interfered. Middle-class houses have thick walls, and stand in their own insulating ground.

In the beginning her name was Orianna. She came from Hungary at the time of the Revolution, to the second grade at Assumption, no heroine to the American children who hated garlic on breaths and thick foreign accents on tongues. Too close to something too close to us still? She was one of the kids whose fathers worked at the seminary, children shamed and shrivelled by their poverty, carrying lunchpails like the one grandpa carried, like the ones all our grandpas or great-grandpas carried; was that why the hatred, the anger, the scorn?

Dolores could torture her with impunity. They couldn't find her baptismal records and so they baptised her again. A conditional baptism, Dolores was quick to emphasise, making it clear that her very existence among us was conditional, further emphasised by the way she was never allotted a full Christian name. Ori-Philomena, Dolores called her, as if she remembered in mid-syllable, and we parroted it after her with fierce, imitative sadism. You were baptised in white as an infant in the arms of your godmother, not standing on your own two feet in your school uniform on an ordinary school day, furtively, conditionally.

Dolores didn't actually beat her.

'Ori-Philomena,' she'd sigh, resignedly. 'Come up here.'

The whole class would stiffen. Silence fell. Ori-Philomena turned red, then white, then red again. She had very white skin with lots of freckles, and her hair hung down, lank and usually dirty. When she went white the freckles stood out in relief, and when she went red her eyes bulged. It was worse because after a while she knew what was coming. Anticipation was another element of suffering.

You never get used to it. You walk on eggs and you know it's hopeless. They'll break. It's fate. Because there's something about you, like a smell; a conditional smell.

Dolores would point to one of the chairs in the front of the room. There were two rows of chairs at the front, four or five chairs in each row. We filed up there to read flash cards.

Ori-Philomena would drape herself over one of the chairs,

with her head hanging down away from us, towards the blackboard. We could only see her twitching bottom covered by her blue pleated uniform skirt and her awkward skinny legs in red socks, ridiculously, ordinary, scuffed American saddle shoes dangling. Sometimes Dolores would have to help her. She was trembling so much she could hardly fold herself over the back of the chair.

Then Dolores would take her map pointer with the rubber tip and bring it down, whistling, past Ori-Philomena's face. She'd let go, her own face purple with rage, striking again and again, the ritual imposing its own control, within which she could release her demon. She never actually hit the child. The map pointer came down with a crash on the chair in front of Ori-Philomena's face. Each time it seemed that it would, that it must, land on her backside humped in the air. The crashes got quicker and harder till Ori-Philomena broke down and sobbed. Then they slowed and finally stopped. Dolores, utterly calm, helped her down.

How many blows hit the target, at home? They came from everywhere; it seemed they must strike home. Home! That high voice like a wind shrieking, out of control, sometimes broke, like Dolores' map pointer sometimes broke. Marguerite yanked at the long brown braids she wove every morning, twisting and pulling till you wanted to scream. She pulled them like bellropes and screamed till your head clanged. There was a sore feeling and a quick forgetfulness afterwards, upstairs in bed alone, till Wall came home.

His hands fumbled you into pyjamas, soothing without saying anything, without ever asking. Conditional existence slipped into sleep, and then it was breakfast and braids and school.

Ori-Philomena left because her house burned down. No one knew what caused the fire. Somehow it had to happen, and it did, and she was gone, a heroine at last, mentioned piously in our prayers, like Joan of Arc, revered only after, rendered down to harmless ashes, a ghost risen phoenix-like and pure. 'Philomena', we prayed for. Years later, that name was scratched from the canon of the saints. Philomena had never existed, or never been holy. Along with Christopher and many others, she was uncanonised. I wondered whether Ori-Philomena was glad, whether she got her own name back, whether she'd already reclaimed it, lived as Orianna and laughed when she heard what became of her conditional saint.

But before she left, we became friends. Inevitably. From what she told me, her life at home was a fairy tale, full of Hungarian warmth; just like mine at school was privileged and perfect, as a good kid, a smart kid, a kid whose father didn't work at the seminary. Our parallel lives met, for a little while.

We made a pact to exchange presents. We would bring our most secret and cherished possessions and hand them over to each other, sealing our friendship forever. I brought my fetish, though I didn't call it that. It had no name. It was too sacred for names.

It was a little cylindrical wooden box someone had given me, painted red and inscribed with little flowers and birds and hex signs in a Pennsylvania Dutch design. Was it grandma's gift? She had a child's knack for picking the best presents, black patent leather handbags with fake fruit on the top, dresses with nylon lace and little fake flowers like popcorn balls, making Marguerite shudder.

I don't remember. Inside I put a piece of black velvet, I don't remember where that came from either, and on top of it a fake yellow rose. The two textures juxtaposed took my breath away, the rose like unmelting butter on the black velvet. I loved lifting the lid, peeking inside and getting that breathless sensation, at the contrast, the mystery.

It was hard to give Orianna the red box – from the moment we were friends, I called her that. I was greedy, though, to see what she would offer me in return.

We stood in the bend in the driveway, our favourite place. Neither of us played jumprope with the other girls. They chanted their rhythmic chants against our backs as we walked. Something about the rope skimming so close to your body was frightening. You might not be able to jump clear of

184

it in time. That fear made me avoid the game, and I suspect it was the same for her, or maybe for her it was the shrill American voices shrieking verses she could make little sense of.

> John and Nora in a tree
> K-I-S-S-I-N-G
> First comes love
> Then comes marriage
> Then comes Nora with the ba-by carriage
> Ten-twenty-thirty-forty.

And so on. The more you jumped, the more babies you had. We walked and talked, instead. That day we walked quickly, both of us clutching our treasures, excited and reluctant. We handed our gifts over, quickly, and bent eagerly over our spoils.

We both straightened and smiled the same uncomprehending, disappointed smiles. She had given me a broken rhinestone necklace. I knew rhinestones were cheap. Not even grandma would wear them for all their glitter and shine, and the clasp wouldn't close.

Orianna looked down at the red box with its silly contents, silly even to me, in that instant. She'd taken it, all right, as I'd tarnished her necklace with my eyes. We walked back to the classroom, dispossessed, still pretending feverishly to ourselves and each other, but lost to each other, our friendship finished.

Once she was gone, Dolores didn't choose another victim. She read us a book instead, a book about a little girl who lived with her grandmother in the middle of a wood. Her grandmother was cruel, the antithesis of mine. It was called *Lisbeth Girl of the Brambles*, and girl of the brambles she was, forever running away to have her bare legs scratched and scarred by the ubiquitous thorns until she got trapped in them and her grandmother came stealthily after, presumably with wire cutters.

There were endless descriptions of scratched and scarred calves. Dolores read them very dramatically, and we listened, riveted. It had the same cathartic effect on her as crucifying

Ori-Philomena on the reading chair and scourging the chair in front with her map pointer. Orianna was gone; in our minds she'd gone down to the janitor and never returned, which we always expected. He spoke Hungarian to her; she was in league with him. In our minds the fire that burned down her house was one with the red glow inside the incinerator.

I wanted to read *Lisbeth Girl of the Brambles* for myself. That was the only way to really read a book. I could read it, Dolores knew that. I could read well; sometimes she let me do the flash cards with the First Graders.

But she didn't want to surrender the book up to me, to take home. Maybe I wanted to bring those two spheres together, somehow. I stayed in the classroom one ill-fated recess, to pester her about it.

She looked at me, listened and sighed. 'You can't get books like this any more.' She smelled strongly of something. Nun. And temper. She lumbered to the back of the room like a bear and something caught in my mind. I wished I'd left her to her own devices. I'd set up my own ruin. I couldn't prevent it.

She paused in front of the cupboard where we kept our lunchboxes in a sort of wall of cubbyholes, a false wall. There was something sticking out between it and the real wall, something she absently reached out to pluck away.

'What on earth is this?' she mumbled, and pulled.

It toppled out. A sandwich. A sandwich that began life at home under Marguerite's quick, impatient hands. Shoved into a sandwich bag, waxed and white. Grudged and small and flat, not full and fat, or so I felt as I took it out of my lunchbox, no plebeian lunchpail for Helena Carnet, and pushed it back behind the wall.

Dolores pulled at the wall and stood transfixed in front of a month's worth of lunches behind it, all in neat white bags, stale bread with peanut butter between like cement, another brick wall, separating school and home? Or Marguerite and me? With bricks of stale bread. The wall falls.

'Good lord,' Dolores sounded as if she'd had a vision. Then

186

she turned to me, quick and shrewd as she was. 'Helena. Are these yours?'

'Oh, no, 'Ster,' I backed away, echoing her own reply to Pat O'Rourke from happier days. 'Oh, no!'

'I won't tell your mother.'

Old witch.

I was resolute. She got Pat O'Rourke to clear out the remains of the wall and then she asked the class for a public confession. The sky had fallen, but I was terribly calm and locked in invincible silence.

'Helena puts her sandwich away every day,' some little snot-nosed creep of a spy says in the pause after she's asked the bricklayer to confess.

Dolores and I lock eyes.

She sends me to the church, to think. It's nice in the church, in the dark, it smells nicer than the classroom, it's a treat. The wall of bread is never mentioned again; as far as I know, Dolores tells no one. I certainly don't.

Soon it's time for First Communion. She thinks the Bread of Angels will heal the wound left by that other wall, that other bread. She probably thinks I'll tell the priest when I make my first confession. But I don't, of course.

A smell of honeysuckle, not mouldy bread comes to mind as I stand by the innocent cupboard. There was a sort of igloo we played in at home, made of bowed honeysuckle bushes. The smell was sweet, in spring. We used to pick the flowers, bite the ends off and suck the honey. I played there with Sally, who lived next door.

Once as we played I felt the urge to defecate and didn't want to go inside, where Marguerite was. Maybe I felt the urge to desecrate, too. I did, by leaving a brown twisty turd like a braid in the white temple of honeysuckle. Something drew her out, just afterwards, as if she'd smelled it, as if she knew.

I blamed Sally, in my terror. But she knew. She sent Sally scurrying home with her denials and dragged me inside, where I got the full treatment. The funny part was, I felt a bolt of triumph through it all. I had done something to merit this, this time; I was getting justice.

When Wall came home I was upstairs in bed with my clothes on and I wanted to tell him it wasn't the same, I'd done something. But I didn't. Partly I was afraid of the disgust on his face and partly I was afraid to speak at all; to break the silence that surrounded all of it, just or unjust. I thought Marguerite probably told him, but he was the same as always.

Once I was out of the classroom, doing an errand, when Dolores performed her ritual with Orianna. I stood in the doorway of another classroom when the sounds came, stood between two conferring nuns who looked at each other, registering the noises. We stood there till it was over, and they exchanged conspiratorial smiles over my head.

'Sister does have Spanish blood,' one of them said.

I pondered that statement afterwards until it became a picture in my mind of Dolores in a white nun's cell with little bottles of blood, Burnt Sienna because it was Spanish, like the bottles of dye Marguerite had taken out on that long-ago day in the Bronx. Like the bottles of amber perfume on her dressing table. Once I found a little bottle somewhere, filled it with her perfume and took it away to my room. She caught me with it as I was tying a blue ribbon around it. She was in a fury, in a moment. It was no use explaining, as I tried to explain, that the bottle was meant for her. But it wasn't just that that seared me through her screams, it was a sense of confusion, that what I was saying was true, but I didn't know how true or with what sort of truth. It was for her; I was for her. Yet I had stolen her perfume, and stolen my own Spanish blood, as she screamed.

The classroom's semi-dark. I walk to the door and leave, closing the door quietly behind me. Where can I go but where Dolores sent me, that day she discovered the wall of bread, to the church? Deciding she couldn't deal with it, leaving it to God. Well, I'm not expecting much in the way of God; there's just nowhere else to go.

Georgia's in the church, sitting quietly, waiting. She wrinkles up her nose at me as I come in, indicating the decor.

It's sort of Italian Wedding Ensemble, all pink and green and painted-on gold chains around the shrines of saints. I make a face at her, defensively.

'Now I know where you get your taste from, kid,' she speaks into the silence.

I jump, almost shhh her out of habit, for talking in church.

'Sorry,' she speaks again in the same soft, rich tone. 'I forgot where I was.'

I have a crazy mental image of us writhing on the dull green carpet in front of the altar. Her laugh's both warning and comprehending.

'I'm going on out to the car,' she says quietly into my ear. 'I'll leave you two alone.'

'Me two?' I only have time to ask before she's turned, genuflecting quite automatically, and there are only the sounds of her feet tapping on the steep flight of steps between the vestibule and the door.

Me two, three, four. Helena-ghosts multiply and scatter. I'm standing in line for the confessional, fearing my turn; how can I confess fifty thousand impure thoughts; kneeling in the confessional, asking if she can be godmother to her own little baby brother, and kindly Father O'Rourke who knows perfectly well who she is despite the all-important secrecy of the confessional, saying yes, yes she may.

A godmother. That's a nun and a mother, sort of. It was Marguerite's doing, bringing them together like that in me, so young. A sort of miracle. She did it because Jimmy had died when I was ten, and I had helped her mother him.

She let me comfort her. She couldn't bear the sympathy of others who believed him better off dead, whatever they might say. I didn't, and she let me comfort her, a little. She let me mother her, a little. It was no accident that my first skimpy period came when I was ten-and-a-half, a few months after Jimmy's death.

He was born with a thyroid disorder that made him slow and small, unsmiling till he died, at nine months. But she'd seen the ghost of a smile so many times we stopped counting, and so, I said, and swore, had I. I said it so many times I

189

didn't even know if it was true; it was like watching my rubber doll turn real at the Jersey shore.

Marguerite couldn't bear the stern, searching looks other people gave him, or the pitying ones they gave her. But I accepted him, and in turn she accepted me. There was more than truce between us, there was peace. I was absolved of hatred for Wally, of injury to him, and to myself through him. I was absolved of all the welling-up unspoken hatred towards her. I loved her, in her frailty, and I loved me in mine, through loving fragile little Jimmy. Was there a savage, sacrificial glee in me too, that a male child should sicken and die while I thrived, at last, in her care?

Perhaps. Even that reconciling light must cast some shadow. But the shadow didn't negate the light. I held him and sang to him and felt my heart surge with love, and when he died I felt that love go out blindly, looking for an object, and finding the one it had sought all along: Marguerite. She suffered bitterly. She was a law unto herself, inviolable, but there were other laws against which she was powerless. Maybe she had met that fact before. I hadn't. She had been monumental, inhuman, monstrous in my sight. She crumpled, when Jimmy died, and became human.

She saw through her own pain to mine, too, and made me the godmother of her next son, sharing her motherhood with me, mothering me with skill and shrewdness, knowing what I needed, as she knew what she needed. We needed the same thing.

We even prayed him into being together, in the months after Jimmy's death. She drove to the dark week-night church, solemn and dramatic, to make novena after novena, and she took me with her, the two of us fitting felt berets on our heads and dressing simply and soberly, driving over the dark roads, hunched together on the front seat of the car. It thrilled me to have those drives alone with her, to stand beside her in the dark church, only a few lamps lit, with the small band of pious, regular novena-folk and us, like strangers in a bar, on a bender, there for a reason. Her beautiful strong soprano rang out, singing the lovely, pleading hymns to

Mary. We pleaded with her together, to be healed, to be whole, to bring a child to birth in health. I knew what we were after; I knew what I was after, when I prayed the urgent prayer we both loved, the memorare:

> Remember O most gracious Virgin Mary, that never was it known that anyone who fled to thy protection, implored thy help or sought thy intercession, was left unaided. Inspired by this confidence, I fly unto thee, o virgin of virgins, my mother.
> To thee I come, before thee I stand, sinful and sorrowful.

Jimmy died three days after Christmas, on the Feast day of the Holy Innocents, the babies Herod slaughtered looking for Christ. Marguerite was feeding him, cooing to him and playing all the little games that sounded so wrong, with a sick, unresponsive baby in her hands, a baby who was sallow and limp instead of smiling, robust, alert, like her other babies; she peek-a-boo'ed and so'o-bigged and one for Daddy, one for Mommie'd him. Then there was a terrible silence and she came racing in to where I sat, ostensibly playing but really listening, perhaps, really, waiting.

'Go get Mrs Finian,' she said hoarsely. 'As fast as you can. Run!'

I ran. Mrs Finian lived down the street. She was a nurse. She still wore her uniform, and had just come off night shift, blinked at me and then looked wide awake.

'Your mother, or the baby?' As if she had been waiting, too.

'The baby.'

We ran. She ran like the wind on her white nurse's shoes, but when she arrived she had plenty of breath still to give, blowing it into Jimmy's nose and throat, furiously, as she'd taught us to do when she came to Girl Scouts. Artificial respiration. As she waved me out of the room I kept thinking, confusedly, that somehow he'd drowned.

The ambulance came and there were big, heavy oxygen tanks to do what she'd done, or tried to do. Then a silence, and the clump of the ambulance men's feet on the stairs, and Marguerite's loud, broken cry.

'He is with the Blessed Virgin,' Mama said, kneeling with us in the next bedroom, and I thought, fiercely, she should give him back. She has her own baby, why take ours?

He looked strange in his little coffin. As if he were blowing bubbles, I thought, and instead of hymns or prayers or even tears that song went through my mind

> I'm forever blowing bubbles
> Pretty bubbles in the air
> They fly so high
> They nearly touch the sky
> Then they fade and die.

The nuns, Marguerite said later, were the only ones who knew what to say, at the funeral. They crowded round her in a circle and talked softly. Whatever they said was inaudible to other ears. She'd always said the nursing sisters at the Catholic hospital were wonderful to her, in labour. So, the nuns and mothers did meet, at the extremities of birth and death.

The night after the funeral, it snowed. That snowfall almost killed Marguerite, as she stood at the window and watched it fall and cried and cried, he'll be cold, poor baby he'll be cold –

It stabbed at me. Her voice, her terrible grief. The terrible Marguerite had been brought up against something she had to suffer. Something that had always shone on her before had turned its dark and bloody beam her way, and when I went with her to the novenas it was to plead with that something to show its other face again.

The church is dark now, as it was the nights of our novenas, not light as it was the day of Jimmy's funeral, or the Sunday after it, when we all went to Mass together, even Wall, and sat stiffly in a front pew. Father O'Rourke turned from the altar to read the parish announcements; then he looked up at us, and smiled.

'We've had another death in the parish this week,' he said, the demonic-looking Irish priest with bushy eyebrows and warts, kind and fiery, more like a warlock than a priest, rocking back on his heels as he spoke, making his early morning, fasting congregation a little seasick. 'The little Carnet (pronounced Karnett) baby died, on the feast of the Holy Innocents, and it is about innocence that I intend to speak.'

Marguerite was wrapped in the fake fur coat she wore that winter. Grief had pared her drawn circles under her eyes, and unsexed her.

'What does it mean, I ask you?' he trumpeted, almost irritably. 'Is it the same thing as ignorance?'

He rocked. 'Ignorance is neither a virtue nor an excuse. Much as we like to pretend that it is.' He glared at us, then softened. Only for a second, though.

'There's nothing much to be said for not knowing anything,' he went on. 'Nothing much at all. Imagine a child whose parents don't send it to school because they prefer their child pig-ignorant.' He snorted at the idea. 'Such a thing would be obscene. Yet there are such parents. We do God no favour if we lump Him with them, as a Father who wants his children in darkness. Who thinks they're cuter that way. To pretend to be ignorant in order to appear innocent is even worse,' he thundered.

I feel as if there's a record playing in my head, but I'm not sure those were his exact words. There was a lot more about ignorance, and then he got down to it.

'Jimmy Carnet was innocent,' he said firmly. 'We hear people call these babies who die baptised without reaching the age of reason little angels. What, exactly,' he asked suspiciously, 'do we mean by that?'

'Unfortunately, what we mean is far from flattering to the angels themselves. We mean they're a band of ignorant infants in nightgowns, that's what we mean. What a surprise it will be to us when, if, we should be so fortunate as to see them! What an eye-opener. Fearsome creatures. Fearsome. Nine fearsome choirs all the way up the line to the Seraphim, pure refined worshipful creatures, pure flame, pure praise. The most fearsome sight in the universe.

'Why does the psalmist say of Adam's sin "O happy fault" I

193

ask you? Because without it, we would be ignorant. Ignorant! And so that sin brought us something. It brought us misery and pain and mortality, that we know. Mortality which has fallen so heavily on the Carnet family, our beloved friends.'

They would put a tape recorder on the altar and record O'Rourke, years later. They would play the tape to the bishop, and O'Rourke would be sent out to Wisconsin somewhere, buried in the snow, like Jimmy. That was after he'd read Camus and tried to share his meditations on *The Plague* with his parishioners.

'God planned the eatin' of that apple, sure enough. He gave us the free choice to eat it because he wanted us to be human, not ignorant. Whatever innocence we have is wrested from evil, is fought for and paid for and won. By Jesus Christ our Lord. By the saints, real human saints. Our little brother Jimmy Carnet —' Marguerite's head went down — 'is not a little angel. He is an authentic human saint. His innocence was won for him by his brother on the cross, in whose death and resurrection we all participate, by the grace of our baptism, like he did. Let us now pray to this brother in heaven, this little brother much bigger and stronger, now than any of us, full member of the Church Triumphant while we struggle on in the Church Militant. Let us ask him to lighten our darkness with a sense of his joy and fulfilment. Let us ask him especially to console his dear mother Marguerite with a sense of his complete human fate. In the name of the Father and of the Son and of the Holy Ghost.'

His voice breaking, he turned back to the altar. But he had done what he could, and it was a lot. He had taken our poor frozen baby and defrosted him as a saint. The magic might not last, but for a moment the sting of terrible waste, of treachery in nature, huge, cosmic treachery, was gone, and such moments were a breathing space. Marguerite was a woman, not to be utterly comforted by any palaver of priests. But it gave her a lifeline to hold while she reached for another umbilical, the real lifeline, while she found her own real, pagan remedy in another child. Like a Hindu dancer, with one hand tilted towards heaven to receive, another towards earth to give, she could balance between the son sainted in heaven and the son dead in the earth, soon to be reborn in her womb.

She mothered him and I stood as his godmother and knew the taste of her pride, as I had tasted her grief. I start to get up from my pew, grateful for what I've recovered, here. Then I stand still as one of the embalmed-looking statues around me. The very last time I was in this church, it seems to me, with horror, the last time I was in this pew it was Wall's funeral and a new, hardset, stupid little priest stood where O'Rourke had once stood, a priest without visible warts, smooth and baby-faced and slick as he bit into us where we knelt, finally vulnerable.

'I haven't seen you in a long time,' he'd said to me at the wake, in a whiny sort of voice. 'But then I haven't seen any of you for a long time,' his eyes narrowing as I began to explain that I lived in England.

'Most eulogists begin by saying the deceased is safe in heaven et cetera,' he began his eulogy, with an unpleasant smile. 'Well, I'm not going to begin like that.

'Perhaps the deceased *is* in heaven,' he went on, his voice making it clear exactly how doubtful he considered that prospect to be.

Wall would've loved it. I could imagine him kneeling there next to me, smiling his shadowy smile. This guy's hot, he'd whisper. What a waste.

He went on to lament the demise of simple faith in our time, and by implication, in our tribe. On and on, about a sugary substance – simple faith – he was convinced could save the world, if only the world would consent to be saved. But it wouldn't and so, he almost pointed at the coffin in the aisle, this was the result.

Now it's time I stood up, and I stand. This unholy holy mother church is one motherfucker I've outgrown, at last. I was too scared and frozen that day to move, and how could I leave Wall there to be insulted, when he was helpless to do what I wanted to do? After all, I had dragged him there in the first place. But I'm doing it now, and I'm taking him with me.

Out, quietly down the steps and out into the soft night air where Georgia's keeping the home fires of her Marlboro burning.

'Let's get out of here,' I suggest with a trace of insistence or passion or, anyway, *heat*, and she's revved up and speeding away, towards Cryon, in a moment.

12

'Even I know what comes next,' Georgia says as we set off. 'Shall we have a drink on the way, or just get it over with?'

'Up to you, darling, up to you.'

'Did you good, h'm, that brush with religion?'

'Oh, it did, it did! Want to hear one last Assumption poem while you make up your mind? You can make suggestions about this one too, if you want. It was written on the occasion of my murdering Pat O'Rourke.'

'You sure murdered a lot of people. Will I be next?'

'I hate to say this, but it was actually at S&M that I wrote it. After Pat and I had gone steady and then broken up –'

Inexcusably old. Not as inexcusably old as I am now, but still.

'The problem was, I was ahead of his time.'

'I see. Well? Go on, kid.'

'We'd broken up and he sent me a Christmas card, a stupid ordinary one –'

'What'd you expect?'

'With just his name on it. No message. No nothing. That's what provoked – this. Ahem.

> 'I watched the smoke that marked the end
> Of all you said to me
> And shed no tears for what love was
> Or what it meant to be.

197

But smiling, thought of grief gone by,
Of days in longing, nights in pain,
Laughed almost, that such an ache,
Cold ashes, could not throb again.

But now a stirring makes me shake
And push aside the jest
That such a note arrive from you
As frozen as the rest

As red and gold and falsely gay

'Falsely gay? I like that —'

With words you never read
To tell me in their mocking way
Not only love, but you, are dead.'

'There's a certain hereditary influence there, something like "old Lem he got so mad/his face looked like a red hot pad." '

'There is. I won't deny it. Kind of like the Sitwells.'

'Kind of. Let's have a drink.'

'Thought you might say that.'

Cryon, New York. You could put it together with a model railway kit, as long as it was an old, dusty kit. One of the last old-fashioned Woolworth's is around here, where, I suddenly remember, I once lost Marguerite. A kind-faced woman was questioning me when I was abruptly found. My feelings were ambivalent when I was parted from her. It makes me smile, now, staring out the window at Cryon, and close my eyes for a second.

Only a second. How can I miss this? Stores leaning against each other for support. The diner where we used to smoke and play the jukebox and feel sleazy and vulgar and bad, like Hannah's friends. Important. Then I notice an unfamiliar shopfront, with unfamiliar lettering carefully stencilled against the glass. 'Ramapough Indians', it says.

'What do you know!' A thrill goes through me. 'They took back their name.'

'What?'

'The Jackson-Whites. That's what they used to be called. It's in William Carlos Williams' 'Patterson'. Wall found it. He was really excited to find it, I guess because they lived right around here. They were called that because a man called Jackson White used to supply Indian women to the mercenaries who fought with the British during the Revolutionary War, and some of them were descended from those women – and those men.'

'Named after a pimp.'

'Only now they're not, you see? Ramapough Indians. That must've been the name of the original tribe, and now they've taken it back.' Oh, how I wish Wall were alive, to find out about this!

'They probably took it back so they could claim money from the government or something,' Georgia says vaguely, and I look at her, aghast.

'Well, why shouldn't they? If it's money due the Ramapough Indians?' My mind skims on to a strange parallel.

'Georgia. I want to tell you a story. I've never told you this particular story.'

'Has it got nuns in it?'

'No. In fact, it hasn't got any women in it.'

'Go on then.' In spite of herself, she's intrigued by the novelty.

'Once upon a time,' my voice shakes a bit as the car rounds familiar bends on the route to S&M, unstoppable, I feel, as if on automatic pilot, 'a certain Republican was running for president. You may remember. Let's call him Sickly Prickly.'

'Oh, let's.'

'Well, Sickly Prickly needed lots of money for his campaign. So he set up a fund, which was called SEEP. Which stood for –'

'I can't wait.'

'Samurai Elite to Elect the President.'

'Huh?'

'You know the Japanese Samurai, the private army, sort of, of the Edo Emperors? Well the president wanted *his* own private army, sort of, too, men who had lots of money and power and would kind of keep everybody else in line, just like the Samurai did. Businessmen with a certain finish to them, ones who might read poetry, you know, occasionally, like the Samurai did.'

'Like William Carlos Williams, for instance?'

'Men whose highest honour consisted in disembowelling themselves, ritually, only they did it with alcohol and overwork, stress it was called. Very effective. He wanted them right in the palm of his hand, just like the Samurai, for all their reputation and their finery, like beautiful tailored suits and –'

'Helena, I get the analogy.'

'Like they were right in the palm of the emperor's hand. And he knew how to get them, too. He knew it wasn't their money, really, that counted. Or even their houses, or even their wives. He knew that deep down it was what it always was everywhere: their names. So he made them all contribute one thousand bucks to his SEEP fund, not much really, and he gave them two thousand when they did, so they'd have something to be ashamed of besides what he took from them; their names. Which went on his list.'

'How'd he make them give the money?'

'Oh, you know, by putting pressure on their bosses to pressure them. They all had houses and wives and all that.'

'Here we are.'

The municipal parking lot. There's no question as to where we're bound. The Lighthouse, Cryon's grand hotel, seedy and decayed like everything else around here. Looks like someone chopped the back of it off.

Oh, I wish I could tell him about the Ramapoughs getting their name back! I wish I could tell him I'd taken my name back. I wish I could tell him prostitution is one thing I understand.

The Lighthouse is just a lighthouse, on the outside. On the inside it's a light house, garish with blinking lights, dancing lights, obnoxious lights. We order a bottle of wine. One sip and I'm drunk.

'Hey –'

'I know,' she nods. 'Me, too. Hey, how'd you like to live in a lighthouse?'

'I'd love it. I love lighthice.'

'You would. You're so corny.'

'You'd love it, too.'

'You're right.'

Pause. Cigarettes. Once, when she came to England, we went to Brighton. It was the only time we chose a bum hotel, where they looked at us and didn't like what they saw, which was far too much. We spent a whole day going furniture shopping, furniture window-shopping, with an air of domesticity so convincing I felt it had to become a reality. It was a rehearsal for reality. I was certain. I still am.

'Brighton,' she says softly. 'The antique furniture.'

What more do you need than that, ever?

'But I hated the hotel,' she says, as if in answer. 'The way they looked at us. What they were thinking. The truth.'

'They weren't thinking the truth. They were thinking something else.'

She shrugs. 'But that's what everybody thinks.'

'You mean, you do.'

'I mean –' she pulls wearily on her cigarette, and we both have more wine. 'I mean I like my life, damnit, I like being normal. It's what I want to be.'

'I hate my life, I hate being normal, it's not what I want to be.'

'You see? We're on opposite sides. Only joined up by – accident. Because neither of us is being – what we are. You're not – you don't want to be married and straight. I'm not –'

'Yeah?'

'Well, all right, it's true,' her voice shakes, but she plunges on. 'I don't want to work for some great big fat chemical company that makes most of its money giving women breast cancer or some damn –'

She's crying.

'Georgia? What is it?'

She waves me away. 'It's all right. Pour, pour. I'll tell you.'
I pour.

'It's my godmother,' she says, sobbing quietly, collectedly.
'She died, six months ago. She –' she takes a sip of wine. 'She
had a mastectomy –'

Dear God. That's how she knew enough about it to talk to
Jody. And I rattled on about godmothers and corpses and,
and.

'She was so brave about it! She was brave all her life, about
everything. She had to take care of her mother, too, and she
did, and she had a sort of career, she – she wanted to play
the piano, you see,' she finishes, quietly. 'She had the most
beautiful hands. She might've done it too, except for her
mother, except for – her.'

Except for her mother, except – for her. So she died
unfulfilled, and became a ghost.

'So she gave lessons.' Georgia shrugged. 'And when she got
cancer, and had her breast off, she laughed and said it made
her an Amazon. And then that was all right, they'd got it in
time, she was fine. Her mother was dead. She was free, she
was seventy-one, she had arthritis and she could hardly play
any more, and she –' she drinks again, hastily gulping. 'She
took all her pills that she'd kept while she had cancer, all her
sleeping pills and painkillers. All at once. Then just to make
sure, she put a plastic bag over her head and fastened it with
a pearl choker that I'd – given her.'

She should've strangled me with one of grandma's
necklaces.

'Let's go,' Georgia downs the last of the wine. 'I want to go
to S&M. I want to stand in that graveyard and cry for her.
Now. My smile's set so hard this past year, I've felt like I had
a plastic bag over my own face. Let's go.'

I pay and hurry out to Georgia. She sobs, in the dark,
outside those winking lights, slow sobs now, the last of the
set. Like waves. I remember those waves of grief. Like
contractions in childbirth.

'She was saying the rosary,' she hiccups, in my arms.
'When she went out. Isn't that –'

Then she's quiet.

'Let's go,' she moves over to her side again. 'I want to finish this in that damned nuns' graveyard.'

Finish her mourning, she means; but her words make me wince. She speeds down the main street towards Stella Maris, a mere five minutes' ride from here.

The off-white old mansion climbs out of the darkness in segments, like a cheshire cat without the stripes. Georgia chugs round the side, slowly, and I avoid looking up at the roof. I'm afraid I'll look up and there we'll be, Georgia Manion and Helena Carnet, embracing each other in our long white graduation dresses, yellowed now and full of holes like Miss Havisham's bridal gown, getting ready to say goodbye, forever getting ready to walk away.

Now we're on the side, by the chapel windows, the saints well and truly guttered out. Whatever once filled that building with helium and made it a magical, mischievous balloon fills it no more. Whatever combination of passions swelled it swells it no more; and here we are, all there is to show for it.

I'm drunk.

Georgia drives round to the back, and parks. We get out and start to walk, slowly, without talking, to the nuns' graveyard. We used to come out here to smoke. Smoke from the graveyard couldn't be seen from the school.

It's pretty, set in cedars, tall skinny ones like nuns, not touching but close, communicating in the darkness as their boughs whisper. But where are the dead nuns?

'Georgia, the tombstones are gone!'

Bridget, Thomasina, I remember two names. Forty or fifty years each in the habit of holy religion. It used to make us shiver to think of it.

Georgia's walking around like a diviner, with a stick.

'I don't understand,' she's saying, 'How could they dig up the graves?'

'Maybe they moved it, when they sold the place? The graveyard?'

'They must've.'

The lack of bones under our feet makes the place more scary, not less. They always felt like benign presences, when when we blew smoke over their resting-place. But now it feels sinister.

Georgia sits down suddenly on the ground.

'The world's going round,' she says plaintively.

'Of course it is, Georgia.'

The woods behind the graveyard are still wild, thick with dark pine and sumac with dark ruby berries. I inhale it deeply, and sit down beside her with my arm around her shoulder.

'She had the right idea,' Georgia's whispering. 'If you just –' she gulps and stops.

'Let's have a cigarette,' this is the place for it, after all.

I light us both one, taking her pack from her neat leather bag.

'She was brave because she thought she was going to die,' she says, in a flat voice. 'She was disappointed, when she was okay. She wanted to die. That's why –'

I hold her again.

'You would've liked her. She might even've liked you, though she would've had her suspicions. She was no dummy. I guess she was right,' she sighs. 'You go on till you can't take it any more. Then you stop.'

She doesn't mean living. She isn't talking about her godmother. She means this. She means us. You go on till you can't take it any more, then you stop. She can't take it any more.

She knows I know, that it's all come together, right here. It's as if we're surrounded by those dead nuns they may or may not have moved, a quiet, compassionate audience, watching and waiting. And praying. It's so quiet; that quiet of presences. I remember that quiet.

'If I could be somebody different,' she says painfully, 'I would, if I could, live – with you. Maybe I could, by staying at Sabine, and lying, and making more and more money – but that'd be the only way I could do it. If I don't –'

More silence. No katydids.

204

'If I'm not with you, then I can quit and not worry about money or respectability or anything, oh it sounds so damn stupid,' her head hurts my shoulder, pounding against it like a brick wall, 'like some sort of sacrifice I have to make to the gods. Maybe it is like that − it is like that.'

Oh, listening presences! Nuns, mothers, dark demons, whoever you are, what do I do now?

You let her go.

But I love her.

But love doesn't mean keep. Or stay. You love Jonathan. But you have to go, and he has to let you go. Sometimes love means:

Go.

'Let's go,' I help her to her feet. 'Georgia. You know.'

'I know. The only thing that comes between good and bye is I love you.'

The old corny line from so long ago. We've been saying goodbye for twenty years. And saying I love you.

We check to make sure our cigarette butts are out, the old conscientious gesture of guilt. Then we walk back to the car, our arms entwined. I have to do it now. If she offers me a night, and I take it, I won't have the strength in the morning. And neither will she.

We stand by the car. The cheshire cat gleams in the moonlight, complete.

'Are you all right to drive?'

'How far?'

The question makes me put my head down on the hood of the car, in shame, and to stop myself saying: Just keep going, let's beat it, let's drive till we've worked out a compromise.

There is no compromise. None that wouldn't leave us, some day, hating each other.

'Just to New York. If you could drop me off at Marguerite's on the way home.'

'Okay, kid.'

She gets in and turns on the radio after the first half-mile. Our hands meet like they did that night at the stoplight, when we came down from Glass Mountain. The radio was

205

playing then, too, and then, too, there was nothing to say. Marguerite doesn't even know I'm in the country. She might not be there. Even if she's home, she might not be there. But I have nowhere else to go. And no money.

No; that's self-pity. I want to finish this there. With her.

The roads are clear, for a Sunday night. I hand her coins for the tolls without noticing. Then we're on the bridge, and I panic. How can we, how —

'What's the address?'

I tell her. We're there the next minute, too fast, much too fast. I've only been here once before, with Jonathan and the kids. I think there's a light in her window.

'Want me to hang around till you get inside?'

'Georgia, if you hang around —'

She nods.

'Okay, Helena.'

She helps me get my luggage from the back, my clothes from England and my Coldwick jewellery. There's still that. We stand there in the street, and just look.

'Georgia — I love you.'

'Helena — I love you.'

That's it, that's the end, the door slams, I'm talking to the doorman, afraid to look behind me to see if she's gone. I don't turn around till I get to the elevator. She's gone.

Fifteenth floor. End of the hall. I take a deep breath and knock. Her dog barks, Val for the Valium the vet prescribes for her.

'She takes it and I don't,' Marguerite says, laughing.

While I'm thinking of that, she opens the door.

While I'm thinking of that and simultaneously thinking, of all things, that I miss my own dog, at home, in England, she's standing there in the doorway for one aghast second, looking as if she's seen a ghost.

'Helena, Helena,' she pulls me into her arms. 'For Christ's sake what are you — I was just thinking of you.'

Then I'm inside and she's dosing me with Jack Daniels. Trust her.

I do. I tell her. The whole thing. She listens and nods. Says almost nothing. I tell her about the first time we ever made love. Valentine's Day. She laughs with me. I tell her how Sam and Mike were sleeping at home and I pictured them there, with the gas fire throwing orange light around them like a Valentine, and I took a cab home at dawn to get back to them, because I had to.

When I stop talking for a minute, an overwhelming tiredness descends on me.

'Come on,' she says firmly. 'We're going to bed.'

For one shocked instant, I don't know what she means. She means just that. She shows me to her bedroom, the only one in the place, and we undress and fall into bed. She's warm against me and, little as I can believe I'm here, and ready to do this simple insane thing, I fall asleep.

In the morning she's up. The washing machine's even whirring, just like it always was. But it isn't just like it always was. Not any more, not since last night, not since that act of acceptance.

I walk into the kitchen, wrapped in a robe of hers, and she looks at me with horror.

'Helena. Something terrible has happened to your face.'

I make my way to the bathroom, to a mirror, but even as I look, I anticipate. The nuns' graveyard, with its scent of pine and its gleaming sumac, had something else growing shiny in the dark. My old childhood enemy, Poison Ivy.

She sits me down in front of toast and coffee, and rushes out for Calomine. I sit, eat, cry, look around. Her apartment's beautiful. Val comes and wags her tail enquiringly, and I pat her on the head, hoping dogs don't get Poison Ivy. Then I pad on my bare feet over to her bookshelf and take down a dictionary.

Ivy. Perh. from the Latin 'ibex', a climber. A widely cultivated ornamental or prostrate or sometimes shrubby vine (Hedera helix) native to Europe and Asia that has evergreen leaves and small yellowish flowers and black berries and that clings to upright surfaces (as of walls, rocks, trees) by means of numerous aerial roots having small adhering disks.

Poison Ivy: a variable colour averaging a dark greyish green that is

207

yellower and duller than Persian green and yellower and paler
than Hemlock green.

Much yellower and paler. I laugh aloud, and the dog looks
up, startled.

My face feels hot. I feel hot all over. Marguerite comes
back, cool and shapely in her jeans and mink coat. I feel like
the Abominable Scarface beside her.

She slathers me with Calomine, and frowns when she feels
the heat of my face.

'Back to bed.'

But I don't want bed, alone, without her, without Georgia.
I want the sofa, at least, and talk.

'Oh, you big baby,' she laughs, 'All right.'

I smile, as she tucks me up on the sofa with an aspirin and a
glass of wine and seats herself in an armchair. I finally have
the answer to her accusations about Wall, to her incestuous
suspicions. Let her so much as dare to mention them again
and I'll silence her forever.

'Yes, Marguerite,' I'll say, calmly. 'You're right. I was in
love with Wall. *And* with you.'

She wouldn't know whether to be flattered or insulted. But
the time for accusations, I sense, is over between us. There's
only one thing I must do, and that's check whether my
version of our past, hers and mine, is right. The things I
remembered at Assumption. But before I can ask her
anything, I doze off only to dream of Wall, and Georgia,
Georgia's face under my hands, caked with pink Calomine,
and Wall under his oxygen tent those years ago, like a plastic
bag, while I yell, trying to make him hear, 'I got my name
back Wall, even if that's all, got my name back Wall even if
that's all, got – ' over and over, till it wakes, not him, but me.

Got my name back, Wall, even if that's all. Guess that's
right, got it back from nowhere. Not from Jonathan. He
didn't take it. I just threw it away, that's all. Jonathan. Here
it comes, now, that last lost chapter of the past, those long,
two years before we married. Before I bullied and blackmailed
him into marrying me. The answer to Georgia's question.

First, though, I got pregnant. Practically on my birthday, God help me. I got pregnant and when it became clear that he wouldn't marry me then and there, I panicked. Had an abortion, and when I came from the nursing home, drained, finished, where did I go? To him.

I went to him and sat on the rim of the bathtub in his flat, behind a locked bathroom door, with the water running in the bath, like a Roman. I picked up a razor blade and made a small horizontal cut in my left wrist. The blood spurted out and I thought, that won't do anything. I made a wider, deeper cut. The blood leapt out then in a great gush, as I imagined the baby had gushed from my womb. I screamed, and when Jonathan hammered at the door, I let him in.

Blood and bathtubs seem to be a theme of our relationship. And bathos. He hailed a cab and took me to a Casualty where the stern young intern seemed frightened by the undeniable nature of what I'd done.

'I have to ask you,' he said after he'd stitched my wrist, 'whether you intend to try again.'

I almost laughed. But he didn't deserve that insult from me, so I just shook my head.

I look at the bracelet of scars now, on my wrist and think about what I was trying to do. I didn't want to die. I was trying to punish myself, and Jonathan, too; but more than that, I was trying to say something. To express something that was happening to me, to get it out of me in the only crude and clumsy language I could find, using a razor blade instead of a pen, writing in blood instead of ink. I was trying to express and so to silence a conflict like the conflict over the child brought before Solomon the Wise, in the Biblical tale. Only the mother who won out, in my case, was the one who wanted the living child cut in two, rather than lost to her, rather than freed to live out a life. I had made the cut and had lived on, divided in two.

Now it's time to go back and choose again, time to be Solomon the Wise and choose, not between Georgia and Jonathan but between those two mothers. The fate of the child is in my hands. It has to be the other one this time, the one who'll let me go, let me make my mistakes and find my way without saying the restraining word that cuts in two, that prevents. But what will that mean?

Marguerite comes in and sits down. I ask her the hard questions, watching her face change, her lovely oval face with its high cheekbones, the witch-face of my nightmares, distorted with rage. It isn't rage that distorts it now, but she answers as calmly as I ask, as dispassionately. It's as if she's been waiting for this.

It's the truth. I forced her life into a mould and she hated me for it. Now the mould is broken, the hatred is past. She doesn't insult either of us with apologies or protestations of love. We both know she's sorry, and also that she's finished with guilt on my behalf, thereby freeing us both. We both know she loves me now, and has for years; that's beside the point, and cannot be used as a sop. This moment is about establishing the truth. The truth, however brutal, makes you free, and we're both freer people when she leaves the room and closes the door. We need a door between us, now, for a bit.

13

Forty-eight hours later I'm over the worst. I'm taking her out to dinner. She's in her denim, and I'm in mine. She with her Clairol hair and mine newly henna'ed. She got some henna for me so I could do it and it never crossed her mind to despise me for wanting it, widowed of Georgia though I am.

'We look terrific,' I say as we stand in front of her mirror, and it's the truth. Not only terrific, but alike. So alike. And so different.

New York looks like a new world. I'd forgotten it existed. I've just come from New Jersey, and fallen in love with it all over again.

And with her? Something different, something that would've happened with Wall, too, if we'd only had time. I like her. She's beautiful, and she's good company. We talk about money and ourselves. She talks about losing Wall, about being alone for the first time in her life.

'I'm looking for a job,' she announces. 'Really looking, this time. I thought it didn't matter, I didn't need the money and why bother? But I do need the money. Money that I earn. Just to have had it.'

'I know. So do I.'

'You'll get it.'

'I know. So will you.'

We walk back through the maze of lights, slightly drunk.

211

Avoiding the eyes. Women alone; I am temporarily alone, soon to be permanently.

And then? Another Bernie?

Never another Bernie.

Another Georgia? Please, God, another –

Never another Georgia.

Another woman?

Maybe. When I'm another woman.

'Did it ever occur to you, Marguerite,' I ask her, laughing, as we sip our nightcaps, ecstatically reunited with Val, 'that penis breaks down into "pen is"?'

'No,' she says dryly. 'But I can see how it would occur to you.'

Time to go. I won't let her drive me to the airport. She has an interview, she needs time to get ready. So do I, so do I. Georgia's okay. I had to call and make sure, before I left. It was a brief conversation. There won't be any more.

I sit with Marguerite for a last Jack Daniels, and I itch. Inglorious but distracting.

'How's Sappho?' she asks, startling me.

Sappho's my dog.

'When I first got her,' I answer, 'I told Georgia I'd finally managed to introduce another female into the house. She said, "You mean, another bitch." '

Silence.

'She's all right. She'll be overjoyed –'

'Yes. And so will I. To see them I mean.' And Jonathan?

'Dogs are such abject dependants,' she says, making me open my eyes. 'Look at Val.' She wags her tail, hearing her name.

'She follows me everywhere. If I get a job, I may have to get rid of her. I can't imagine her being able to live alone all day.' She shakes her head.

'No. Well, she can't imagine it either. But if it happens, she'll manage it.'

'I guess,' she looks at me.

We laugh. Frauds, the two of us.

Then we look away.

I stand, finish my drink, grab my suitcase. She comes to the door, and Val, of course, looking anxious, wagging her tail.

'Are you sure –'

'I'm sure.'

'You've got enough money, now,' she laughs at me.

'Plenty.'

'And the boys' presents.'

'And the boys' presents.' Which we picked out together.

'Well.'

'Goodbye. I hope you get that job – if you want it.'

'Me too. And that you – get what you want.'

I walk down the hall towards the elevator, and wave to her as I get in. Then the door slides shut and she's gone. No, I am. Down, with a clutch at the stomach.

Smile at the doorman, walk across the lobby, you can do it. There's a taxi, gliding by as if sent.

He stops. I give him my bag and say Kennedy, he smiles, it's a good fare.

I look up.

Something old, something new, something borrowed, something blue, goes through my mind, maybe because this is a threshold, because I'm leaving my mother. Or both.

Blue denim, new. Coldwick snake bracelet, old. Something borrowed, a slapdash prayer:

Old mother, old necromancer, stand me now and ever on my head.

Marguerite waves from her window as I pull away, as I do from mine. More a salute than a wave.

Other new fiction from Virago

UNION STREET
Pat Barker

Union Street could be any street, anywhere. But in this powerful novel it lies at the heart of a city in the industrial North-east of England, a wasteland of decaying streets and partly demolished houses. It is the winter of 1973, a cold winter of unemployment, the year of the miners' strike.

This is the story of the women – and their men – who lived in that street, in that year, at that time. There is Kelly, eleven years old, bright, funny, engaging, a tough child of the streets; there is Joanne, eighteen, pregnant, unmarried; there is Lisa, mother of two, pregnant again, her husband out of work. Then there is Muriel, breaking her heart over her dying husband, comforted – but not for long – by her growing children. Central to the story are Iris, formidable mother and grandmother, the matriarch of the street, and Dinah, the local prostitute, knocking on sixty but still on the game. Last of all there is Alice, seventy-six now, fighting for that last and most precious freedom: the right to die in her own home.

Other new fiction from Virago

BLOW YOUR HOUSE DOWN
Pat Barker

A killer is roaming the streets of a northern city, setting off a wave of terror. He singles out prostitutes, and the face of his latest victim stares out from every newspaper and billboard, haunting the women who walk the streets.

But life and work must go on. Brenda, with three children can't afford to give up, while Audrey, now in her forties, desperately goes on 'working the cars', protecting herself as best she can. A city and its people are in the grip of a deep sickness, and when another woman is savagely murdered, Jean, her lover, can only find the strength to counter evil with evil. It is Maggie, the survivor of an attack, who finally outlasts the malign and terrifying presence, and recovers her capacity to love.